THE FAMILY HOME

Lorraine Mace is the critically acclaimed author of the DI Sterling thrillers, as well as two standalone thrillers, *The Guest* and *The Family Home*. Lorraine lives in the warmer and sunnier clime of southern Spain.

THE FAMILY HOME
LORRAINE MACE

ACCENT

First published in 2024 by Headline Accent
An imprint of HEADLINE PUBLISHING GROUP

2

Cataloguing in Publication Data is available from the British Library

ISBN 978 1 4722 8394 8

Typeset in 11.25/15.25pt Bembo Std by Jouve (UK), Milton Keynes

Printed and bound in Great Britain by Clays Ltd, Elcograf S.p.A.

Headline's policy is to use papers that are natural, renewable and recyclable
products and made from wood grown in well-managed forests and other
controlled sources. The logging and manufacturing processes are expected
to conform to the environmental regulations of the country of origin.

HEADLINE PUBLISHING GROUP
An Hachette UK Company
Carmelite House
50 Victoria Embankment
London EC4Y 0DZ

www.headline.co.uk
www.hachette.co.uk

For Chris, who is always there to encourage and support me whenever I feel like giving up.

Prologue

Sally's eyes opened to complete blackness. Where was she? *Did it matter?* She was so tired, so very tired. She'd just close her eyes for another few moments and then try to work out what was happening. When she woke again, she was still in the dark. A voice in her head was yelling, trying to tell her something. What? Something crucial to remember about where she was, but she couldn't grasp the thought. Maybe it wasn't important. She just wanted to sleep, but the voice wouldn't stop yelling.

Wake up! Wake up!

But it was too hard. She needed to go back to sleep.

Wake up! Wake up!

Sally attempted to sit up, but she couldn't. She tried to move her hands, but they seemed to be tied together. She struggled to lift them, but they didn't reach very far. Something was in the way. It felt like material. Was she wrapped in a blanket? The soft drowsy feeling crept over her again, so she

1

closed her eyes. She'd figure everything out later, when she woke up properly.

Wake up! I must wake up!

Her eyes opened again. It was still dark. Where was she? Then she felt herself being dragged. Someone was moving her.

'Help me!' she cried, again and again as she was bumped over uneven ground. Suddenly, there was a falling sensation. The breath left her body as she landed with a jolt.

Sally screamed, 'Let me out! Who are you? Why are you doing this to me?'

She could barely move. The blanket was all around her. She was in a cocoon. Who put her here?

Lifting her hands as far as they would go, she tried to rip her way through the material, but it wouldn't give.

'Oh no you don't! You're staying down there.'

Sally knew that voice. Her memories returned with sickening clarity. She had to escape now or she would die in this hole, but she couldn't move. Couldn't get her hands free.

And then she felt clump after clump of earth land on her body.

Chapter One

Two weeks earlier – Friday 6th June

S ally dropped the frozen peas into her trolley and re-
adjusted her sunglasses. Pushing the trolley onwards, she
prayed there wouldn't be a long queue when she got to the
checkout. Gordon never believed her when she told him she'd
had to stand in line for more time than he thought was needed.

She picked up a sliced loaf and turned the corner of the aisle
only to see her worst fear confirmed. Only two of the checkouts were manned and long queues stretched back from both of
them. Which one to choose? She was sure to pick the wrong
one. Heart pumping, she steered her trolley to the left and got
in line behind an elderly couple. The woman glanced up and
smiled. Instinctively Sally reached up to her cheek where she'd
carefully applied extra make-up this morning before work.
Had it worn off? Was that why the woman seemed to be staring at her?

Sally half turned and pretended to be moving the items in
her trolley so that she didn't have to make eye contact. Through

a blur of tears and the darkness of her shades she lifted the bags of frozen vegetables and moved them from one spot to another.

Come on, come on, she urged silently as her queue showed no signs of moving, unlike the other one which was going forward at a rapid rate. She'd picked the wrong line. Gordon would be looking at his watch now, wondering why she was taking so long.

At long last her turn arrived. She rapidly packed the shopping and paid, almost running from the store in her haste to get to the car before Gordon got upset over how long she'd kept him waiting.

She needn't have worried. As she approached the car, she heard Gordon laugh. It was one of his good laughs. Deep, throaty and carrying just a hint of flirtation. By the time she reached the sound, an elderly lady was looking up at Gordon as if he was her saviour.

He glanced over at Sally. 'At last, hon,' he said. 'I was wondering where you'd got to. Fortunately, I was able to while away a few minutes with this lovely lady. I know you're going to be jealous, but I couldn't help myself.'

As he finished speaking, he lifted the last of the lady's shopping bags from her trolley and put them into the boot of the car parked next to their hatchback.

'I'll just put this trolley back. Won't be long,' he said, then turned to grin at the elderly lady and winked. 'As for you, try not to miss me too much.'

The lady watched him walk away before turning to Sally.

'You're so lucky,' she said. 'Your husband couldn't have been kinder. There I was, struggling with my heavy bags and he leapt out of your car to help me. My Bert, bless his soul, even when he was young and fit, never lifted a finger to carry the bags from the car to the house, far less come shopping with me to make sure I didn't have to do all the heavy lifting myself.'

Sally smiled. 'He likes to help,' she said, wishing she could tell the truth, but Gordon had charmed the woman so completely she probably wouldn't believe it even if Sally uncovered her bruises, which she would never do.

The lady smiled as she got into her car. 'I hope you take care of him. Good men like that are hard to find. Have a lovely weekend.'

She shut the car door and waved. Sally waited until the old lady had reversed out before opening the hatchback and picking up the first of her shopping bags, keeping a wary eye on Gordon as he walked back across the car park.

If he was in a good mood he'd help her. If he wasn't . . . *Don't think about it*, she told herself. He didn't speak as he reached the car, opened the door on the driver's side and got in. Sally put the last of the bags into the car, carefully closing the boot so that it didn't slam. She wheeled the trolley over to the building and slotted it into the line of others and headed back to the car.

As she opened the door and saw his face, she knew whatever she said was going to be wrong. Maybe it was better to keep quiet.

'Well?' he said, holding out his hand for the credit card. 'What kept you this time? Or should I say *who*? Come on, who were you talking to?'

Sally shook her head. 'No one. There were only two checkouts open and long queues at both of them.'

He started the car. 'You expect me to believe that? You are

such a liar. Never mind, you'll tell me the truth later. I'll get it out of you one way or another.'

As the car moved out of the supermarket car park Sally began rehearsing in her mind what she could say to placate him. The truth wouldn't work. He never believed her when she said she hadn't spoken to anyone. Maybe if she pleaded stupidity, saying she'd picked up the wrong items and had to go and change them, he might accept that, or maybe she could say there hadn't been the right coffee on the shelf and she'd had to ask one of the stackers to go and get some. No, that wouldn't do. That would prove him right because she'd have spoken to someone. She'd go with the stupidity story.

The drive home was torture. She kept stealing glances at his face and could see how angry he was. Should she speak? No, safer to keep quiet and hope he'd come round by the time they reached the house.

Gordon turned into their drive and switched off the engine.

'Get out,' he said. 'I'll bring the shopping in. I don't want to look at you until you're ready to tell me the truth. Go on, get inside and wait for me.'

She climbed out of the car and walked to the house, legs trembling so much she stumbled as she reached the front door.

She heard him sigh. 'Stupid clumsy bitch. I don't know why I put up with you.'

Leaving the front door open for him to bring in the bags, Sally went through to the kitchen and tried to compose herself. Hearing voices, she moved over to the window and saw their neighbour, Janet, had pulled up on the adjoining drive.

'Well, just look at you,' Janet cooed, as she walked to stand

6

next to Gordon. 'If only I could get George to help bring in our shopping, but he's probably asleep in front of the TV.'

Sally's stomach heaved as Janet grinned and moved towards Gordon. *Oh, dear God, no!* she thought. *Please don't flirt with him. He's already so angry.*

Sally didn't catch Gordon's reply, but it must have been funny because Janet burst out laughing, moved up close, and put her hand on his arm.

'You can come and lift my bags any time,' she said and winked. 'I doubt George would even notice.'

Sally could feel her heart pounding. Gordon hated women who acted like their neighbour. He said it proved that all women were whores at heart.

'Now, Janet, you know very well I only have eyes for my lovely wife,' Gordon said, smiling in a way that would once have melted Sally's heart, but that now filled her with fear.

He turned away from Janet and walked towards the house, carrying two bags in each hand. Sally could see by the look on his face that tonight was going to be bad. She knew now there'd be no placating him. He had already been angry with her and now Janet had made it worse. But what had she done this time? Sally wracked her brains trying to work out what could have caused him to go from smiling at her and saying not to be too long as she climbed out of the car, to over-the-top fuming by the time she got back. It couldn't just be the amount of time she'd taken to do the shopping. There must be something else.

She jumped as he spoke behind her.

'Don't stand there blocking the way. The least you could have done was pour me a drink. Why do I have to do every-thing around here? Isn't it enough that I take care of you?'

He dumped the bags on the floor.

'Well,' he snarled, 'aren't you going to answer me?'

Sally panicked, not knowing which question to answer first. 'Gordon, please, what have I done to upset you?'

'*Gordon, please,*' he mimicked. '*What have I done?* I'll tell you what you've done, you cheating bitch, you've arranged to go out to pick up some man, that's what you've done.'

She shook her head. What was he talking about? 'I haven't. I promise.'

He kicked at one of the bags and the shopping flew across the floor. A white haze filled the kitchen as the flour bag exploded.

'Now look what you've made me do!' he yelled.

'I'll clean it up,' she said, turning to reach for the broom from behind the kitchen door.

'Leave it!' he snarled, pulling her back to face him. 'When were you going to tell me about your night out?'

'I'm not having a night out. I promise I'm not going anywhere.'

'*Oh, no, Gordon, I'm not going out,*' he said in a squeaky voice. '*I promise!* Except you're a liar, aren't you? Did you think you could keep it a secret from me?'

'What?' she begged. 'I don't know what you're talking about. I don't keep any secrets from you.'

'Really? What about this?' he said, pulling her phone from his pocket. 'This went ping while you were in the shop, so I read the message. "See you at 7:30," it says. Who's it from? Who the hell is CT and why is he sending you messages about going out? When were you planning to tell me?'

Sally relaxed slightly. He might not like what she had to

say, but at least she could explain this. 'That wasn't meant for me,' she said. 'One of the girls at work, Carly Tanner, has arranged a night out for everyone. She set up a WhatsApp group and put us all on it. I've already told her I can't go.'

'I see,' he said. 'You told her you can't go, not that you didn't want to go.'

'I don't want to go,' Sally said. 'That's what I meant.'

'It's not what you said though, is it? You said you can't go. You wanted to, but you told her you can't. Why did you want to go? So you can whore around with some other man?'

She shook her head. 'No, Gordon, you're all I want. All I've ever wanted. You know that.' She smiled and reached out to touch his arm. 'Let's not fight.'

He pulled his arm away and shook off her hand. Throwing her phone to the floor, he stamped on it again and again until the pieces were mixed in with the flour.

'Now you can't make plans to go out and whore around with your slut friends. Get this mess cleaned up.'

'I'll just put the shopping away and then—'

He grabbed her, his hands circling her throat as he pushed her against the wall.

'No! Get my dinner ready. I'm starving. You'd think a man working hard all day would be able to come home and relax, but no, you have to go and spoil our weekend before it's even started.'

'I'm sorry,' she whispered.

He let go and looked her up and down. She could feel his eyes burning into her.

'You always say sorry, but then you do something else that

means I can't trust you. Right now, I can't bear to look at you. I'm going to watch the news. Call me when dinner's ready.'

As she moved around the kitchen preparing the bolognese sauce and boiling the pasta, all Sally could think about was what had happened the last time he'd been this angry. That evening had ended with a visit to the hospital to set her broken bones. Maybe she should put the sleeping powder she'd hidden at the back of the drawer in his dinner and leave tonight instead of waiting until she'd saved enough money, but where could she go? She couldn't contact her half-sister until Monday when she went back to work. She'd tried so hard to build up a running-away fund and Alison had offered her a temporary place to hide, but if she left tonight, without a phone she had no way of contacting her sister and nowhere near enough money even if she could get hold of her secret bank card, which she couldn't because that was in her desk at work. Even if she could somehow get to the office, she had no way of getting in until the cleaners arrived on Monday morning.

'That smells delicious,' he said, coming up behind her and kissing the back of her neck, making her heart sink. 'Are you having wine?'

She used to think Gordon being nice after he'd lost his temper meant the danger was over. She knew better now. She turned round and he waved the bottle, giving her one of his winning smiles, which disappeared when she shook her head.

'Not tonight, thank you. I don't fancy any.'

'Yes you do,' he said, moving to the table and pouring some into her glass.

She moved to the table and sat down, desperate to placate him, but couldn't help giving a gasp of fear as Gordon reached across the table and patted her hand.

'I'm sorry for yelling at you, Sal, but you make me so mad at times I can't help myself. You never seem to learn, no matter how many times I put you right.'

Sally gave what she hoped was a forgiving smile.

'Why aren't you eating?' he said.

Brought back to earth, she shrugged. 'I'm not very hungry.'

'You're not sulking, are you?' Gordon said, reaching out again but this time gripping her left wrist so tightly she knew there would be yet another bruise.

She picked up a fork with her right hand and moved the food around on the plate. 'No, not sulking,' she said.

'Good,' he said, letting go of her wrist. 'Because you've got nothing to sulk about, have you? You've got a lovely home and a husband who adores you. What more could any woman want?'

Sally knew she had to head this off before it went any further.

'You're right,' she said. 'I'm one of the lucky ones. Would you like more bolognese?'

Gordon smiled and nodded. 'That's my girl.'

Sally moved across to the sauce. Keeping a careful watch on Gordon, she thought about opening the drawer containing the bag of crushed sleeping tablets, but her hands were shaking too much. She knew she couldn't do it without him noticing. If he found the powder, he'd go berserk.

She took his full plate back to the table and watched as he refilled her wine glass, this time to the brim. She only took tiny sips, knowing she had to keep her wits about her.

'Do you know what that stupid bastard said to me at work today?'

Sally stayed quiet. When Gordon was in one of these moods, it was safer not to speak.

'He thinks just because he's my foreman he knows it all. Well, take it from me, he doesn't know his arse from his elbow.'

He swallowed the last of the wine in his glass, looked at hers and glared.

'Why aren't you drinking? You know I don't like to drink alone. Are you trying to upset me? Is that what you want? Is it?' he said, his voice rising on each question.

Sally shook her head and picked up the glass, taking a tiny sip before putting it back down again.

'It's bad enough I have to work with idiots without having to live with one. Why don't you answer me? Cat got your tongue?'

'I was listening,' Sally said. 'What did Mr Peters say to you?'

'Ah, fuck you. I don't know why I bother telling you about my day. You're too thick to understand what I have to put up with.'

Sally knew this would go in one of two directions. Either he was going to lash out at her, as if his bad day was her fault, or he would decide she wasn't worth the effort of explaining how unfairly everyone treated him. She breathed a sigh of relief when he got up and staggered through to the lounge without saying anything else, leaving her to clear away the dishes.

She waited until he'd gone, then turned to the shopping bags she hadn't had chance to unpack. Each time she moved, she hurt. *She had to leave soon, but with what money?*

Shaking, she put the sugar into the container and threw the empty packet in the bin. Would she have more bruises to cover up before going back to work on Monday? Weekends were always the worst. At least during the week she could get away for most of the day. She loved her job and the women she worked with, but they were beginning to shut her out because she could never join in with the events they planned.

Gordon said she couldn't go anywhere without him because other men would be after her, but he also didn't want to spend time with her workmates. He said they were a bunch of tarts, which was unfair. All of them were either married or in a steady relationship. Their husbands and partners often went out with them in big groups. Gordon refused though because he said he loved her so much he wanted her all to himself. What was that old Tina Turner song? *What's love got to do with it?*

When she'd finished packing everything away, she went through to the lounge to find out if Gordon wanted coffee.

'Why the fuck would I want coffee when I've got this?' he said, lifting his glass in her direction.

She saw he'd already had quite a few glasses as the bottle of brandy she'd bought in the supermarket was only half full. Knowing what would happen if he drank any more, she forced herself to speak.

'I just thought you might like some coffee to go with the brandy,' she stammered.

It was the wrong thing to say. He jumped up from the chair and lashed out. His fist caught her cheek and she fell backwards, landing in a heap against the wall.

'You thought? You thought? You're not capable of

thinking. Too stupid to know when to speak and when to shut the fuck up,' he yelled, reaching down to grab hold of her hair and dragging her back up from the floor. 'Who are you to tell me what to do?'

'Gordon, please,' she pleaded. 'I didn't mean you should stop drinking. I thought you might like a coffee to go with the brandy. You like that sometimes, don't you?'

Sally knew the next few seconds would decide her fate. He was either going to beat her to a pulp or apologise. Holding her breath, she forced herself not to move.

He smiled. 'Sally, Sally, Sally, you drive me insane, but you know I love you, don't you?' he said, letting go of her hair. 'You're right. A cup of coffee with a slug of brandy in it would be perfect.'

She went back into the kitchen and made a cortado coffee. Strong, just the way he liked it. Then she opened the drawer and took out the sleeping powder, stirring some into the coffee. It was now or never! He was on the point of losing it completely. She couldn't go through another night like the last time. He almost killed her then.

'Aren't you coming to sit with me?' he asked as she put his coffee on the small table next to him and turned to go back into the kitchen. 'You know I like you to be in here where I can see you.'

Sally moved to the couch and sat down at the end furthest from his armchair. Out of range – just in case he lashed out again.

'Not there,' he said. 'Come up this end.'

She got up and moved closer to him, keeping a wary eye on his face for any sign he was about to make a sudden move, but he smiled and turned his attention back to the television. Sally sat, quietly watching as he downed the coffee in three quick gulps. *Please make the powder work*, she prayed silently. *She had to get away!*

Sally was so deep in thought that she jumped when Gordon started snoring. The level of brandy in the bottle was down around the one third mark. He'd knocked back nearly a full bottle of wine, two thirds of a bottle of brandy and a cup of coffee laced with sleeping powder. His mouth was hanging open and he was out for the count.

His wallet was on the small side table between the sofa and his armchair. Sally stared at it, wondering if there was enough money in there to cover a few days, hotel expenses. She only really needed enough to tide her over until she could get to work on Monday to pick up her bank card. Keeping a watchful eye on him, she reached out with a shaking hand and picked it up.

There was a thick wad of notes. Would it be enough? She looked wistfully at the bank cards, but there was no point in taking most of those. He'd never told her the PIN numbers for any of the cards, other than for the one she used in the supermarket once a week. She could take that and draw some money from a cash machine. Did she dare? No. He'd be able to track where she was if she used it.

Gordon twitched and shuddered. Sally froze.

What would he do if he woke up and caught her with his wallet in her hand? She knew the answer to that would be more broken bones and went to put the wallet back, but realised she might be giving up her only chance to escape. Placing the wallet on her lap, she slid the notes out and quietly stood up, shoving the money into the back pocket of her jeans. She'd count it later.

Gently she put the wallet back onto the table, then inched away from the couch so as not to disturb him. She should go upstairs and pack a bag, but he might wake up while she was doing it. If he caught her, he might be so angry he'd . . . what? She couldn't bring herself to think about what he might do.

She crept to the front door and opened it, praying it wouldn't make any noise. Standing on the doorstep, she hesitated. If only she still had a phone, she could call Alison to let her know she was coming. Go or stay? Did she really have a choice? She had to leave. Her half-sister had said she was welcome at any time. Sally could only hope she meant it.

She listened, relieved to be able to make out the rise and fall of Gordon's snores. She softly pulled the door closed behind her, took a deep breath, and ran.

Chapter Two

Ten minutes later, gasping for breath, Sally slowed down to a walk. Even if Gordon had woken up, he wouldn't realise straightaway that she'd left. It probably wouldn't even cross his mind until he'd searched the entire house for her, she thought. But could she rely on that?

Sally looked at her watch. It was already nearly ten o'clock. Close to tears, she forced herself to think. Who would take her in around here? One of the girls from the office would probably offer her a bed for the night, but she had no idea where any of them lived. She just needed somewhere to hide until Monday when she could email Alison and arrange to go to her. Without her phone Sally couldn't even search for a cheap hotel.

The last time she had seen her sister had been at their old family home in Rutland. Alison had wanted to help her then and had made it clear in her recent emails she still felt the same way. For weeks now she'd been begging Sally to come, saying there was no reason for her to stay with Gordon a moment longer. Even if Sally couldn't let Alison know she was coming, she could still head over to Rutland and find a hotel to stay in overnight.

She had to go somewhere Gordon either didn't know about or wouldn't think to look even if he did know. At least in Rutland Sally would be miles away from Gordon and he wouldn't have any idea where to find her. Feeling better now that she had a destination in mind, she looked around and realised she'd run in the direction of the train station. She could get a train to Oakham and a taxi from there if she had enough money. But did she?

Moving into the light shed by a streetlamp, she pulled the notes from her jeans back pocket. Opening her fist, she counted the money she had snatched from Gordon's wallet. Just under £300. That was more than enough for the train and taxi. Gordon wouldn't think to look for her in Rutland because he'd never wanted to know anything about her life before she became his. He said he'd spoken to her father on the phone once, but had never met him or Alison.

She choked on a bark of laughter and realised she must sound hysterical. Back then she'd been only too glad to lose contact with her family. All she'd wanted was for Gordon to love her. He'd made it clear she didn't need family or friends. He was going to be her whole life.

Sally stopped as she thought about what she might find in Rutland. The house wasn't her sister's. It belonged to their father. Even though Alison had said in her emails that Sally could stay in the house, what if her father refused to let her in as he had once before?

Stop with the negative thoughts, she scolded. *Move! Now, before Gordon comes to find you!* Just the thought of him finding her sent shivers through her body. There was no time to waste. Whatever she found when she got to Rutland she'd have to deal with. The only thing that mattered tonight was to get away from Gordon. She began a brisk walk, but after a few strides she quickened her pace and ran.

When she reached Nottingham station, she realised she had no idea whether or not there would be a train to Oakham. The ticket office was closed, but there was a machine in the foyer. There were no direct trains to Oakham, but the last train to Peterborough was coming in five minutes. It was an hour's journey, and then she could change at Peterborough for a train to Oakham. If she'd missed the last one, she would have to find a cheap hotel for the night. Sally keyed the details for the Peterborough train into the machine and fed a twenty-pound note into the slot. Once she had the ticket, she looked around for somewhere to hide until the train arrived, but there was nowhere. She edged backwards and tried to blend into the shadows against the station wall.

As the train came into view, she let go of the breath she'd been holding. Surely once she was on the train, she'd be safe. She waited until the doors opened before moving away from the wall and climbing into the carriage. *Come on, come on*, she silently prayed, as the train remained stationary. Then, with a jolt, it pulled away from the station, taking her to a new life.

Sally peered through the window, convinced she'd see Gordon striding onto the platform, but there was no sign of him or anyone else. Her reflection in the glass came as a shock. She'd forgotten to pick up her sunglasses and a new colourful bruise under her left eye showed vividly against the whiteness of her face. Maybe that would be enough to soften her father's heart so that he would forget the past and allow her to stay for a while.

Closing her eyes, she leaned her head back against the seat cushion and tried to remember her early years in the Rutland house. She'd only been seven years old when she'd had the accident that had left her in a coma. She'd been told afterwards that Grandma Fletcher, her mother's mother, had been at the hospital every day by her bedside, but not her own mother. When Sally had finally come out of the coma and was later able to leave the hospital, she went to live with Grandma Fletcher. Much later she found out that her mother had left home. She hadn't loved Sally enough to take her.

Her grandmother died shortly after Sally had turned seventeen. She'd gone to her father's house, hoping to be made welcome. She remembered him coming to Cornwall for tea each year on her birthday. Grandma Fletcher had always made excuses as to why he didn't visit more often, probably to save Sally from feeling hurt. Or maybe it was to compensate for her own feelings of guilt because it was her daughter's running off with a lover that had caused a rift in the family.

Sally had gone in all innocence that day to the Rutland house, expecting to be taken in. She hadn't even made it over the doorstep. He must have seen her from the window as she walked up the drive because he refused to even open the front door, simply shouting at her from inside.

'No, you can't stay here,' her father had said. 'I'm sorry, it's just not possible. You have to go back to your grandmother's. I believe she left the house to you. She said she was going to do so and that you would have a comfortable allowance until you were twenty-five and inherited everything. You don't need me.'

Sally had stood on the doorstep, stunned and unable to believe what had just happened. She heard a noise and looked up to see Alison leaning out of one of the upstairs windows.

'Wait for me,' she'd whispered. 'I'm coming down.'

A few minutes later she'd appeared from around the side of the house.

'We need to be quiet,' she said, 'so that he can't hear us.'

'Are you living here?' Sally asked.

Alison nodded. 'I've always lived with Daddy. Well, on and off.'

Sally felt again that punch in the gut. If Alison, who was only seven years older than she was, was allowed to live at home, why didn't her father want Sally in the house? Almost as if she'd heard her sister's unspoken question, Alison reached forward and clutched Sally's arm.

'You look like your mother, you know. That could be why he doesn't want you here.'

'Because she left him?' Sally asked.

Alison nodded. 'That was the day you nearly died. Daddy thinks you were running after your mother, maybe begging her to take you too,' she whispered.

Sally felt bile rise into her throat. So her mother hadn't wanted her. She'd guessed as much, but it hurt to have it confirmed.

'Why don't you wait in the boathouse while I convince Daddy to let you move in with us?' Alison said. 'Do you remember where it is? Round the back of the house at the far end of the lawn. I could bring you food and whatever you

21

need. I'm sure I could get him to change his mind within a day or so. He always listens to me.'

Sally felt such a rush of gratitude she moved to hug Alison. As she did so, the front door opened and her father's voice thundered out.

'Alison, get inside. As for you, Sally, go away. I told you you're not welcome here. Go on, go! And don't come back! If you do, I'll have you arrested for trespassing.'

Tears falling unchecked, she'd trudged into the village and found a pub where the landlord was kind enough to call a taxi for her. She'd returned to Grandma Fletcher's house and lived alone until she met Gordon six months later. What had he called it? A whirlwind romance. He said he'd never felt about anyone the way he did about her. Gordon had dealt with probate for her and, after Grandma Fletcher's house was sold, they'd moved away from Cornwall to Nottingham. She lost touch with everyone she'd known growing up. Gordon had said he wanted her all to himself. She hadn't realised then how much he intended to keep it that way.

On the day she turned eighteen, three months after they had bumped into each other at the library, they were married.

In her emails, when Alison insisted Sally come to live in Rutland, Sally had reminded her sister of what their father had said when she'd last tried to move in, but Alison insisted it would be fine. Their father wasn't the same man he was back then. As long as Alison lived in the house, Sally would have a safe refuge, for a while at least.

She barely remembered Alison from childhood but recalled her kindness that dreadful day after Grandma Fletcher had died and she'd gone to Rutland to find somewhere to live.

Her sister must be about forty-four now. She'd never married. Alison had made it plain in her emails that she longed to get to know Sally now that they were both adults. She'd wanted her to come home from the hospital when she came out of her coma, but Sally had been sent to stay with her grandma instead.

Sally shifted in her seat, trying to find a comfortable position, but her bruises made it difficult to settle.

Would her father turn her away again? It was possible, she knew that, even though Alison said otherwise, but she had nowhere else to go. None of her old friends from her teenage years even knew where she and Gordon had moved to after they'd got married. He'd said it was to make a fresh start in life, but Sally realised now it was to isolate her. He'd only allowed her to go out to work because they needed the money after her inheritance from Grandma Fletcher had run out. Gordon had never earned a great salary. He always said it was because others at work were jealous of him and blocked the promotions he deserved.

He'd put a wall around the two of them and not allowed anyone in. She'd become completely dependent on him in every way. But not any more, Sally vowed. There was no way she'd ever go back to that life. Twenty years of fear was enough.

As the train pulled into Peterborough, the magnitude of what she was about to do hit home. She was relying on Alison to convince their father to allow her to stay. The father who not only didn't want her around, but had threatened her with the police if she ever came back.

Chapter Three

S ally stood on the platform at Peterborough close to tears. There wouldn't be an Oakham train until morning. The thought of trying to check in to a hotel without any baggage or identification felt like an impossible task, but she had to do it. She wandered outside, determined to find somewhere to stay the night. As she walked along Station Road, she saw an illuminated sign for a taxi rank. Of course, she had enough money to get a taxi. It would probably be cheaper than a hotel room and she wouldn't have to explain to a stranger why she had no proof of who she was. Nor would she have to put up with pitying looks because of her bruises or try to make up a story for why she didn't even have a toothbrush to her name.

Sally climbed into a taxi and gave the driver the Rutland address. As the car pulled away, she let out a sigh of relief. Whatever happened tonight, she wouldn't have to worry about what kind of mood Gordon was in, or how much he'd had to drink.

As the car approached Rutland Water, Sally looked out, trying to pinpoint places she might have known as a child, but either it was too dark or she simply didn't recognise anywhere. Eventually, the taxi slowed down and turned onto what was little more than a narrow track. It felt like forever before they stopped.

'Is this the right place, love? It looks a bit deserted. Are you sure you've got the correct address?'

Sally looked out of the taxi window and saw why the driver was asking. The house stood a long way back from the track, surrounded by a large expanse of lawn. The driver had pulled off the uneven lane onto a long, paved drive which led up to the house. The building was in complete darkness.

Was it the right place? It was dark, and it was so many years since she'd been here. It looked forbidding and enormous in the moonlight. It was much bigger than she remembered.

'Well, love, what do you want to do? I can take you back to Peterborough if you want, or into Oakham. It's your choice.'

Either place would probably be better than getting out of the car if no one was home, but then Sally thought she could sleep overnight in the boathouse as Alison had suggested so many years before. She'd said it was at the back of the house, so Sally knew it wouldn't be visible from the road.

'Sorry to push you, love, but I can't sit here all night.'

'No, of course you can't,' Sally said. 'I'll get out. What do I owe you?'

'That'll be sixty pounds, love. Look, here, take my card. If you need me, give me a bell,' he said. 'I'm sure I shouldn't be leaving you in the dark like this. Are you certain you don't want me to drop you off in Oakham? No additional charge!'

Sally smiled and shook her head. She had no phone, so couldn't call even if she wanted to, but it was good to know there were some decent men in the world after all. They weren't all like Gordon. She handed over the fare and took his card in return, slipping it into her jeans pocket.

'I'll just wait here until you're in the house,' he said.

Sally shook her head. She didn't even know if anyone was home.

'No, thank you. You go. I'll be fine,' she said.

As the tail lights of his car disappeared down the lane, Sally thanked the heavens there was a partial moon. Without it she'd have been standing in pitch-black darkness. There were no street lights. She looked up at a sky so full of stars it felt like she'd stepped into a sci-fi film. Shaking herself, she looked around. There was another drive at right angles to her father's with a house much closer to the track. She tried to remember who had lived there when she was a child, but her mind was blank.

She started walking along the drive. It seemed much further than when she had last come to her father's house. Should she try to raise Alison? What if her father opened the door? What could she say? Would he know who she was? Alison had said in one of her emails that he was suffering from Alzheimer's, so he might not even recognise her. No, it would be better to go round the back and hope the boathouse wasn't locked.

She took a step off the drive towards the side of the house. There was no point in dithering. As she crept across the lawn, she suddenly remembered going into the boathouse as a small child and getting into trouble for it. How odd, she thought, for that memory to return when she had forgotten so much of those early years.

She turned the corner of the house and saw a dark structure

at the end of still more lawn. Compared to their own tiny garden, with a minuscule patch of ground where Gordon grew vegetables, this felt as if she was in a park. Gordon complained about having to look after their garden. He'd have a fit if he had to tackle this. Maybe her father hired someone to care for the grounds. She tried to work out how old he must be, and realised he had to be about seventy-one. There must have been eleven years between her father and her mother because Maggie had only been twenty-two when she'd had Sally.

Reaching the boathouse, she saw it was more rundown than she'd expected. The house and grounds seemed to be in a much better state than the ramshackle wooden building in front of her. She tried the door, hoping it wouldn't fall off its hinges. The handle moved with a squeak, and she instinctively turned to see if anyone in the house had heard the noise and turned on a light, but the building was still in darkness.

Sally opened the door. There was a hint of moonlight coming in through the Velux window in the roof, but the glass was dirty, as if it hadn't been cleaned in a long time. The interior was too dark to make out anything other than vague shapes in the shadows. Worried that she might fall over something and wake someone in the house, she wished she still had a phone so that she could turn on the torch app. As she moved into the interior, she felt a rush of dread so overwhelming she started to retch. Leaning forward, she clutched her stomach until the nausea passed.

That earlier vague memory of coming here as a child grew stronger. She'd seen something bad, something that had frightened her, but what?

She turned back and closed the door. There was no boat to

be seen, but she realised she hadn't expected there to be one. Somehow she knew there hadn't been a boat here for a long, long time. Probably since before she'd even been born.

She looked around for somewhere to settle, but the mattress was gone. Mattress? How could she have known there was once a mattress in here?

Shaking off the question, she spotted a tarpaulin in the far corner. She could spread that out to cover the floor. There was nothing she could use as a blanket, so she would have to curl up to keep warm. She shivered from the cold. Or maybe she was just exhausted. Or scared. She was scared of the boathouse. *Stop it!* she ordered her mind, but the fear remained.

Forcing herself to ignore the alarm bells ringing in her head, she moved over to the tarpaulin, praying there wouldn't be spiders lurking, or worse, snakes. This was out in the countryside after all. Who knew what she might disturb when she picked it up and opened it out.

She felt the wooden walls closing in on her and gasped for air. As she battled to breathe, she heard a noise outside. She turned to face the door. It flew open and a bright light shone full in her face, blinding her to everything but the torch held by whoever was blocking the doorway and her way out.

Chapter Four

'M aggie! Maggie, you've come back to me. Oh, Maggie, I've missed you.'

As he spoke, the man lowered the torch and moved forward. Sally was stunned by how old he looked. Her father seemed to have aged beyond belief in the twenty years since she'd last seen him. The front of his dressing gown hung open to reveal paisley pyjamas. He had nothing on his feet.

'I'm not Maggie,' Sally said. 'It's me, Sally.'

For such a fragile-looking man he moved surprisingly quickly. Sally found herself clasped in his arms with kisses raining down on her head.

'Maggie, my Maggie, I thought I'd never see you again. Why did you leave me when I loved you so much?'

Sally pushed against his chest, but he held her even tighter.

'I'm not letting you go. Why should I, when you've only just come back to me?'

Through the open door Sally saw someone running across the lawn towards the boathouse.

'Dad!' Alison yelled from just outside the door. 'Let her go!'

'No! She's come home. We thought she was gone forever, but she's here. I've never stopped loving you, Maggie. Never!'

'That's not Maggie,' Alison shouted. 'That's Sally! Let her go!'

Her father drew back a little and stared into Sally's face. She saw a change come over his appearance. From looking at her with adoration, his expression changed to one of anger.

'Where have you been? I tried to find you so many times, but you'd sold up and moved from your grandmother's. You have a damned cheek turning up here like this in the middle of the night!'

Sally stepped backwards and tripped over the tarpaulin. She stopped herself from falling to the floor by clutching at the wall.

'Please, Father,' she said. 'I need somewhere to stay. Just for tonight. Please, I have nowhere else to go.'

He shook his head so violently she feared he'd have a stroke.

'So now I'm good enough for you? After all these years when you didn't even have the decency to tell me where you were?'

Alison moved forward and took his arm. 'You need your medication, Dad. Let's go into the house.'

'Let go of me! I want to know what's going on! Alison, did you know she was coming?'

Alison shook her head. 'No, I didn't know, but it's okay. I'll deal with it.'

He shuddered, his voice becoming childlike. 'Why am I out here? What's happening? I'm cold!'

'Come, Dad, let's go back. Wandering in the garden at night on your own is too dangerous. Anything could happen. You might fall, and we wouldn't want that, now, would we? Come on, let me take you back into the house. I can make you some Horlicks. You'd like that, wouldn't you?'

Sally watched as Alison gently turned him around and steered him out. At the doorway, she turned back to Sally and mouthed, 'Stay here. Don't move. I'll be back.'

As they trudged across the lawn, Sally slumped to the floor. If Alison was prepared to help her, maybe she'd found a safe haven after all.

It felt like an eternity before Sally heard the sound of Alison running back to the boathouse.

'Come on,' she said, gesturing to Sally to get up. 'Let's get you into the house and find you a bed.'

'You must be wondering what I'm doing here in the middle of the night,' Sally said, clambering to her feet.

Alison shook her head. 'Looking at the bruises on your face it doesn't take a genius to work out you've finally run away from that husband of yours. But why didn't you tell me you were finally ready to leave? I'd have come to pick you up.'

Sally sighed. 'I couldn't. He smashed my phone, but even if he hadn't, I didn't put your number in it. Gordon goes through my phone and I was scared he'd find it. I'm sorry, I owe you an explanation for turning up like this.'

Alison held the door open for Sally. 'Hey,' Alison said, placing a hand on Sally's arm as she was passing through the door. 'I'm just glad you're here. Really glad.'

As they walked over to the house Sally cast a look up at her half-sister. Alison was looking straight ahead with a dreamy smile on her face. She was being so kind to someone who was to all intents and purposes a stranger when she already had so much on her plate. Sally wished she'd been able to keep in contact with Alison over the years, instead of only reaching out to her a few months earlier when she'd first begun to plan her escape from Gordon.

'You must have realised that Dad isn't all there,' Alison said. 'As I mentioned in my emails, he developed dementia a couple of years ago. He's going downhill quite rapidly. He frequently gets up and wanders around the grounds at night. I often find him here in the boathouse. During the day he spends most of the time in the past, muttering all sorts of strange things, often about your mother. The rest of the time he's sort of here, with us, in the present.'

'Only sort of?' Sally asked.

'Yes,' Alison said as they reached the house. 'He's here, but not really. He usually knows what day of the week it is and has a good grasp of day-to-day stuff, but then he'll go off somewhere in his head for an hour or so. When he comes back, he could be in the present, or off on a trip down memory lane. The only problem with that is that the memories are not necessarily true. Sometimes they're what he wants them to be, rather than what actually happened.'

She stopped at a door at the rear of the house and caught hold of Sally's arm. Her grip was firm and Sally winced. The years with Gordon had made her more sensitive, and Alison was obviously very strong. Had to be to be able to deal with their father.

'I'm telling you all this so that you know what to expect while you're here.'

Following Alison into a massive kitchen, gleaming pans hanging from a rack overhead and a well-scrubbed oak table in the centre of the room, Sally stopped on the threshold.

'I remember this room! The pantry is through there,' she said, pointing to a door next to the alcove where an Aga was sending out welcoming heat.

As she closed the door behind her, Alison's words sank in. 'What do you mean "while I'm here"? Is it okay for me to stay for a few days? Dad made it clear all those years ago that I wasn't welcome, but then tonight he said he'd tried to find me.'

Alison shrugged. 'As I said, often what Dad says after he's been off to wherever it is he goes in his head, isn't the truth. It's what he believes at that moment. Or maybe it's what he wants to believe.'

Sally glanced over at Alison, choosing her words carefully. 'So you don't think he looked for me?'

Alison frowned. 'He might have, or he might think he did once he realised who you were. The bottom line here is that you can stay for as long as you want. It's been a lonely life looking after Dad on my own. It will be good to finally have you here.'

Tears filled Sally's eyes, blurring her vision. 'Thank you,' she said, 'but I don't want to cause any problems.' She hesitated. 'The last time I was here he threatened me with the police if I came back.'

Alison nodded. 'I remember. I think it had more to do with your mother than with you, but he's always refused to talk to me about it.' She shrugged. 'I also tried to get in touch with you a few months after you'd been here, but you'd moved and not left any forwarding address.'

'I didn't have chance to,' Sally said. 'Gordon, my husband, insisted we sell Grandma Fletcher's house and move to a cheaper area. We didn't have much money.'

'Oh, I always thought your grandmother was rich.'

Sally shook her head. 'So did I, but Gordon said she was deeply in debt and lived beyond her means, so most of her estate went to clear her financial obligations. It's why I . . . um . . . don't have much money on me, but thanks to Brenda in HR at work, I have a secret bank account. It doesn't have a fortune in it, but at least it's a start.'

'Yes, you said in your email. I was so surprised to hear from you at the time, but then I realised Gordon had kept you from us.' She pointed to Sally's eye. 'I knew from that first letter that your life must be bad, but not quite how bad. Was it your friend at work who told you to write to me?'

Sally nodded. 'Brenda does voluntary work for a women's charity, so knows how hard it is for women like me to leave their husbands. She told me to reach out to you and set up a bolthole. She also helped me open a new bank account. I got a raise a few months back, but I didn't tell Gordon. The extra money went into that account.'

'It sounds like she was a good friend to you, but you've got me now. You can stay as long as you want. I'd love to have you here. As I said, half the time Dad won't even know you're around. We'll have to deal with him if he gets upset and tells you to leave. Come on, you must be desperate to get into bed. Let's go upstairs. You can have your old room back.'

Alison led the way through a door on the far side of the kitchen. Sally followed into a large entrance hall. There was the front door she hadn't been allowed to come through all those years ago. If only Alison had been able to convince their father back then, how different her life could have been.

She walked into the hall and looked around. The only

thing that she remembered was the staircase. It dominated the hallway, rising up through the centre. Sally tried to picture what was behind the many closed doors on either side of the hall, but her mind remained blank.

She followed Alison up the stairs to a wide landing with small hallways branching off to the left and the right. Instinctively turning to the right, she realised Alison had turned left.

'Oh, sorry,' Sally said, stopping and coming back. 'I don't know why I went that way.'

Alison smiled. 'It's because your old room is that way. You remembered! Your bed doesn't have any covers on it, so we need to get some from the airing room.'

She opened a door off the hallway to the left and passed Sally some bedlinen.

'What else do you remember?' Alison asked.

'Nothing really,' Sally said. 'Somehow I knew my room was along there, but that's about all. I wish I could remember more.'

Alison smiled. 'Well, let's see what happens. In the meantime, let's get your bed made up so that we can both get some sleep.'

They walked across the landing and Alison opened the door Sally had almost gone towards earlier. Instead of being pleased she'd made the right connection, Sally shivered. There was the echo of a memory of something happening up here. Something bad. But what could it have been?

Once the bed was made up, Alison said goodnight and left. A few moments later she tapped on the door and opened it.

'I thought you might need some toiletries,' she said, putting a nightdress, a washbag and two towels on the bed. 'I always keep a supply of new toothbrushes and various other things, so you should find everything you need in there. Unfortunately, this isn't one of the rooms we added an en-suite to when we did the renovations. Can you remember where the guest bathroom is?'

Sally shook her head. 'Not really, no.'

'Across the hallway, second door on the right. Sleep tight, little sister. I am so pleased you're here.'

Sally waited until Alison had gone before opening the washbag. It really did contain everything she needed. Feeling grubby after her long journey and the time in the boathouse, what Sally wanted more than anything was a shower, but she didn't feel it would be right to disturb the house at this time of night. She'd have to make do with a good wash and hope for the best.

She quietly opened her door and tiptoed along the hall to the bathroom. Fifteen minutes later, feeling better than she'd believed possible, Sally crept back towards her room.

As she passed the opening to the staircase she shivered again. There *had* been something. She knew she'd fallen down the stairs, but not how it had happened. She remembered the sensation of running before falling. Had she been trying to get away from someone, or running for help? She didn't know. Just that she'd been running, running, running. And then she must have tripped and ended up in a heap at the bottom of the stairs.

Chapter Five

*S*he had to get away! She had to leave! Gordon was going to kill her. Sally sat up with a start, the sweat-drenched night-dress clinging to her body. She'd been having a nightmare but could only remember wisps of it. She had been chased and the shadow behind her was gaining ground, getting closer and closer. She knew that had it caught her, whatever it was, she would have died.

Was that what woke her up? The feeling she was about to die? She shuddered. Maybe it had been that partial recollection from last night that had triggered the nightmare. *What happened the night she fell down the stairs?* she wondered. Maybe Alison knew something and would tell her, but Sally didn't want to start asking questions and upsetting her sister after all her kindness.

Sally looked around. She didn't remember the room from her childhood, even though she'd known instinctively where it was. It didn't look in the least like a young girl's bedroom, but then why should it? She hadn't lived here for almost thirty years. Of course, over the decades many of the rooms would have been upgraded and they would have redecorated at least a couple of times. Alison had said as much the night before.

She tried not to feel hurt at being unwanted by her father, but she couldn't help it. When she'd been ready to leave the hospital, he hadn't fought for her to come home. She'd seen him once or twice a year during her childhood when he came to visit at her grandmother's. Grandma Fletcher had always said it was because he went abroad so often on business trips and couldn't look after a child, but he hadn't wanted her as a teenager either, although maybe the fact that she was the image of her mother was to blame for that. Had that been the reason? It had certainly been a shock when he'd turned her away, as during his visits to see her in Cornwall he'd always been kind, if a bit distant.

Sally knew there was little point in trying to work out what had gone on in her father's mind. One thing that was clear was how much he still loved her mother. Last night he'd truly believed she'd come back to him and had been overjoyed.

Where did she go? Sally wondered. Why did Maggie leave her behind? Unwanted by both parents, no wonder she'd fallen so hard for Gordon's words of love and devotion. She wished she'd realised in time that his love had come with so many conditions she no longer existed as a person in her own right, only as his possession. If she had understood the way his mind worked, she might have escaped sooner.

Sally threw the covers off. She couldn't stay here forever, but at least she had a place of safety while she figured out what to do next. Reaching for her jeans, she pulled the bank notes from the pocket and counted them. She had a little over two hundred pounds to her name. No clothes; no means of income; no plans. But once she got her bank card sent to her from the office, she would be able to buy clothes, find a job and make plans. For the first time since getting married, she was free to make her own future.

She'd just finished getting dressed when there was a tap on the door.

'Come in,' she called.

The door opened and Alison stuck her head round. 'Morning! I was thinking that maybe we should go shopping to pick up some stuff for you. What do you say?'

Sally thought about how little money she had. She needed to get a job, but couldn't do that without first buying some new clothes. She also had to buy a phone.

Alison must have seen her indecision because she came into the room and sat on the bed.

'Look, you don't have to tell me anything about your finances that you don't want to, but what if I lend you whatever you need and you pay me back when you can?'

'Oh, I couldn't do that,' Sally said.

'Why not? You'll need a change of clothes. You're shorter than me so mine won't fit you, or I'd let you rummage through my wardrobe. I can offer you a few tee-shirts, but my jeans and shoes would be useless.'

She reached over and grabbed Sally's arm. 'Come on, say yes. We could go into Oakham or Stamford, whichever you prefer. No, I've got a better idea. We can go to Peterborough. The Queensgate Centre has more shops than we could possibly need.'

Sally smiled at the thought of shopping without Gordon's

restrictions stopping her from going into certain shops or buying clothes he didn't like. But she didn't want to impose on Alison any more than she already had.

'Thank you. If you can lend me some money until my bank card arrives, that would be great. Unfortunately, I wasn't able to save much and it won't last forever, so I'll need to get a job. Are there any employment agencies in Oakham or Stamford?'

'Of course there are,' Alison said, 'but you're not going to them today, even if they were open on a Saturday, which they might not be. We're going out purely for pleasure.' She grinned. 'Come downstairs when you're ready. We'll have some breakfast and then head out.'

Alison hesitated. 'Uncle Peter comes over to be with Dad if I need to go out. He'll be here later.' She shrugged. 'He can be spiteful. Don't let him get to you. Believe me, he'll do his best to upset you.'

'Not one of your favourite people?'

Alison shuddered. 'No, he isn't.'

She walked over and opened the door, but then looked back. 'I thought I heard you cry out this morning. I don't want to pry, but if you need to offload, I'm here to listen.'

She went out and closed the door behind her. Sally sat on the bed and fought against the tears that threatened to fall, partly because of the wretched situation she found herself in and partly because of the gratitude she felt towards Alison. Once she had control of her emotions, she stood up. Breakfast and then a shopping trip. She couldn't wait.

Sally approached the wide marble staircase and looked down. How on earth had she survived that fall? All she could see were unyielding solid-looking steps leading down to an unforgiving tiled floor with a few scatter rugs, but at the base of the stairs where she must have landed there was nothing to soften the impact. Maybe there had been more rugs back then.

She went down, clinging to the handrail while telling herself she was stupid to do so. She was no longer a child likely to trip. She was a grown woman. Her pep talk didn't make her feel any more secure and she was relieved when she reached the downstairs hall. She looked around. It was vast. On one side a small side table held a fabulous flower arrangement. Directly opposite, on the other side, was another small table, this time showcasing a statue of a horse in motion. Sally walked over, fascinated by the fact that the bulk of the statue was balanced on one slender leg. The skill of the artist was apparent in the horse's muscles and facial details.

The front door opened, and she turned to see a man come in. He looked across at her.

'You!' he said. 'What the hell are you doing here?'

The man was uncannily like her father, but he had a more aware expression and looked much younger. Even if Alison hadn't warned her, she would have easily guessed who he was. However, unlike her father the night before when he'd thought she was her mother, there was no affection in this man's voice. Maybe he'd disliked Maggie.

'I'm Sally,' she said.

'I know who you are. You look even more like your mother than you used to. You are *almost* the image of her, but not quite so beautiful. You have the same dark hair and Elizabeth Taylor violet eyes, but you've always lacked something of her charm, even as a child. But I repeat, what are you doing here?'

41

'Alison invited me to stay for a while.'

'I'm sure she did,' he said in a low voice, sounding anything but pleased about it.

He walked across the hall and stood next to her, running his fingers over the horse's back.

'It's exquisite, isn't it?' Turning to face her, he frowned. 'Champion was your mother's horse. John commissioned the bronze as an anniversary surprise, but she was more than a little ungrateful because she left him the month after he gave it to her.' He laughed. 'You haven't a clue who I am, have you?'

Sally returned the frown.

'Alison told me you're Uncle Peter. You look so much like my father, but it's strange . . . I don't remember you.'

He shrugged. 'Please don't call me uncle. It makes me feel a zillion years old.'

'What should I call you?' Sally asked.

'You can call me Peter.'

'Do you live here?'

He shook his head. 'No. Alison wouldn't like that at all. Neither would John. At least, he wouldn't when his mind is okay. When he's off with the fairies then he doesn't care one way or the other.' Peter finally smiled. 'Let's go and see what Alison has rustled up for breakfast, shall we? She called me this morning and said she needed me to watch John, but she didn't mention you. She also said your father is in one of his happy moods, so we should be okay for the time being. If he comes back to the present, we might both be thrown out. Which might not be a bad thing for you.'

'What do you mean?'

He opened his mouth to answer, then shrugged. 'How much of your childhood do you remember?'

Sally shook her head. 'Very little.'

'Really? I wonder if you're telling the truth.'

Deciding to ignore his cryptic comments, Sally smiled. Not knowing how much influence he might have, she couldn't afford to antagonise him.

'As I said, I don't remember you.'

'I'm surprised. I was often in the house when your mother was alive. In fact, I was one of her many admirers. Of course, after you came out of hospital, you moved away to live with your grandmother, so I never saw you again.'

He hesitated and Sally thought he seemed to be weighing his words before speaking.

'You're not welcome here,' he said, quiet and menacing. 'There's no place for you in this house.'

Feeling as if the ground had shifted beneath her feet, Sally struggled for the right words. 'Why? Wh—What do you mean?'

He took a step forward, seeming to tower over her. 'I'll tell you—' he broke off as the kitchen door opened.

'Maggie!'

Sally looked over to see her father standing in the open doorway. Before she could answer, Alison appeared behind him.

'That's not Maggie, Dad. It's Sally. She's come to spend a few days with us. You saw her last night, remember?'

'Not Maggie?' Sally watched in horror as tears slid down his face. 'Not Maggie?'

'No, Dad. Not Maggie. Peter, would you help Dad upstairs

please? He's finished his breakfast and could do with some rest now.'

'Come on, John,' Peter said, walking across the hall and taking his brother's arm. At the foot of the stairs, he turned to Sally and hissed, 'Get out! You're not wanted here!'

Chapter Six

Sally waited until Peter and her father were well on the way up the staircase before crossing the hall and going into the kitchen. Alison was busy at the Aga, but turned around as she came in.

'Sit wherever you like, Sally. I'm just finishing up the scrambled eggs. Help yourself to cereal and toast.'

'Should we wait for Peter?' she asked.

'No need. I'll make some fresh eggs for him if he doesn't come straight down. Sometimes Dad is easy to manage, but at others he can be difficult, and it takes more time to get him settled.'

Sally reached for a cereal bowl and filled it, wondering if she should tell Alison what Peter had said. Deciding she shouldn't keep anything from her, she waited until Alison had finished at the Aga.

Her sister put a bowl of scrambled eggs onto the table. 'Sorry, it's a bit of a basic breakfast.' She looked across the table. 'Everything okay, Sally? You look concerned.'

'It's something Peter said about my being here.'

'What did he say?'

'Just that I should leave. He said I wasn't wanted, but he didn't say why. I'm guessing it's because I might be upsetting our father. I know I look so much like my mother.'

'Peter can mind his own business,' Alison said with more force than Sally expected.

'He seems to have taken a dislike to me. He was quite adamant. He made me feel like an intruder.'

'He's a nasty, spiteful man, always interfering. I want you to stay, and as I'm the one who takes care of Dad, I have the final word.' She smiled. 'Peter isn't here that often. I called him this morning to say I would be going out and needed him to Dad-sit. When I need to go out for any length of time he comes over and stays with Dad until I get back.' She shrugged. 'But we don't get on most of the time, so I only ask him when I really have to, like today.'

Sally smiled. 'I'm sorry to be causing so much trouble for you.'

'You kidding? Having you here feels like a dream come true, trust me. I just wish I'd been able to lay on a celebration breakfast to give you a proper welcome. Dad and I eat very simply most days.'

Sally looked across the table that seemed to be laden with enough food to feed an army. If this was simple, how would Alison view the way she and Gordon used to shop? He would never allow her to bring home anything that he didn't con-sider essential.

'John has settled down to watch one of his recorded televi-sion shows,' Peter said, coming into the kitchen and sitting at the table. He frowned at Sally as he reached for the bowl of eggs. 'How long are you planning to remain?'

'Peter, enough!' Alison said. 'Ignore him, Sally. He has no say about what happens in this house.'

Sally looked from one to the other. From the looks on both faces, it seemed as though there was a long-standing battle taking place. Alison was the first to look away.

'Just remember, Alison,' Peter said. 'Everything that takes place here is my business, and you, of all people, cannot afford to forget that.'

There was something in the way he said the words that made Sally glance up from the eggs on her plate. Alison looked scared and as if she wanted to say something, but she must have caught Sally's concern, because she smiled before turning back to Peter.

'Let's keep things civil, shall we?'

'Of course,' he said, turning away from Alison. 'Tell me, Sally, how did you get those dreadful bruises?'

Sally instinctively put her hand up to her face, annoyed that she must have missed a spot when she'd used the make-up Alison had donated.

Peter studied her face. 'Oh, you have bruises there as well? I hadn't spotted those, but now you've pointed them out I can see them. I was asking about the dark marks just above your wrist.'

Sally looked at her arms and saw the bruises left by Gordon's fingers when he'd gripped her the night before. Was it really only last night? So much seemed to have happened since. Before she could answer, Alison stepped in.

'Really, Peter, they are not questions you should be asking. All you need to know is that Sally needs a safe haven. I've told her she can stay as long as she wants.'

Peter frowned. 'A safe haven? Here? Maybe John will have one of his rational moments and remember he's still the owner of the house and not you, Alison.' He shrugged as a flush stained Alison's face. 'I really don't feel Sally should stay if John doesn't want her here.'

Sally's mild feeling of dislike morphed into something much stronger as Peter turned to her.

'Do you honestly remember nothing of your childhood here, Sally? You really were an inquisitive little thing. Always into places where you had no right to be. Isn't that right, Alison? Annoying little monkey, wasn't she? Poking and prying? No secrets when Snoopy was around. Did you know that's what Alison used to call you?'

Alison stood up. 'I was fourteen to her seven, Peter, of course I called her names. Ignore him, Sally. Shall we go and enjoy ourselves?'

Sally pushed her plate to one side. 'Yes, I'd love to, but let's clear the table first.'

'No, you can leave that to me. You go upstairs and grab your things.'

Sally ignored her and started collecting the plates together. 'I'm not going to let you wait on me hand and foot.'

As she spoke, Peter threw his napkin on the table, got up and left the room without another word.

Alison sighed as the door closed behind him.

'Was he deliberately trying to upset you?' Sally asked.

Alison nodded. 'He does that sometimes. He likes to wind people up. If you let him get inside your head, he'll drive you nuts. He knows that I don't like asking him over, but I need him to help me when Dad gets too aggressive to cope with on my own. You haven't seen the worst of his behaviour yet. When you do, you'll understand more.'

She turned to stack the dishwasher, leaving Sally wondering which of the two brothers she meant regarding the bad behaviour – Peter or her father.

Chapter Seven

Sally clutched the armrest as Alison took yet another bend far too fast. From the moment they'd set out Sally's stomach had been churning. A couple of times she'd not been able to hold back a gasp of fear as Alison had overtaken another car on one of the twisty country roads. She'd laughed at Sally's reaction, telling her she knew the roads too well for them to be in any danger, but Sally wasn't so sure. By the time they reached the Queensgate Shopping Centre in Peterborough Sally felt she'd survived enough near-death experiences to last her a lifetime.

'Do you drive?' Alison asked as she manoeuvred the car into a parking space.

Sally shook her head, too embarrassed to explain that Gordon had never allowed her to take lessons.

Alison nodded, as if she'd suspected as much. 'That's why you reacted as you did. Don't worry. We'll be fine.'

Sally smiled, not trusting herself to say the right thing when her mind was yelling at her to tell Alison exactly how unsafe she'd felt, especially when other drivers had been hooting at Alison, to show their displeasure when she cut them up.

As they walked from the car park to the centre's entrance, Sally's spirits rose. At last, she could buy some clothes without Gordon watching her every move and accusing her of choosing clothes to attract other men.

'Let's find a cash machine first, so that I can draw out some money for you,' Alison said.

Sally started to speak, but Alison held up her hand. 'We've already discussed this. You can pay me back later. Okay?'

Sally nodded. 'Okay – and thank you.'

They entered the shopping area and Sally gasped. She'd never been allowed inside one of these and was astounded at just how many shops there were on different levels. All her shopping had been done in local stores where Gordon felt comfortable and could control her choices.

'What do you want to do, Sally? Shall we split up or would you rather I came round with you?'

The thought of wandering from place to place on her own was too precious to give up easily, but she didn't want to offend Alison. Fortunately, she didn't need to worry.

'Tell you what,' Alison said. 'After we draw out the cash, why don't you have a good look round and we can meet up back in this spot in a couple of hours? Then we can find somewhere nice for lunch and, if you want or need my help afterwards, I'll come round with you. How does that sound?'

Like heaven, Sally thought.

'That would be great,' she said. She looked at her watch. 'Shall we say back here at one?'

Alison nodded. 'There are boards up all over the place saying what shops are on each level. Put my number into your phone. If you need me, you can just call and tell me where you are.'

'I don't have one, remember?' Sally said. 'Gordon smashed mine. Buying a new phone is top of my list.'

'Okay, I'll be here at one. Don't worry if you're late. I'm not going anywhere.'

She followed Alison as they walked to the cash machine on the ground floor.

Alison drew out five hundred pounds and handed it to Sally.

'That's far too much. I don't have anywhere near that amount in my bank account. I won't be able to repay you until I get a job.'

Alison laughed. 'That's fine. I don't need the money back anytime soon. Having you near is all I want.'

Sally thanked her with tears in her eyes and watched through a blur as Alison strode away. Whatever happened, she made a silent vow to somehow make it up to Alison for everything she'd done for her. For a moment, the tears threatened to fall. It had been such a long time since anyone had shown her so much kindness. It brought home just how much Gordon had controlled every aspect of her life. No friends, no family allowed into their private circle, but that was all in the past. She was going to be her own woman from now on. First things first, she thought. She would buy a cheap phone, then get on to the happy job of shopping for clothes and toiletries.

The two hours seemed to fly past. As Sally was carrying her many bags back to the meeting point, she stopped outside a sports clothing store. As a teenager living with Grandma Fletcher, and even during the first few months with Gordon, she'd been a keen runner. It'd been years since she'd put on running shoes, but the urge to go in was overwhelming. She looked at her watch and saw that she still had a quarter of an hour to spare. She went in and spent the next few minutes picking up tops and shorts at random and putting them into a basket.

Shoes were a different matter though. She remembered how particular her grandmother had been about her having the right footwear. Looking at the vast array of running shoes she had no idea where she should start. Luckily a saleslady came over and offered to help. Ten minutes later she was laden with two more bags to add to her collection.

As she left the shop, she glanced across the atrium and saw a woman staring at her. She'd spotted the same woman watching her a few times while she'd been shopping, but hadn't thought too much of it. Now, though, the woman was looking at her so pointedly from the other side of the mall, Sally wondered who she was.

She turned away and headed for the spot where she'd arranged to meet Alison. She only had a minute to spare when she saw her sister standing by the doorway. Sally sped up a bit so as not to keep Alison waiting.

'I'm sorry I'm late,' she said.

'You're not. I was early. Wow,' Alison said, smiling. 'We'd better put all your bags in the car before we go for something to eat.'

Sally nodded. 'Good idea. I don't fancy carrying these everywhere we go.'

They were about to enter the car park when a woman's voice rang out.

'Alison, how are you?'

Sally turned and saw it was the woman who'd been staring at her earlier.

'Hello, Mrs Carstairs,' Alison said. 'I'm fine, thank you. How are you?'

'Very well, my dear. I must say, I saw your young friend a little while ago and couldn't believe my eyes.' She smiled at Sally. 'I thought at first it was Maggie. You, my dear, must be her daughter. I'm afraid I cannot remember your name as it is so many years since I saw you as a child, but you are so much the image of Maggie that I know I'm not mistaken. Are you staying with Alison and John?'

Sally smiled back. 'I am for the time being, but I'm not sure how long I'll be there.'

'Oh, my dear Alison, you must bring her for tea before she disappears once again.' She turned her penetrating gaze on Sally. 'I won't take no for an answer. I live right next door, so you won't have to risk your life by having to get into the car with Alison. You must have nerves of steel to be willing to let her drive you here.'

She laughed, but it sounded forced to Sally's ears.

'There's nothing wrong with my driving, Mrs Carstairs,' Alison said. Sally could hear the irritation in her voice.

Mrs Carstairs smiled and patted Alison's arm. 'No, my dear, nothing at all if you were on a racetrack. I hear you zooming along our country lanes and fear for any small animal who might get in your way. I prefer to drive at a much more sensible pace, but you young people are so foolhardy and believe you will live forever. I must be off. I'll let you know when to come for tea.'

Once she was out of earshot, Sally laughed. 'What an odd woman.'

Alison shook her head as they walked towards the car. 'Nosey old cow, I suppose she's harmless as far as I'm concerned, but *you* need to watch your step.'

'Me? Why? I've only just met her.'

'I forgot,' Alison said, clicking the key fob to open the car doors. 'You don't know who she is. Your mother was her husband's secretary. That's who your mother ran off with. She's been bitter ever since, so her super-friendly act is just that – an act.'

Sally was stunned. 'So why invite me to tea?'

Alison shrugged. 'Who knows? Maybe she thinks you're in touch with your mother and can tell her where she and Mr Carstairs are holed up.'

Sally swallowed a lump in her throat. 'She'd be out of luck. I haven't seen my mother since the day she left. I received birthday and Christmas cards with money inside every year until I left Cornwall after Grandma Fletcher died, but she never came to see me. The messages in the cards in the early years made me think she would come back one day, but after a while, I gave up hope of her ever coming to see me.'

They stood in silence beside Alison's car.

Alison touched Sally's arm. 'Oh, Sally,' she said. 'I'm sorry. I really didn't mean to rake up painful memories.'

Sally was glad when Alison turned to open the boot and couldn't see her face.

'I don't have any memories to rake up. I can barely

remember my mother. She chose to leave me behind, so I'm not going to waste my energy in getting upset over her. I gave up on that years ago. Shall we go and have some lunch?' she said, putting the last of her bags into the car. 'My treat.'

As they walked back into the shopping centre, Sally thought about what she'd said to Alison. She'd been lying when she said she'd given up on feeling anything regarding her mother. It still hurt that she'd been abandoned by both parents. She doubted if that pain would ever go away.

Chapter Eight

Monday 9th June

S ally woke on Monday morning wondering what time it
was. She'd meant to switch her phone on last night but
had forgotten to do it. It was a lowering thought that she had
no one to call, or a friend who would call her, so it didn't matter
that it was off. The only people she knew were her work col-
leagues and she'd never been allowed to get to know them
outside of the office. Maybe in this new life she was living
she'd be able to make friends.

She was relieved the weekend was over. It was draining
living in her father's house, even though Alison had gone out
of her way to make her feel welcome. Her father alternated
between believing she was her mother come back to him and
recognising her as his daughter and demanding to know
where she'd been hiding. Sally had spoken to Alison about it,
trying to reconcile the memory of him turning her away with
the man now angry with her because she hadn't kept in touch.

'I think it's best if you don't mention what happened when

you came here all those years ago,' Alison had said. 'He clearly doesn't remember it, or has somehow blocked it out. His illness is hard to understand, but I sometimes wonder if he had the first symptoms years ago, but we didn't realise what was going on.'

'He seemed focused enough back then, Alison. His words and actions were unequivocal.'

Alison sighed. 'I know. I remember. All I'm saying is that he's struggling with his memories, so it would be cruel to make him recall something he clearly wants to forget. Maybe he's ashamed of what he did.'

Sally nodded. 'There is that, but it's hard not to remind him when he gets so angry and accuses me of hiding away.'

Alison squeezed Sally's arm. 'Let it go. He can't help it.'

Sally smiled and promised to do her best.

Fortunately, after that conversation, most of the time their father seemed to be living in the past where he'd been happy with Maggie. The rest of the time he became so aggressive towards Sally, she feared upsetting him even more, and so she followed Alison's advice.

The previous afternoon, she had been sitting in the lounge trying to work out how she could stretch her meagre resources when he'd come in and seen her counting the notes she had left.

'Why did you leave me, Maggie? Did I not give you enough money to squander?'

Sally stood up as he came towards her waving his fist.

'Dad!' Alison shouted.

Sally jumped at her sister's stern voice. She'd been so taken up with her father's obvious distress, she hadn't realised Alison had followed their father into the lounge.

'Don't you dare interfere, Alison. You know what she did with that man. Don't pretend!'

'I don't know anything of the sort, Dad,' Alison said. 'I was just a child when Maggie left.'

He turned away from Alison and glared at Sally. 'I gave you everything, Maggie, and it still wasn't enough, was it, you bitch?'

Sally saw Alison move behind their father and inject something into his arm. He relaxed almost immediately.

'I think it's time for you to go and rest. Come on now, Dad,' Alison said. 'Let's go upstairs and we can talk about Maggie and how much you loved her.'

'I hated her.'

'Yes,' Alison said. 'We can talk about that as well.'

Sally was in awe over the ease with which Alison was able to guide him towards the door. When she came back down again a few minutes later, Sally commented on her expertise.

'I've been looking after Dad for so long now, it's second nature.'

'What was in that injection? It took effect almost instantaneously.'

'It's just a sedative I have to use when he gets agitated.'

'It's me, isn't it? I remind him too much of my mother. I should go. I upset him every time he lays eyes on me.'

'Try not to take it to heart,' Alison said. 'I have no idea what's going on in his head half the time. I wish I did. It would make my life so much easier.'

'Whatever the reason, my being here clearly upsets him, which must make everything harder for you. I should leave. I've worked out I have enough cash to spend a week in a cheap hotel in Peterborough while I job hunt. I think I should go tomorrow.'

'Rubbish!' Alison said. 'You're not going anywhere. I don't want you to. We've only just connected again. Don't worry about Dad. That injection will sedate him for a few hours. He'll be as right as rain when he comes round again.'

Sally was thankful that Alison had insisted on her staying because using the last of her money on hotel bills wouldn't have made sense.

That reminded her. She needed to call HR this morning and tell them she wouldn't be coming back. She owed it to the company to be honest about the reason why she couldn't give them a month's notice, but she would explain that she hadn't had a choice.

Getting a new job was priority number one. Even if she could drive, she couldn't commute from here to Nottingham. Learning to drive was something she intended to put right once she had a regular income, although that was still a long way off. But she was getting ahead of herself. She had to get a job and then somewhere to live before she could think about driving lessons.

She'd been stressing so much about her future, but one good thing about the weekend had been early Sunday morning when she'd gone out for a short run. She hadn't ventured far for two reasons: firstly, she didn't know the terrain, so she resolved to ask Alison for some advice. Secondly, she should have bought a running light to wear as it had still been dark when she'd set out. As it was, she'd walked cautiously along the narrow track connecting the drive to the country road.

As she'd stepped off her father's drive onto the track, she'd looked down the drive alongside his and realised that must lead to Mrs Carstairs' house. She was just about able to make out the building in the gloom. If anything, it looked as if it could be even bigger than her father's mansion.

Finally, Sally climbed out of bed and smiled at the clothes hanging from the wardrobe door handles. She'd been so excited at the thought of putting on new clothes for her trip into Peterborough to sign on at job agencies that she'd been unable to resist sorting out what to wear before going to sleep.

She headed for the bathroom. Today really felt like the first day of her new life.

Breakfast was a quieter affair than it had been on Saturday thanks to Peter not being there, but he was coming over later to be with John while they were in Peterborough.

Once again Alison had put on a fabulous spread.

'You have to let me help you with this, Alison. It's not right you doing it all.'

Alison laughed. 'No chance. This is my domain. I don't allow anyone to mess with my kitchen.'

Sally sat down and began buttering some toast. 'Have you always lived here with our father? Were you here when I lived here?'

Alison shook her head, her expression hardening. 'Ha! No, I wasn't as lucky as you were,' she said, and then took a moment to recompose herself, before continuing. 'I fluctuated between living here and living with my mother. It's a long, complicated story. I'll tell you about it one day. Today we have to get you into Peterborough.'

'I need to make a phone call before I go,' Sally said and explained about wanting to let her old company know why she had left without warning. 'I'm just hoping they won't give me a bad reference because of it.'

She finished her breakfast and headed upstairs to the bedroom she was beginning to think of as hers. Sitting on the bed, she switched on her phone and called her old office.

'Hi, could you please put me through to HR?'

After a few seconds, her call was connected.

'Brenda Massington here. How can I help you?'

'Brenda, it's me, Sally Watson.'

'Sally! I am so glad to hear from you. Are you okay?'

'I am. I'm sorry to let you know like this, but I won't be coming back.'

'I guessed as much. You've finally left your husband, haven't you?'

'I have, but how did you know?'

'Because he was here first thing this morning, raising hell and accusing everyone of hiding you from him. I had to call the police in the end as he wouldn't leave.'

'Oh God. I am so sorry.'

'Don't you worry about that, Sally. I'm just relieved to know you're not with him. Obviously, you will want your outstanding pay. Where should Accounts send it? Or shall I instruct them to pay it into the new bank account?'

'But I haven't worked off my notice period. I don't have any pay to come.'

'I've already cleared it with Accounts. You'll be paid your outstanding salary and holiday pay. Extenuating circumstances have been approved.'

Sally felt the tears welling up. 'I can't thank you enough, Brenda. Please have it paid into the new account. My bank card is in the top drawer of my desk. Please could you get it and send it to my sister's house?'

'Of course. What's the address?'

Sally gave her the details and ended the call. Thank goodness Brenda was on her side. At least she'd have a bit more money coming in. Without Brenda's advice and support she wouldn't have had any money squirrelled away and certainly wouldn't have thought of reaching out to Alison and asking for asylum.

After another hair-raising drive with Alison at the wheel, Sally only exhaled when Alison finally parked the car in the Queensgate Shopping Centre car park, thankful to have arrived in Peterborough in one piece.

'You've got the list of employment agencies and addresses?' she asked.

Sally nodded and got out of the car. All the agencies she had written down were within easy walking distance of the parked car.

Alison smiled at her across the roof of the car. 'I'm off to do some window shopping. Text me when you're on your way back and I'll meet you for coffee in that place where we had lunch on Saturday.'

'Sounds like a plan,' Sally said. 'Let's hope one of the agencies will have something for me. If I need to go for an interview, would you be able to take me? I hate being such a drain on you, but the sooner I get a job the sooner I'm out of your hair.'

Alison laughed. 'You're forgetting I don't want you to leave. In fact, if it was up to me, you wouldn't leave ever again. We need time to get to know each other.'

'We can still do that,' Sally said, 'but I must at least try to find a new job.'

Alison smiled. 'If you say so, but part of me hopes it will take a while. Off you go on your quest.'

Sally waved goodbye and headed for the first agency on her list.

Nearly two hours later, she texted Alison to say she was on her way back to the shopping centre and desperate for a coffee. Filling in the same information forms and giving the same answers to the same questions in four different places, only to be told there was nothing available at the moment, had been demoralising. Only the fifth place had offered a glimmer of hope that something might be coming up in the next few days.

Her phone pinged and she saw she had a reply from Alison.

Chatting to someone. Might be a bit late.

Sally shrugged. She might as well go to the restaurant and wait. Once inside the centre, she headed straight for the escalator and went up to the first floor. Only after she'd walked around the full level did she realise the restaurant must be on the ground floor. The place was so huge that she'd completely lost her bearings. As she walked to the escalator, she spotted Mrs Carstairs coming towards her. Remembering Alison's warning, Sally quickly changed direction. She could go to the next escalator and walk back once she was at ground floor level.

As she turned, she thought she saw Alison on the other side of the atrium, but knew she must be mistaken because the woman she saw was dressed in blue and Alison had been wearing a red jacket. Sally stopped and studied the woman. She really did look very much like her sister, but she could see now that she was much older.

Sally shrugged and continued on towards the escalator, amazed at how long it had taken to find her bearings. She hoped that she wasn't now keeping Alison waiting. She was almost at the escalator when she felt the strap of her new handbag being wrenched off her shoulder. Without thinking, she raced after the youth who'd taken it and launched herself at him.

She missed the jacket sleeve she'd been reaching for but managed to catch hold of the strap of her bag. Before she knew what was happening, the youth turned and shoved her away. She lost her balance, fell backwards and hit her head against the plate glass window of a shop.

Chapter Nine

Sally opened her eyes, trying to work out why she was surrounded by a sea of faces. Her head was thumping, and she couldn't think straight. As she moved, a sharp pain shot along her side. Gentle hands helped her to sit up. Groggily, she looked around and tried to focus. As her vision cleared, she recognised Alison's concerned face as one of those peering at her.

'Sally, can you hear me? Are you okay? Oh my God, you gave me such a fright. What happened? Can you hear me? You've probably got concussion. Should she go to hospital?'

Sally realised the last question was aimed at the kind-looking man with the gentle hands who'd helped her to sit up. He was dressed in some kind of uniform.

'I think it would be a good idea to get her checked over,' he said. 'She doesn't appear to have broken anything, but it won't hurt to be careful and get that bump on her head checked out.'

'Can you stand?' Alison asked.

Sally noticed Alison had two handbags.

'You got my bag back,' she said, wincing at the pain darting behind her eyes.

'I didn't,' Alison said. 'That young man over there is the one to thank. He not only rescued your bag, but he also held the youth who'd snatched it until the police arrived to arrest him.'

Sally looked across and saw the youth being held by two police officers. One of them came over.

'How long have I been out?' Sally asked.

'Not long, but I'd advise you to go straight to the hospital to get that bump checked out,' he said.

'I need to stand up.'

She climbed to her feet, helped by the nice man who she now saw was a security guard. 'Thank you. I'm sorry to have been so stupid.'

He smiled. 'Not at all. It's my job to look after people in the centre. Let's see if you can walk okay.'

As he held her arm and led her away from the crowd that had gathered around her, Sally caught a glimpse of a man standing on the far side of the mall. Gordon! But that wasn't possible. He didn't know where she was. She stumbled as she strained to look back in the direction where she'd seen the man and Alison's arm came round her waist to hold her up.

'Let's get you to the car,' she said. 'I'll drive you to A&E for a check-up. Even if you feel okay, you probably have concussion and should be examined.'

Sally nodded and then wished she hadn't. It felt as if a drum solo was being pounded out in her head. She looked all around the mall as she walked but couldn't see any sign of the man. It couldn't have been Gordon. Maybe she really was concussed.

'Who are you looking for?' Alison asked.

'I thought I saw Gordon, but I must have been wrong,' Sally said. 'He can't have any idea I've come to you. I never mentioned our family after we got married.'

'Why not?' Alison asked.

'Dad's rejection was too painful. I didn't want to think about it.'

'So you never told Gordon where we lived?'

'I put the address on the wedding invitation I sent to you and our father, but that was so long ago. I can't believe he'd remember. God, I hope not!'

'Dad never mentioned receiving the invitation. But let's not worry about that. We need to get you to the hospital. That's all that matters right now.'

Walking the distance to the car park felt like forever. Alison kept her arm around Sally's waist the entire time. Sally would have liked to pull away to see if she could manage, but didn't want to upset her sister.

As they reached the car, Alison finally let go of her and Sally gave a sigh of relief. She sank onto the car seat and pulled her legs inside.

Sally waited for Alison to get into the driver's seat and then carefully turned in her direction. The slightest movement made the pain in her head feel ten times worse. At least she'd come round this time, not like her childhood accident which had left her in a coma for weeks. Grandma Fletcher had never wanted to talk about that time, so she knew next to nothing about what had actually happened that day.

'Do you know who found me when I fell down the stairs as a child?'

Alison stopped with the key midway to unlocking the ignition. 'What on earth has made you think of that time?'

Sally shook her head and then wished she hadn't. 'It was you saying I might have concussion. I was thinking how lucky I was not to end up in a coma like before and it made me wonder who had found me.'

'It was me, and one hell of a fright you gave me. I'd just come in from the garden and found you at the bottom of the stairs. Do you really not remember?'

Sally shrugged. 'No. But getting that knock on my head and passing out made me think of how many blows to my head I must have had when I fell down the stairs back then. I've seen how hard the marble is and the floor is the same. It's a wonder I wasn't killed. How come I was all alone when it happened?'

Alison put the key in the lock and started the car. 'Yes, it is a wonder. That day was chaos. It was like Piccadilly Circus with everyone in and out. It was the day your mother ran off with Mr Carstairs.'

Sally nodded, looking down at her hands. 'That I remember. Was I chasing after her? Is that how I fell?' she asked.

Alison pulled out of the parking space and drove the car towards the exit.

'I really don't know. I'd only just been dumped back home yet again, my mother having decided she couldn't cope with me. There was so much shouting and people were having hysterics. My mother was the cause of most of the noise. She was having one of her breakdowns.'

'Your mother was there?'

Alison nodded, but kept her eyes on the road. 'Yes, she'd

brought me back to the house and insisted your mother look after me. You were too young to know what was going on, but just before your mother moved into the Rutland house, our father bought my mother a place in Peterborough for us, me and my mother, to live in. The only problem was that my mother was prone to fits of depression. I suppose now she would have been diagnosed as bipolar, but back then she didn't get the help she needed. When she was well, she'd insist she couldn't be without me and I had to live with her, but when she was unwell she'd drive to Rutland and dump me on Dad and your mother. Often, she'd hang around for hours yelling abuse at your mother for stealing her husband, until Dad would have to call a doctor to sedate her.'

Sally didn't know how to react to the image this conjured up. It seemed that Alison's mother had had extremely good reasons to dislike Maggie.

'How did my mother meet our father?' she asked.

Alison laughed. 'The same way she met Mr Carstairs. She was Dad's secretary until they married and then she stopped work for a couple of years after she had you. Then she started working for Mr Carstairs in his office in the grounds of their house, which was convenient because it was next door to our house. She spent most of her days over there.'

Sally was at a loss for words. It seemed her mother had broken up not only the Carstairs' marriage, but had also ousted her father's first wife. She shuddered, then realised Alison was still speaking.

'It must have been galling to Mrs Carstairs because it was so obvious they were having an affair right under her nose. That's why she was there that day as well. She had come over to try to find out if our father knew where Maggie and Mr Carstairs had gone, but Dad was away on what was supposed to be an extended business trip, so he didn't even know at that stage that they had run off together.'

'So your mother and Mrs Carstairs were both in the house when I fell?'

Alison didn't answer for a while. Sally wondered why she'd gone quiet, but then realised she was negotiating her way into Peterborough City Hospital. It wasn't until Alison had parked the car that she turned to face Sally.

'I can't remember where everyone was when I found you. It was a pretty upsetting day all round. My mother had been having hysterics because Dad wasn't there. Apparently, he had left early that morning to fly to France. She was screaming she couldn't cope with me and that it was all your mother's fault I was so out of control. I ran out into the garden to get away from everyone, especially my mother, who was making me feel like a burden she needed to offload. I hid in the boathouse. I don't know how long for. When I came back in you were lying at the foot of the stairs and I couldn't find anyone to help you until Peter turned up. Then, as I said, Mrs Carstairs arrived looking for Dad. She took charge and called for an ambulance. Peter followed the ambulance to the hospital and I stayed with Mrs Carstairs in her house until Peter came back.'

Sally felt that familiar sensation of being kicked in the stomach. 'My mother left me on the floor?'

Alison sighed. 'I can't answer that because I don't know exactly when you fell. By the time I came back in from the boathouse everyone had gone. My mother didn't bother to say goodbye to me. Even though she knew Dad was away, she still

71

left me.' She stopped and put her hand over her mouth, looking stricken. 'Oh God, Sally, I didn't mean to sound whiney. I know your mother left you behind that day, which was far worse than what I had to deal with.'

Sally shrugged. 'It's okay. I'm used to knowing my mother didn't want me. Did you live with Dad all the time after that?'

Alison laughed. 'If only! No, my mother came to take me away while you were in hospital, but she dumped me back again on a regular basis. When you came out of hospital you went off to live with your grandmother until she died, so you probably had a more stable upbringing than mine. Dad was away so much of the time, I was either with my mother or being looked after by a variety of women Dad hired. None of them lasted very long though once they realised Dad wasn't in the market for another wife. In truth, I probably had a really volatile upbringing, but I survived, as we all do.'

Sally wanted to ask questions but didn't feel now was the right time to discuss Alison's mother's illness.

'I've never thought about it before now,' Sally said, 'but you could be right about me having a better childhood than yours. My granny was a lovely person. Do you see much of your mother?' Sally asked, remembering the woman she'd seen who'd borne such a striking resemblance to her half-sister.

Alison nodded. 'Yes, quite a lot now that she's on the proper medication for her condition. In fact, I had coffee with her this morning. When you told me you were going to go to sign on at the job agencies I called her to see if she felt like meeting up. That's who I was with when I got your message to say you were on your way back. I didn't bring her to meet you because . . . well, because I didn't want to upset her. You really are the image of your mother and I wasn't sure what effect seeing you would have on her.'

The more Sally learned, the more she wished that she didn't look so much like Maggie. Had Gordon been right constantly accusing her of wanting to go off with another man? It seemed her mother had done it more than once. Was it in her genes? Sally wondered how long Maggie had stayed with Mr Carstairs before finding someone else's husband to seduce.

'Are you okay?' Alison asked. 'You looked as if you'd gone off into space for a moment there. Is your head hurting?'

'No, I'm fine,' Sally said, not wanting to cause a fuss, but wishing the pain in her head wasn't quite so agonising.

'You don't look it! Come on, let's get you checked out.'

As they walked to the A&E department, Sally wondered if her father had left her with her grandmother because he couldn't cope with such a young child on his own. In that case, why hadn't he hired a nanny to look after her as he had for Alison while she was living in the house? Or was it because she was too much of a reminder of what Maggie had done? Maybe, when Sally had turned up on his doorstep after Granny died, she'd looked so much like her mother he hadn't been able to cope with the memories it had stirred up for him. Maybe it wasn't that he hadn't wanted her, but more that he'd done what he believed was best all round. *Yeah, and if you believe that you'll start believing in the tooth fairy and Father Christmas*, Sally scolded herself.

She had barely sat down after giving her details to the receptionist when she heard her name being called out.

'Shall I come in with you?' Alison asked.

Sally smiled and shook her head. Alison had already done more than enough. She'd never be able to repay her kindness.

'No, it's not necessary. I feel fine now. Just a few aches and pains from where I made contact with that plate glass window.'

Finding out their father had cared enough to hire someone to look after Alison, but wouldn't do the same for her, had hurt more than she would have believed possible, but she shouldn't have been surprised. Every time he saw her, she reminded him of her mother so much that he appeared to suffer an unbearable sense of loss all over again.

Chapter Ten

Gordon sat in the car park of the Queensgate Centre and punched the steering wheel. He'd almost had her. Knowing she had nowhere else to go other than her family in Rutland, he'd raced there after that bitch at Sally's office had called the police. He'd got there just as Sally and the woman he presumed was her half-sister were driving away from the house. He'd followed them to the shopping centre, but couldn't find her inside.

Then she seemed to appear out of nowhere and he could only watch from the upper level as the crowd gathered round her after the kid had tried to snatch her bag. By the time he reached the lower floor, the crowd had grown, and he'd had to hang back until the police finally moved away from Sally. Then her sister had helped her out to the car park, and he hadn't been able to get to his own car before they drove off. Not that it mattered, he'd heard the woman say she was taking Sally to the hospital.

He only had to get over there and take Sally home, then life could get back to normal. Gordon thought of the beatings he'd given his first wife which should have tamed her, but she'd fought back, the bitch. He'd come home from work one day to find she'd run away again. Tracking her down that final time had been hard, but he'd done it. He hadn't meant to kill her but he'd been so angry he'd lost control. Her body now lay submerged under a layer of peat on Fox Tor Mires.

He'd been beside himself with rage and grief after losing her. But then he'd moved to Cornwall and met Sally.

Sweet young Sally had looked on him as her knight in shining armour. She'd adored him and he'd adored her. At least, he had until he'd seen her flirting with the guy manning the checkout till in the supermarket. Sally had wept and promised she hadn't been flirting, but he'd watched her through the store's window as she'd laughed with the man while he was scanning her items.

It had taken a few hours teaching her a lesson before she'd finally admitted that she'd led the guy on. She should have known if she'd made a joke about something the man would take that as a sign she wanted more. He forgave her that first time because she was too young to understand that men will always know when a woman is sending 'come and get me' signals. Sally was so beautiful, all she had to do was smile at a man and they'd be sniffing round her like a dog who'd found a bitch on heat.

But she never learned. That's what drove him to hit her each time. She never learned not to smile, not to laugh, not to speak. She always made excuses. That the man had spoken to her first and she was just being polite by answering him, but if she hadn't sent out a vibe showing she was easy then the man wouldn't have known to talk to her. If Sally had learned to be modest, keep her eyes down and not flirt, then he wouldn't have had to teach her the same lesson over and over again.

Gordon felt the rage building in his chest. He'd find her, take her home, teach her a lesson she'd never forget and then never let her out of his sight ever again. All he had to do now was drive over to the hospital and wait until she came out.

Chapter Eleven

Half an hour later, having been given masses of advice over what to do if she developed any of the symptoms described on the piece of paper the young doctor had given her, Sally went back to the waiting room to find Alison.

'I can go home,' she said, 'but I have to watch out for everything on this list.'

Alison stood up, looking concerned. 'Hey, how are you feeling? I'm glad they're not keeping you in. That way I can look after you. Come on, let's go home. I've had several WhatsApp messages from Peter complaining about how long we've been out. The last one came just a couple of minutes ago, even though I'd told him what had happened to you and where we were.'

Sally caught a note in Alison's voice that made her look closely at her sister's face. Did she imagine it, or did Alison sound scared? She was about to ask what Peter had written to cause that reaction when she heard the sound of an argument raging in the distance. The man's voice sounded so much like Gordon she turned in the direction of the sound, but the argument was taking place on the far side of the car park.

She must be imagining things. She was being ridiculous, she knew that; it couldn't possibly be Gordon. He had no idea where she was.

Sally tried to shake off the fear that he might have found her, but only Alison's presence enabled her to keep walking and not go over to make sure it really wasn't him.

'Did you hear that man shouting just now?'

'No, why do you ask?' Alison said as she opened the car door and helped Sally to climb inside.

'I must be imagining things. First I thought I saw Gordon at the shopping centre and just now I thought I heard his voice. Sorry, Alison, the knock on my head must have been harder than I'd realised. I'm hallucinating.'

'All the more reason to get you safely home. Buckle up!'

As they approached the road to Rutland Water, Alison turned to ask Sally once again if she felt well enough to walk unaided when they got home.

'Really, I'm fine,' she said, wishing Alison would concentrate on the road and stop glancing in her direction. 'I don't even have a headache any more, for which I am really thankful. For a while it felt as if someone was drilling into my skull.'

'I can imagine,' Alison said. 'When I saw the crowd around you, with you lying there as if dead, I thought I'd lost you again. This time for good.' She slowed down and turned the car onto the drive. 'Damn!'

'What is it?' Sally asked, realising the last word wasn't meant for her.

'Peter's car isn't here. He must have got fed up waiting for us and gone home. We'd better get inside in case Dad is having one of his turns.'

Alison had barely stopped the car before jumping out and running towards the front door. Sally climbed from the passenger seat and followed her inside, but turned back when she heard a car approaching. Peter's dark hatchback pulled into the drive. Sally didn't care for cars, but decided, when she eventually learned to drive, a small hatchback would probably be the best choice. On the other hand, Gordon always chose the latest version of his hatchback whenever he upgraded, and the last thing she'd want would be a constant reminder of the many times he'd verbally abused her while driving.

Peter stopped his car close behind Alison's, and Sally watched him get out, thinking how sullen he looked. She barely knew him but didn't like what she'd seen so far. When she moved into her own place, she would make sure to avoid him like the plague. She couldn't put her finger on why, but she felt as if he had something to hide, something she was certain she would one day remember from her childhood. He made her skin crawl.

'Oh, so you've finally decided to come back, have you? I've got better things to do with my time than waste it watching over my demented sibling.'

Before Sally could answer, Alison appeared at the front door.

'Peter, where were you? We agreed that Dad should never be left on his own. You locked him in his room. He was going frantic. Fortunately, I didn't have to sedate him.'

'Alison, you sedate the poor bastard every chance you get. He's probably got more sedative in him than blood these days. I was gone for a matter of minutes. I needed to go to the shop and, as you know, that means a car ride to get there.'

'What was so important it couldn't wait until we got back?'

'My needs are none of your concern, Alison. You can't control me, so don't think you can.'

Sally saw a deep flush rise up Alison's throat and wash over her face.

Feeling guilty over causing the argument, Sally stepped forward. 'I'm sorry. Don't blame Alison. It was my stupid fault for not taking better care of myself. I got mugged.'

Peter shrugged. 'Don't think that throwing yourself in as the sacrificial lamb will carve you a place in this family. The sooner you leave, the better for everyone,' he said.

'Why are you so determined to get rid of me?' Sally asked, wishing her head didn't ache so much, making it impossible for her to gather her thoughts.

'Because you don't belong here and never will.'

'Leave her alone,' Alison said.

Peter glared at her. 'You look more like your crazy mother every day.' He turned to Sally, looking her up and down in a way that made her want to slap him. 'As for Sally, she's grown up to be the image of her mother, and we all know what sort of nature her good looks hid, don't we! I wonder how much you're like her in character.'

Sally stepped forward. 'Peter, you know nothing about me. Just because you had reason to hate my mother after what she did, that doesn't give you the right to speak to me like that.'

Sally stumbled back from the rage on his face.

'You don't know me, and you don't know this family either. You should get out while you still can.' He turned back to Alison. 'As for you, you should remember that I know all your guilty secrets and might just let them out one day.'

'Maggie? Maggie? Is that you? Don't go away and leave me again, Maggie. I love you.'

Sally turned to see her father stumbling down the last few stairs and crossing the hall towards her, his arms outstretched. Alison moved between them.

'No, Dad, that's not Maggie. She's gone and isn't coming back. Come on, I'll take you back to your room.' As she tried to turn him round, Alison flicked her hand at Sally, indicating she should leave the hall so that she would no longer be in her father's eyeline.

'I don't want to go to my room. I'm not a child. Where did she go?' he yelled.

Sally made it into the kitchen and peered out to see Alison gently urging their father back towards the stairs. Peter was standing near the front door and Sally wanted nothing more than to run out and slap the look from his face as he watched Alison grappling with his brother.

As she considered what to do next, the voices in the hall reached a crescendo.

'Maggie only wanted to love you, but you wouldn't let her. Your mother poisoned your mind against her.'

'Dad,' Alison's voice had taken on a pleading tone, 'that was all so long ago. Maggie has gone. She isn't coming back.'

'She wouldn't have left me. I know she wouldn't. I'd have killed her first. I didn't, did I? Did I kill her? Where did she go?'

Sally turned to look at Peter, not sure what to expect, but was stunned to see a look of horror on his face. Had her father murdered her mother? Did Peter know more about what had happened back then? She peered out into the hall to see that Alison had managed to manoeuvre their father to climb the stairs. Once he reached the top, Sally stepped out into the hall. Peter was still standing next to the open front door, staring up at Alison and his brother.

'I'm out of here. My advice to you is to leave and never come back, but I doubt you'll listen to me.'

'Why do you want me to go so badly?' Sally demanded. 'Why don't you want me here?'

He shrugged. 'All you need to know is that this is not your house. This is not your safe haven. You don't belong here. Why can't you simply accept that you're not wanted?'

He was gone before she could ask him anything more. She went back to the kitchen and sat at the oak table, waiting for Alison to come back. The voices from above had gradually become softer and then moved further away as Alison had convinced their father that a nap was exactly what he needed. Once again, Sally was in awe of the way Alison could manage their father, but it also made her wonder what Peter had meant about over-sedating him. Surely she could only give as much sedation as his doctor prescribed.

A few minutes later Alison came into the kitchen. Sally jumped up.

'Shall I make us some tea?' she asked.

Alison nodded. 'But to be honest, I need something a bit stronger. There's some brandy in the cupboard. Pour a slug in our cups. I take it Peter has gone?'

Sally filled the kettle and set it to boil and then turned back. She nodded. 'He's a strange one, isn't he?'

Alison frowned. 'He likes to cause trouble whenever he can.'

'Alison, Alison, where are you?' The yells from above sounded desperate.

'Shall I go up? Or would that upset him even more?' Sally asked, wishing she could do something to help instead of making the situation worse. 'I can try to calm him down.'

Alison shook her head and stood up. 'No, he might take you for Maggie again. I'll go and do it. You make the tea. Don't forget to add some brandy.'

By the time Alison returned Sally had everything ready on the table. She looked up as Alison came in.

'Was it something serious?' Sally asked.

'No, he wanted to watch television and couldn't find the remote. It was on the bedside table next to him, but that's the one place he didn't look.'

'Does that happen often?'

Alison shrugged. 'He forgets even what he's looking for sometimes, or can't see what's right in front of him because he gets confused. Anyway, he's calm enough for now so we can relax for a while. How are you feeling? Any headache or other bits hurting? Oh, you probably shouldn't be having brandy just in case you did have a concussion after your fall.'

Sally smiled. 'It's okay. I only put it in your cup.' She hesitated, but decided to ask anyway. 'Do you think my mother might be dead?'

'What on earth makes you ask that?' Alison said, her eyes fixed on her mug.

'It was partly our father asking if he had killed Maggie, but mainly the expression on Peter's face when he heard what Dad had said. He looked horrified, as if he might know something. Is it possible that Peter . . . no, I'm being stupid.'

'You think Peter hurt your mother?'

Sally nodded. 'Either that, or he thinks his brother did.'

84

'Well, Dad was away on business when your mother left, so it's highly unlikely he did anything to her. As for Peter, he adored your mother. Almost worshipped her, if I remember rightly, so I doubt he would want to hurt her either. Besides, she didn't leave on her own. She went with her lover. Sorry, Sally, I know it would almost be easier for you to take if she hadn't left of her own free will, but I don't think anything happened to her. Dad rants and raves, but although he sometimes asks if he killed her, it would have been impossible as he wasn't even in the country. Besides, didn't you say your mother sent you birthday and Christmas cards every year?'

'You're right,' Sally said. 'Of course you are, but the look on Peter's face was so stark.'

'Peter is many things, but I don't think murderer is one of them. If I could stop him coming over, I would, but he's the only other person that Dad will allow to stay with him. If it wasn't for Peter, I wouldn't be able to leave the house at all.'

'Can I ask you something? It's about Peter.'

Alison frowned, but nodded.

'Has Peter hurt you in some way?'

Alison appeared to freeze on the spot.

'What an odd question. Why are you asking me that?'

Sally wished she hadn't voiced her concern, but knew there was no going back now that she had.

'A few times you've had a strange expression on your face in response to things he's said to you.'

Alison shook her head. 'You're imagining things.'

Sally knew she wasn't, but didn't want to push Alison when she clearly didn't want to talk about it. Time to change the subject.

'I could stay with our father so that Peter didn't need to come over so often,' Sally said. 'That way you could get a few hours to yourself without having to call on him.'

Alison took a sip of her tea and sighed as she put the cup down. Sally could see there was something on her mind and waited to hear what it was.

'Don't take this the wrong way, but you look so much like your mother I don't think it's a good idea. You being here has stirred up all sorts of memories I thought Dad had long forgotten, but he's getting them muddled in his head. I don't know if you heard, but he accused me of not being nice to Maggie.'

Sally nodded. 'I couldn't help but overhear. He was yelling at you by that point.'

'Well,' Alison said, 'he certainly got the wrong end of that particular stick.'

'What do you mean?' Sally asked.

Alison picked up the brandy bottle and poured a drop more into her mug. 'He thinks I was unkind to Maggie, but he couldn't be further from the truth. I thought she was wonderful. She was everything my mother wasn't, and I was in awe of her. She was stunning to look at. Do you remember how beautiful she was? But it wasn't just that, she had this amazing presence, didn't she? If she was in the room then no one else stood a chance of being noticed, not just by men, but by other women as well. Everyone was mesmerised by her, including me. I tried everything to make her like me, including looking after you whenever she wanted to go off and do something. I was your regular babysitter during the times I was living here.'

'And did she?' Sally asked. 'Like you, I mean? I can't remember . . .'

Alison laughed. 'Not a bit. She made it quite clear that this was her house and she didn't want me in it. I was a burden that she had to put up with whenever my own mother lost her marbles.' She sighed. 'I'm sorry to have to say this, Sally, but although your mother was lovely on the outside, she was a mean bitch on the inside.'

Chapter Twelve

S ally would pay and pay dearly for what she'd put him through since she'd deserted him.

Slumping onto the sofa, his mind drifted to the accident at the hospital earlier that day. He'd just caught sight of Sally leaving with the same woman who'd taken her from the shopping centre and was turning his car in her direction when some stupid bitch driver had come out of nowhere. He hadn't had time to take any avoiding action before she'd driven into the side of his car.

To make it worse, *she'd* accused *him* of dangerous driving. *Him!* As if any woman could be trusted behind the wheel. She must have seen his car before she hit it, but did she try to avoid it? No! What's more, he was certain that Sally had looked over in his direction. She must have heard his voice, but had she come over to make sure he was okay? No! She'd carried on walking and ignored him. He could have been badly hurt for all she'd cared.

It was time for her to come home so that he could teach her a much-needed lesson.

Chapter Thirteen

Alison had insisted that Sally should rest, so she went up to her room and lay down on the bed, going over in her mind Alison's words about her mother. She desperately tried to remember what her mother had really been like, but could only recall a few instances and each time she searched in vain for a sense of warmth. She couldn't bring to mind any occasions when they might have been happy. A visit to a wildlife park when her father had also been there felt like a good memory. A circus outing, but this time just with her mother and some man she didn't know, didn't bring any feelings of happiness. There had been a trip on a boat along a river with both parents, but she couldn't recall which river or who else had been with them, just that she'd upset her mother in some way. She remembered her father holding her close against the rail as the boat moved and telling her everything would be okay. He pointed out something in the distance, but what it was or where they had been going, was beyond her recollection.

Even though she'd always resented Maggie for leaving her behind, until today she'd never had a sense that she was unkind, although what could be more unkind than to walk out on your child? Sally felt even more confused than she had on the day her father had sent her packing when she'd tried to return to Rutland after Grandma Fletcher's death. What was the truth about her parents? She tried to remember her mother loving her, but had she? She'd walked out and never come back. She recalled clearly her father telling her she wasn't welcome, but now he seemed even angrier with *her* for not keeping in touch with *him*.

As for Peter, she must have seen him when she was young, but had no recollection of him at all. He'd said that was down to her mother not liking him, but Sally wasn't sure she could trust a word he said. He gave her the creeps.

She sat up. Whatever the truth of the past, whether her mother had been a bitch to Alison or not, clearly Alison had felt unwanted. Sally wanted to make up for Alison's hurt. Her sister could easily have turned her away, but instead she had been the closest thing to a friend Sally had had since Gordon had come into her life.

Had it really been his voice she'd heard in the hospital car park? It had certainly sounded like him, but the man had been on the far side of the car park, heavily involved in an argument, so she couldn't be sure. Besides, how could he have known she was at the hospital? Unless the man she'd briefly glimpsed in the distance at the shopping centre had been Gordon and he'd followed them to the hospital? No, that didn't make sense. She'd been there for the best part of an hour. He wouldn't have waited outside and not come in. Unless he had and not seen her because she was in with the doctor. That was possible. On the other hand, maybe he'd waited outside so that he could follow Alison's car to see where they lived.

Enough! Gordon was in the past and she was not going to let him ruin the present. She got up and tested her balance. Her hip ached a bit from where she'd hit the ground, but not so much that she wouldn't be able to run. Her head was fine. Resolving to put Gordon out of her mind, she walked to the door. Maybe she should join a running club. She could get to know new people without Gordon accusing her of trying to seduce any of the men.

Wondering if Alison knew of a local club, Sally went downstairs to find her.

Alison was in the kitchen preparing dinner, but looked up and smiled as Sally came in.

'What are you doing downstairs? I thought I told you to go upstairs and rest,' she said, gently scolding Sally.

'You did, but I feel fine, so I thought I'd come down and help you get dinner ready.'

Alison laughed. 'Not a chance. This kitchen has been my domain for so many years now, I get edgy if anyone tries to do anything. If you're not going to rest, you just sit yourself down over there and chat to me while I get on with these vegetables.'

Sally sat down, wishing there was something she could do to ease the burden on Alison. It seemed as though she was so used to being the workhorse of the family that she didn't know how to let anyone help.

'When did you come here to live permanently?' Sally asked.

Alison turned from the range, frowning. 'Let me think. I started working for Dad not long before you came here after your grandmother died. What year was that?'

'She passed away at the end of 2002, early in November, so I must have come here later that month.'

Alison nodded. 'That's right. I'd only been living here a few weeks then.'

'What did you do in our father's business?'

'I worked as his private assistant. I loved being in the office and then having Dad to talk to about the business when he was here, which wasn't very often.'

'He still travelled abroad a lot then?'

Alison nodded. 'He did, but nowhere near as much. In fact, Peter took over a lot of the overseas aspect of the business. They were partners, you know.'

Sally shook her head. 'No, our father never spoke to me about his business whenever he came to visit me in Cornwall.'

'Sorry, I assumed you would know. Did your grandmother never speak about him?'

Sally shook her head. 'Not much. I've always thought Grandma Fletcher felt guilty because it was her daughter who'd caused so much anguish in the family.'

Alison reached out and gripped Sally's arm. 'I can understand that. I think I'd feel the same.'

'When did he sell the business?'

'It was just after his symptoms started. As soon as he was diagnosed, he put everything in place to make sure all went as he wished. While he still had control of all his faculties, he arranged for me to have power of attorney regarding his health.' She frowned. 'He should have signed for me to control his financial affairs as well – it would have made things much easier – but as I said, Dad and Peter were business partners, so it made sense at the time for Dad to put financial matters into his hands. Peter and I don't see eye to eye over money, but there's little I can do about it.'

'No, I guess not,' Sally said, feeling uncomfortable talking about money when she hadn't been part of the family for most of her life and wasn't in a position to contribute. Maybe that was why Peter was so keen to get her to leave.

Alison shrugged. 'As long as Peter signs off on all the bills for the house, we manage to get along. Anyway, let's not talk about any of that now. How are you feeling? That's a nasty bruise you have forming on your forehead.'

Sally felt a bubble of hysteria rising. The bruise was nothing compared to many others, much worse, that she'd needed to cover up over the years.

'I'm not feeling too bad at all. In fact, I think I need to do a bit more exercise. You aren't letting me help you and I feel I'm turning into an unfit blob. I was thinking of joining a running club. Is there one near here? Within walking distance, I mean.'

'Not that I know of, but then running isn't really my thing,' Alison said. 'I've seen plenty of people jogging around the perimeter of Rutland Water, though, so maybe there's a club on the other side of the reservoir. Why don't you have a look online while I finish up here? But don't think I'm going to allow you to go out running until I'm certain you're completely okay.' She grinned. 'This is your big sister talking.'

Sally laughed. 'I know, and it feels so good to have you taking care of me. Be careful or I might never move out.'

Alison waved a wooden spoon at Sally. 'That would suit me just fine. Now, go and have a look for a club. Dinner is going to be at least another half hour. Longer if we stand around chatting.'

Sally walked through to the study trying not to limp. Alison was right, she probably shouldn't run until her hip stopped hurting completely, but she could still find a club to join for when she did feel up to it. She had just powered up the laptop when she heard the front door open.

Alison must have heard it as well, because the next sound was her voice. 'What are you doing back again?' she said.

'I realised I forgot to make a transfer to settle the household accounts when I was here earlier,' Peter said. 'Where is Sally? She needs to get out of this house.'

'She's in the study. Leave her alone. You know I want her here.'

Peter's voice dropped so low Sally couldn't hear what he said next, but Alison's voice came through clearly.

'You wouldn't dare! You have more to lose than I do!'

'Get out of my way,' he said.

Knowing he would be coming to the study, Sally shut down the laptop and stood up. She didn't want to be told yet again that she should leave. Now that she knew he controlled the household funds, she felt even more of a financial burden. She got to the doorway just as he reached it from the other side.

'I hope I haven't interrupted you,' he said.

'I'd finished what I was doing,' Sally lied, waiting for him to move out of the doorway. He stood his ground.

'I need to go and help Alison,' she said, hoping that would be enough for him to allow her to leave.

'As if Alison would allow you or anyone else into her hallowed domain.'

He stood to one side, giving her enough space to pass.

'Tell Alison I'll be in to see her shortly. She's been rather extravagant recently. I'll have to get her to rein in her spending.'

Once through the doorway, Sally had to force herself not to run to the kitchen. Was that last comment aimed at her? Surely her being here wasn't adding that much to the cost of running the house.

Alison glanced up as Sally entered the kitchen.

'I can see by the look on your face that Peter has been his usual self. What did he say to upset you?'

'Nothing! I mean nothing I could complain about. It's the way he speaks rather than the words used. Do you know what I mean?'

Alison laughed, but Sally couldn't hear any humour in the sound. 'Don't I just?' Alison asked. 'I've been putting up with his comments and snide remarks for years. He knows exactly how to get under my skin and never misses an opportunity.'

'Did you give Alison my message?' Peter's voice sounding directly behind her made Sally jump. 'How nervous you are,' he said, 'terrified of the slightest sound.'

Sally turned. 'I'm not, it's just that I didn't hear you come into the kitchen.'

'What message?' Alison asked.

'Just that you need to cut back on your extravagant spending, Alison. Your father's accounts are taking too much of a hit. We're in a recession, in case you hadn't realised, and the investments are not bringing in as much as they were.'

'I'm not spending any more than usual,' Alison said.

'Oh, but you are! Now that Sally is here, all the bills, including shopping, have gone up.'

95

Alison must have seen how Sally was feeling because she pointed the kitchen knife she was clutching at Peter.

'Pack that up,' she said. 'Sally is welcome to stay for as long as she wishes. If Dad were in full control of his faculties, he'd say the same. There's enough money to go round.'

Sally wished she were anywhere other than in the kitchen. Peter's words had hit home hard. If she were going to stay here, she needed to get a job so that she could contribute to the household expenses. She looked up and saw Peter staring at her. He must have intended to make her feel bad. Well, he'd certainly succeeded.

'I don't know you very well, Peter,' Sally said, 'but you seem to take great delight in upsetting people. What a sad life you must live.'

His face darkened and Sally instinctively took a step back as his fists clenched. Then, as suddenly as it had appeared, the anger left his face.

'Well done, Sally. A direct hit. Maybe there's more fight in you than I'd given you credit for. You're going to need it. Is that how your pretty face got ruined? Did you fight back? Does that make you feel strong? You're not! Pack your bags and get out. No one wants you in this house.'

Chapter Fourteen

'Peter! That's enough! You might not want Sally to stay, but I do, and you know it.'

Sally wanted to reach out and slap Peter's face, but found a way to hold back. She was astounded by how much rage filled her body. Whenever Gordon had attacked her all she'd wanted to do was hide, but the goading from Peter had made her want to hurt him. But this wasn't who she was. She'd lived with violence for so long, no way was she going to be the one dishing it out.

Peter must have read the indecision on her face because he smiled.

'For the first time I saw a family likeness between you and Alison. You have more self-control, but when you glared at me just now you looked exactly like your big sister.'

'Give it a rest, Peter,' Alison said. 'You've had your fun. Now go home.'

Peter turned his attention to Alison. 'She may have looked like you briefly in her rage, but if I were writing a pantomime, you'd be the ugly sister. I can't believe there's only seven years between you.'

'Leave her alone,' Sally said, turning towards the doorway as a shadow darkened it. Her father had shuffled into view.

He moved so quickly that Sally didn't have chance to avoid his hands as he grabbed her arms and began shaking her violently.

'Why have you come back to haunt me? Haven't I suffered enough?'

Suddenly his grip on her loosened and Sally was able to draw in a gasping breath. Alison had hold of their father and was guiding him to one of the chairs around the table.

'Peter, don't just stand there, take this thing away,' Alison ordered.

Sally realised Alison still had a syringe in her hand. She must have sedated their father while he'd been shaking Sally.

Peter took the syringe and put it on the kitchen work surface.

'Come on, John,' he said, 'let's get you up to bed.'

Alison moved forward to help, but Peter waved her back.

'Not you,' he said. 'You've done more than enough.'

'Don't be stupid, Peter,' Alison said. 'You can't manage him on his own when he's been sedated. Take his other arm.'

Sally watched helplessly as Alison and Peter manoeuvred her father upright and half walked, half dragged him into the hall.

'Let's lay him down on one of the sofas in the drawing room,' she heard Alison say.

After a few minutes, fierce whispers drifted across from the front door.

'She needs to leave,' Peter hissed.

'No! She stays.'

'I'll make her go,' Peter said.

'You leave her alone,' Alison said. 'Don't forget I have the evidence to get you put away for a long, long time.'

'So you keep telling me, but you never produce it, do you? You want to watch what you say, Alison. You might find it gets dangerous if you're anywhere alone.'

'Are you threatening me?'

Sally heard Peter laugh. 'If that's how you want to take it, then yes.'

Then the door slammed shut and a few moments later Alison came back into the kitchen.

'Dad will be out for at least an hour, so we might just as well eat,' she said.

'I couldn't help but overhear what Peter said. He really wants me out, doesn't he?'

'We don't need to take any notice of anything he has to say.'

'Is that because of the evidence you have?'

Alison looked shaken. 'What evidence? What are you talking about?'

Sally wished she'd kept quiet, but had to go on now she'd shown she'd been eavesdropping. 'I heard him threaten you and you telling him you had evidence.'

'I don't know what you're talking about, Sally. You must have misheard.'

Alison looked close to collapse. Clearly Peter's words had really hit home and now Sally was making the situation worse.

'I'm sorry, Alison. You're right. I must have misheard. Look, I'm adding to your troubles,' Sally said. 'Clearly, I'm causing Dad a lot of grief and, as Peter pointed out, adding to the cost of running the house. I should leave, but at the moment I just don't have enough money to stay anywhere else.'

Alison sat down. 'I want you to stay,' she said. 'I need you to stay. Having you here is such a comfort. If you leave me, then I'll be back to having no one to talk to about Dad. No one understands what it's like living with him.'

Sally slumped into a chair opposite Alison.

'I want to help you, but it seems as if I'm doing more harm than good. If you could lend me the money, I could move somewhere nearby, so that you could call on me whenever you needed a break. If Dad was sedated, then I could come over and stay with him.'

Alison sighed. 'If that's what you really want, then I will lend you the money, but please, I'm begging you, please stay. You don't know how much I need you here. Why don't you think it over before making a decision?'

Sally nodded. 'Whatever is best for you,' she said. 'I'll stay for a bit longer. Thank you for giving me this safe haven. I just wish I could do things for you in return. There must be something that would make your life easier, or make it more enjoyable, even in a small way.'

'No problem!' Alison said and grinned. 'If you want to give me a treat, you can take me out to lunch with your first pay packet. For now, let's eat. I'm starving.'

Sally realised she hadn't checked her phone to see if any of the job agencies had sent her a message regarding an interview. Unless she got a job, she'd never be able to leave. Even with the money in her secret account, she didn't have enough for a month's rent, far less a deposit and everything else she would need to pay for.

Peter was out of luck if he thought he could force her out.

Later that night, just as she was drifting off to sleep, she recalled the conversations she'd overheard. Alison had definitely mentioned evidence and Peter had sounded furious. It seemed there were family secrets that went back many years.

What did Alison know about Peter that could get him locked away for the rest of his life?

Chapter Fifteen

Wednesday 11th June

Sally sat on the edge of the bed and picked up her phone. She smiled as she checked for messages, knowing there wouldn't be any threats from Gordon waiting to ambush her. She'd constantly had to check in with Gordon while at work so that he could be certain of where she was at all times.

Gordon had only allowed her to use her phone for calls and messages from him. The only reason she'd had WhatsApp on the phone he'd smashed had been because she'd had to admit to the other girls in the office she didn't have it installed when they'd wanted to set up the group chat for nights out. Carly had helped her download it and then added her to the group. Knowing she couldn't go out with them, she had never even looked at the app, but Gordon must have been checking it every time she left her phone with him while she was in the supermarket. In some ways, she was glad he'd found the group chat. If he hadn't, would she still have left that night?

No, she wouldn't have run out without money or letting Alison know she was on her way. She'd planned to leave once she had built up a bit more cash to cover her living expenses for the first couple of months. She'd only intended to stay with Alison for a few days at most. But after Gordon had attacked her with the same ferocity that had landed her in hospital more than once before, she'd had no choice but to leave.

Although finding the WhatsApp group chat was why he'd gone for her that evening, there probably would have been something else to fire him up. He never seemed to lack a reason to attack her.

Shuddering, she stood up. Dealing with Gordon's rages was all in the past. Whether she stayed here or moved to a place of her own, her marriage was over. She was never going back to a life of constant fear.

Searching through her handbag, she found the cards for the job agencies she'd signed up with. Feeling like she'd won the lottery just by being free, Sally called each of the agencies, hoping at least one of them would have an interview to offer her. The first three had nothing, but there was better news on her fourth call.

'Hi, thanks for checking in, Sally,' Carola from Rutland Careers said. 'I was just about to call you to let you know I've set up an interview for you next week. It's a bookkeeping position in Oakham, well within your capabilities. In fact, you're more than over qualified for it, but as there is so little on offer at the moment, I thought you might want to go along.'

'Carola, that's wonderful,' Sally said. 'Hold on while I grab a pen to take down the details.'

'Do you have WhatsApp?' Carola asked. 'If you do, I can

send you all the necessary information so that you have it on your phone.'

'I do! That would be great, thanks,' Sally said, smiling as she realised she was now able to use the app without fear.

Sally closed the call and slipped the phone into the back pocket of her jeans, thankful that she'd been able to buy clothes suitable for an interview. She couldn't wait to tell Alison the good news and almost skipped from the room. Life was really looking up.

She went downstairs, hearing her father's voice as she crossed the hall towards the kitchen. Hesitating, she thought about going back upstairs, but as she turned to remount the stairs the front door opened and Peter came in.

'Still here, Sally? You really should take my advice and run. You never know what might happen to you if you stay.'

As always, Sally had no idea how to respond to Peter's words. She felt the colour rush into her face, making her feel like a gauche schoolgirl.

'Are you threatening me?' she stammered. 'It won't work. I'm not going anywhere.'

Peter scowled. 'That's up to you, but don't say I didn't warn you.' He stopped as John's voice piped up. 'Why don't we go and see what John has to say? Don't you want to spend time with your father? How mean of you when you're taking advantage of his hospitality. As you're so determined to stay, the very least you can do is go in the kitchen and wish him a good morning.'

As he said the words he lifted his elbow, clearly expecting her to take it and walk with him. Sally ignored the gesture and strode ahead.

She heard him chuckling behind her. 'So easy to wind up, Sally. Where's the sport in it for me if you don't fight back?'

Sally had barely made it to the kitchen door when the front door bell pealed across the hall. Her stomach heaved and she nearly threw up when she heard Gordon's voice calling from outside.

Chapter Sixteen

'I know you're in there, Sally. Come out. Please. I just want you to come home.'

The doorbell pealed again and again as Alison came out of the kitchen, closing the door behind her.

'What the hell is going on?' she asked. 'Why haven't you answered the door?'

'It's my husband,' Sally said. 'I don't know how he's done it, but he's found me.'

'Shall I let him in?' Peter said. 'I'm sure between us all we can calm the beast. Or maybe you would be better off returning home with him. He doesn't sound that ferocious, does he? In fact, he sounds more like a loving pussycat than a savage tiger.'

'No!' Sally said, louder than she'd intended. 'I mean, no, please don't let him in.'

'Peter,' Alison said. 'Go into the kitchen and see if you can keep Dad calm. If necessary, there's a sedative in the cupboard in the larder. Sally, you don't have to be here. I'll deal with your husband.'

'You can't!' Sally said. 'You don't know what he's like. He'll come across all sweet and charming at first, but he can turn in an instant. He might hurt you.'

Alison laughed. 'He won't lay a finger on me. Bullies only attack people who show fear. I'm not scared of some loud-mouth lout who thinks he can throw his weight around. Sally, go into the drawing room. You're safe here with us. We won't let him hurt you, but I don't think it's a good idea for him to see you. That might be too much for him to cope with.'

'Sally! Sally, open the door. I need to see you.'

'You're not going to let him come in, are you?' Sally said as Alison walked towards the door. 'Please don't,' she pleaded.

'He won't cross the threshold, I promise. I'm just going to open the door on the chain. Go on, now, go!'

Sally ran to the drawing room and closed the door, pressing her ear to it so that she could hear if she needed a more secure hiding place. If only Alison would listen to her. It was crazy to open the door, even with the chain on. There was no telling what Gordon would do in one of his rages.

But the voice she heard wasn't Gordon's angry tone. It was Gordon at his charming best.

'Hello, you must be Sally's sister. I'm so pleased you took her in. She's been troubled recently and I've been so worried about her since she disappeared.'

'You don't have to worry,' Sally heard Alison say. 'She's safe here with us.'

'May I come in? I'd like to see her.'

'Not at the moment. She's resting upstairs. I can tell her you were here though. Maybe we could arrange for the two of you to meet somewhere nearby.'

'Thank you,' Gordon said. 'That would be wonderful, but if you could just ask her to come outside for a few minutes, that would be even better. I've driven all the way from Nottingham to be here.'

'I understand. I'm sure she'll want to meet up with you, maybe we can sort something out for tomorrow. By the way, how did you know she was here?'

Sally heard Gordon chuckle. 'It wasn't difficult to work out. She told me about her family when we were first together. When she ran off . . . When she had her funny turn and disappeared, I was frantic, but then I remembered she had family in this area. I knew her maiden name, so it wasn't difficult to look you up. You and your father are both on the electoral roll.'

'But you didn't come straight here?' Alison asked. 'She's been with us for a few days now.'

Again Sally heard that false laugh. 'I didn't want to bother you, so I waited until I saw you leave on Monday and followed your car to the shopping centre. I was about to reach out to Sally when that bastard tried to rob her. Then she was surrounded by people and I couldn't get close.'

'So Sally was right! She said she thought she'd seen you, but she was concussed so we thought she must have imagined it.'

'Was that why you took her to the hospital?'

This time Sally heard Alison laugh and her heart sank. Laughing at Gordon was never a good idea.

'Yes, that was why she went to the hospital. She heard your voice, you know. She was sure it was you yelling at someone, but I didn't believe her.'

'I was coming over to her when some stupid woman caused

108

our cars to collide. Look, all that has nothing to do with today. Please, I just want to see my wife. I love her and want her to come home.'

'I understand and I'm sure Sally will want to talk to you, but not today. Does she have your number? I'll get her to call you.'

Sally heard the chain rattle as Gordon's fist must have connected with the door.

'You stupid stuck-up bitch. Who the fuck do you think you are? Are you going to get Sally to come out or not?'

'Not!' Alison said, then Sally heard the front door slam.

Sally shivered in the drawing room as Gordon began banging furiously on the front door.

'Open this fucking door! I want my wife.'

'Peter! Peter! I need you!' Alison called.

Sally heard him come into the hall. 'John is getting very agitated in here,' he said. 'This is not good for him.'

'I know,' Alison said. 'Call the police. I doubt Sally's husband will leave of his own free will.'

Sally stood rooted to the spot listening to Gordon's ranting outside. She heard footsteps as Peter crossed the hall and went back into the kitchen, closing the door behind him. The drawing room door opened and Alison looked in.

'Sally, I think it's best if you go upstairs.'

The last thing she wanted to do was leave her sister to deal with Gordon, but Alison insisted.

'Go on, go!' Alison said. 'The sooner I deal with him the better. Our neighbour will be listening to the horrible man sounding off.'

Sally turned and ran to the top of the stairs. She then knelt down so that she could peer through the balustrade at the top. If Gordon tried to hurt Alison, no matter how scared she was, she'd go back down and fight to protect her sister.

She watched as Alison checked the chain on the door and opened it slightly before stepping back as Gordon's hand shot through the gap.

'Why don't you go home and wait for Sally to call you?' Alison asked. 'We've already established that she doesn't want to see you at the moment.'

'Open this fucking door!'

'I want you to leave our property,' Alison said.

Sally could see her sister was standing a safe distance from Gordon's outstretched hand, but she still feared for her safety. If the chain broke, Gordon would think nothing of flattening Alison to get to his wife.

'I want my wife. I'm not leaving without her. Tell that bitch to get out here now! We're going home.'

'She doesn't want to go with you,' Alison said. 'And I want you to leave my property. If you don't go, I'll have you arrested for trespassing.'

Sally was stunned by how calm Alison sounded. Why couldn't she be as brave as her sister? But she knew the answer to that. After so many years of being too scared to do anything without Gordon's approval for fear of what he'd do if she stepped out of line, there was no way she could react as Alison was doing. Ashamed of her cowardice, she hung her head as the battle of wills between Gordon and Alison raged.

'Open this fucking door,' Gordon yelled. 'You have no right to keep my wife from me.'

'You know, you are a very stupid man,' Alison said, 'if you

think this is the way to get Sally to come back to you. You need anger management and a lot of counselling.'

'Fuck you, you cow,' Gordon snarled. 'I want my wife. I bet she's been whoring around and you've been helping her. I won't give up. Tell her I'm not going away.'

Alison put her head to one side, as if listening for something. Then Sally heard the faint sound of a siren in the distance.

'I think you should do yourself a favour and leave now,' Alison said.

'Fuck you! Get Sally before I break this door down.'

'I wouldn't recommend that,' Alison said. 'Can you hear that? It's a police siren. My uncle called them, so I suggest you take yourself off if you don't want to be arrested for disturbing the peace.'

'Screw you, you dried-up cow. You don't tell me what to do. I'm going, but you tell Sally, I'll be back.'

'Okay, Arnie Schwarzenegger, but off you go now. Although, it might be better if you stayed. The police are almost here. They can make sure you leave my sister alone.'

Sally saw Gordon's arm disappear from the gap in the door, stunned at how easily Alison had dealt with him. As Alison closed the door, she looked up and smiled.

'It's safe to come down now,' she said. 'I can understand why you've been scared of him; he really is a nasty piece of work, but as long as you're staying here, he can't hurt you.'

Sally stood up and staggered to the top of the stairs. Holding on to the banister for support, she walked down.

'I can't thank you enough,' she said as she reached the bottom. 'I hate the fact that he found me. It shows I'm not even safe here.'

The siren sound was now deafening as the police car pulled into the drive. As the last notes faded, Alison held out her hand.

'I promise you, he cannot hurt you while you are here with your family. It's time to report him, Sally. Let's get some advice from the police. You don't have to live in fear.'

Alison opened the door and walked to the police car.

'We called you because my sister's husband was here threatening to hurt anyone who stood in his way. My sister needs some advice on how to deal with him. Could you spare a few minutes to give her some information?'

Sally wasn't sure whether to be glad or not when the officer nodded. The idea of dealing in any way with Gordon scared her so much she began to shake, but she knew deep down that one way or another, she had to find a way to get him out of her life for good.

The officer got out of the car, saying something to his colleague, who nodded, but remained in the car.

'I'm PC Robinson. I'd be happy to point the way forward for you. Shall we go inside?' he said.

Alison turned back to the house and led the way, squeezing Sally's arm as she passed.

'Come on, Sally. Let's deal with this issue once and for all.'

Sally followed the police officer and Alison into the drawing room and sat in the armchair facing the one the officer had taken.

'First things first,' he said, taking out a notepad. 'I know your sister says he was threatening, but are you, or have you been, the victim of actual domestic abuse?'

Sally nodded, feeling ashamed, but knowing she had to be honest.

'In that case you can apply for an injunction,' PC Robinson said.

'What does that mean?' Alison asked. She was perched on the arm of Sally's chair, as if trying to protect her.

'An injunction is a court order that falls into two categories. Does your husband live here?'

Sally shook her head. 'No, I left him. My sister took me in.'

PC Robinson nodded. 'In that case, you need a non-molestation order which will protect you from being harmed or threatened by your husband.'

'What happens if he doesn't obey the order?' Sally asked, trying and failing to imagine Gordon doing as he was told by anyone, even the court.

'If he breaks the injunction, he'll be arrested.'

'Is it expensive to get one?' Sally asked, thinking of her rapidly diminishing funds.

'There's no fee when you apply, but if you wish, you can pay for legal advice to help you. You might be eligible for legal aid.'

'What's the next step? How do we apply?' Alison said.

Sally felt her sister's hand on her shoulder, glad of the support. This all seemed like an impossible hill to climb.

'You can apply online,' the officer said. He scribbled down a few words and tore out the page, handing it across to Sally. 'You can use the RCJ Citizens Advice CourtNav service to prepare an injunction application online. You'll need to create an account where you outline what's happened to you, giving as much detail of the abuser as possible – his name, address and so on.'

Sally nodded, feeling overwhelmed, but determined to see this through. 'What happens once I've done that?'

'You'll have a hearing, which can be via video or a phone

call if it's hard for you to get to court, but you would need to explain your reason for not being able to be in court in person when you apply.'

'I'll take you to the court,' Alison said. 'We'll make sure Gordon can't get anywhere near you.'

'What if he comes back before I can get this injunction?'

'Do you feel you need immediate protection?' the officer asked. 'If you do, you can ask for an emergency order when you apply. In that case, you don't have to tell your husband that you're applying. The court will hold a hearing, but that's one which you *must* attend. It may issue an order at the hearing. You'll still have to tell your husband about the application, but only after the order has been issued.'

'What do you mean? Why do I have to tell him?'

'Because he has to be able to defend himself. If you're worried, then getting an emergency order is the way to go. Once you get that and your husband is told about it, you will have protection until the full hearing.'

He stood up. 'Is there anything else I can help you with?'

Sally could barely see him through eyes blurred with tears. She shook her head. Instead of feeling reassured, the mountain felt even harder to climb. She'd have to tell Gordon she was applying for a restraining order. The thought of that churned her stomach. She was vaguely aware of Alison and the officer leaving the room as she stared unseeing at the wall opposite.

She jumped when Alison's voice sounded next to her.

'Okay,' she said. 'Now we know what to do, let's get to the computer and make a start.'

Sally looked up. 'Alison, I'm going to have to tell him what I'm doing. I don't think I can face him and say that.'

'You won't have to face him. I can do that for you. The officer didn't say *you* had to tell him. He said Gordon has to be informed. Didn't you know, that's what big sisters are for? Besides, if we apply for the emergency order or whatever it's called, you won't need to tell him until after that's in place.'

Sally stood up. Alison was so capable, the complete opposite of herself, but maybe it was time to be more assertive.

'You're right,' she said. 'Let's get the application underway.'

'That's my girl. We'll need to turf Peter off the computer. I saw him go into the study when I was seeing the officer out, so he must have taken Dad upstairs. At least, I hope he did. We'd better check first that he hasn't left Dad on his own in the kitchen.'

Chapter Seventeen

Gordon pulled into his driveway still seething. He opened the car door and climbed out, slamming it hard behind him. Sally wouldn't get the better of him. He'd get her back if it was the last thing he ever did on this earth. Who the hell did she think she was, running away from him? As for that sister of hers. That was a sour hag if he'd ever seen one. No self-respecting man would want that in his bed.

Opening the front door, he caught sight of himself in the hall mirror. Fuck! He looked every one of his fifty-eight years. Is that why Sally ran off? Was she looking for a younger man? He'd kill her if he thought she was climbing into the sack with someone new.

He kicked the door closed and headed upstairs. The bedroom felt cold and empty without his wife. Pulling open Sally's wardrobe door, Gordon grabbed a handful of hangers and dragged them from the rail. He'd teach her not to run off again. When she came back, he'd only allow her to wear clothes that covered her from head to toe.

Holding the hangers in his left hand, he felt in his pocket

for his penknife. Flicking it open, he smiled. She'd have nothing to wear other than rags by the time he finished. He dragged the knife through the material again and again until all that was left were shreds hanging like pennants.

Feeling worse instead of better, Gordon slumped back onto the bed. No way was he going to allow her to escape him. He had to get her back! It was time to make a plan.

Chapter Eighteen

S ally followed Alison towards the study, still shaking from all that had happened with Gordon. Could she really go ahead with this? Would Gordon obey the injunction even if she could get one in place? He always believed she was his to control as he wished. Would it really be any different just because a judge told him to stay away?

She stopped midway across the hall. Alison must have realised Sally had come to a halt because she also stopped and looked back.

'What's wrong?'

'I don't know. It just came to me that Gordon has never obeyed anyone other than himself. What if I start the legal proceedings and it makes him so mad, he tries to find a way to attack me? Or worse, what if he comes after you because he knows you're standing in his way.'

Alison walked back and put her hand on Sally's arm. 'You have to do this. Don't you see? If you don't, then he will continue to be a threat to you. You'll never be free of him. As for me, I'm not scared of him. If he comes anywhere near this house, or me when I'm out, I'll call the police. You have got to stand up to him, Sally. It's the only way. Come on, I'll be with you every step of the way.'

Sally nodded. 'Taking this first step is just so terrifying. You don't know what he's capable of,' she said.

'Why don't you tell me, so that I know who and what we're dealing with? Just bear in mind, I said *we*. Not *you*. We're together in this.'

Sally nodded. Maybe by talking about it some of the fear Gordon had induced over the years would begin to fade.

'You saw how charming he was when you first opened the door?'

Alison nodded.

'He was like that with me in the beginning. Always loving and kind. I met him just a few months after Grandma Fletcher died. Not long after . . . after our father turned me away.'

She sighed. Alison took her arm and turned her around. 'Let's go back to the drawing room and sit down for a bit. We can't talk out here in the hall. You'll feel more comfortable in there.'

Sally shrugged. 'I'm not sure I'll feel comfortable anywhere talking about my marriage, but you're right. This isn't the right place for it.'

She trailed behind Alison back into the drawing room and settled herself into one of the armchairs. Alison sat on the sofa at right angles to her chair.

'As I said, he was all charm in the beginning. I had a part-time job in our local library. He used to come in most days and chat about all sorts of things. I was so impressed with his wide range of knowledge. Many years later I realised he actually knew very little about the topics and must have done a bit of reading up so that he could bring out scraps of information to make himself appear well read.'

She shrugged. 'I fell for it. I was so young and really didn't know much about men. Grandma Fletcher's male friends were all ancient in my eyes and she wouldn't let me mix with our local groups. She said they were louts. They probably were, but I don't think they were bad at heart.' Sally shook herself. 'Anyway, the point is that I was very naïve and saw Gordon as a cross between a superhero and a god. In no time at all we were seeing each other outside of the library.'

'Didn't he work?' Alison asked. 'How could he have so much time on his hands?'

'He said he was self-employed and his hours were his own. That was another lie I discovered much later. He had no business and no money. I think he must have heard about Grandma Fletcher dying and targeted me as a means of getting some cash, but that's not how it seemed at the time.'

Sally used her fingers to wipe away a tear as it fell down one side of her face.

'Here,' Alison said, passing her a tissue.

'Thank you. Gordon used to bring me small gifts to show how much he loved me. Nothing important, little stuff, like a bar of my favourite chocolate, or a single rose. I was head over heels in love with him by then and he said he was with me. Funnily enough, I think he was and probably still is, but it's a twisted kind of love.'

Sally thought back over the years, wishing she'd never taken the job in the library, but it had seemed like a lifesaver at the time, giving her a focus after the death of her grandmother.

'Go on,' Alison said. 'He charmed his way into your life and you fell for him. Apart from being after your grandmother's money, it sounds as if he treated you well at first. What changed?'

'It was after we'd been married for a few months. I'd got a job in a small accounting firm. There was a young man working in the post room. I think he had a crush on me and I made the mistake of telling Gordon about the way he kept trying to flirt. It made me feel so uncomfortable. I'd expected . . . I don't know what I expected, maybe for Gordon to show me how to deal with the situation. You know, how to put the young man in his place without causing a scene.'

'And did he?' Alison said. 'Did he tell you what to say to the guy?'

Sally shook her head. 'No. He blamed me. He said I must have been leading him on. He said that no man goes after another man's wife unless the woman has made it clear she wants him to do so.' Sally choked back a tear. 'And then he slapped me hard across the face and called me a whore.'

'Why didn't you leave there and then? Why stay?'

Sally looked up. 'You don't understand. It's easy to judge.'

Alison shook her head. 'Oh Sally, I'm not judging you. Far from it. I'm just trying to understand.'

'He was so sorry. Immediately after, he was full of apologies. He said it was fear of losing me, that I was everything to him and he couldn't bear the thought of me wanting to be with someone else, someone younger. By the time he'd finished, he'd convinced me that it was all my fault for telling him about the guy in the first place. He promised he would never do it again. But that set the pattern. He'd lose his temper and lash out, then he'd apologise and bring me gifts to make up for it.'

She shuddered. 'It got worse as the years went on. No matter what I did or didn't do, he'd lash out with his fists, sometimes with his feet as well. There were times when I couldn't go to work for weeks at a stretch, but that made him even angrier because it meant I didn't get paid and we really needed the money.'

'Didn't you have sick pay at your company?'

Sally nodded. 'Of course, but only so many weeks per year. I used mine up most years and then some.'

'So what made you finally decide to leave? What made you reach out to me?'

'I told you. It was Brenda in HR. She used to give me little pep talks, adding scraps of information on how to deal with abuse, how to get away, how to squirrel money away so that I would have an escape fund, but most importantly, she made me reach out to you. And now here I am having brought Gordon into your life as well.'

Alison shook her head. 'No, you didn't do that. He did. And I'm not going to allow him to bully you any longer.'

Sally wondered if she could ever make Alison understand what it felt like to be too scared to speak in case what she said was wrong, or stupid, or out of place, or any one of so many things that made Gordon lose his temper.

She felt Alison squeeze her arm. 'He will never stop unless you make him accountable, Sally. He'll keep coming back if you don't get this restraining order in place.'

'And if he does?'

'Then we'll have the law on our side. Let's see how brave

he is after spending some time in a cell with people who aren't in the least bit scared of him. He might find out what it feels like to be the one taking the blows instead of dishing them out.'

Sally knew that Alison was right. Taking a deep breath, she nodded again. 'You're right. Let's go and do it before I change my mind and back out.'

'Good girl!' Alison said.

Sally stood up. With Alison on her side, she felt she could do anything. They walked across the hall, arm in arm. Sally had never felt so ready to fight back. They reached the study, just as the door opened and Peter came out.

'Well, well, well, what a dark horse you are, Sally, having the ability to reduce your poor husband to a gibbering wreck. Although, to be fair to you, I can understand your reluctance to return to him.'

'Not now, Peter,' Sally said. 'I don't need your snide comments.'

Alison smiled at Sally. 'Let's get this application underway, shall we?'

'Always trying to control the situation, aren't you, Alison?'

'Leave her alone!' Sally said, surprising herself as she stepped between her sister and Peter. 'Alison doesn't deserve your nastiness and neither do I!'

Sally felt as if she was under a microscope as Peter looked her up and down.

'The timid mouse has found her voice. Encounters with you are going to be so much more interesting from now on, but don't go fooling yourself into thinking you know Alison. She is far more devious than you can ever imagine and totally untrustworthy.'

Sally felt Alison's hand on her arm stiffen.

She sighed. 'I don't believe you.'

'You deserve what's coming to you, if you insist on staying here. I'm off.'

'Wait!' Alison said. 'Where's Dad? Did you have to sedate him?'

'If you bothered to open your eyes and looked into the study, you'd see that my beloved brother is sitting on the sofa. Unlike you, I didn't have to sedate John. He fell asleep while I was sorting out the accounts on the laptop. The money situation is getting out of hand. This excessive spending has to stop.'

Sally squeezed past Peter, feeling guilty. She was costing Alison and her father money, but couldn't move out until she had a job. Peter smiled as if he knew he'd scored a hit, and then left the room. Sally was relieved when she heard the front door close.

Alison sat at the desk and signalled to Sally to take the armchair closest to her. Sally didn't remember this room from her childhood and wondered if it might have had a different use back then. Now it was a cross between a comfortable working environment and a small sitting room. In fact, she thought it was nicer than the more formal drawing room. Cosier and very inviting. If the employment agencies didn't come up with any concrete job offers, maybe she'd be able to do some bookkeeping from home. Thank goodness she had the interview next week. That might result in a job offer. At least then she'd be able to pay her way, even if she couldn't immediately move out. Maybe she wouldn't need to move.

'Sally!'

She jumped, realising she'd drifted off into a pleasant day-dream where she could stay here and be safe.

'Sorry,' she said. 'I was miles away.'

Alison smiled at her, but it looked strained. Sally guessed the situation must be taking its toll on her even if she tried to disguise it. 'I guessed that from the abstract look on your face, that and the fact that I've asked you the same question three times without getting an answer. What is your husband's full name and date of birth?'

Sally apologised again and spent the next twenty minutes answering Alison's various questions. Grateful beyond words that Alison was taking control of the situation, Sally vowed not to be a burden to her sister.

As Alison slammed the laptop shut, Sally told her about the interview she'd be going to the following week.

'The only problem is that it's in Oakham. Is there a bus service from anywhere near here?'

'Don't be daft, I can take you. I have business to deal with in Oakham, which I can arrange for the same day as your interview. When is it?'

Sally opened WhatsApp on her phone to look at the details the agency had forwarded, but before she could share them with Alison, their father woke up.

'What are you doing here?' he said.

Sally wasn't sure if he was talking to Alison or herself, but as her presence always seemed to upset him, she kept quiet.

'Sally! I asked you a question, what are you doing here?'

'She's staying with us for a few days, Dad,' Alison said, getting up and walking over to the sofa. She sat down next to him and took hold of his hand. He shook his head and threw her hand off.

'Don't patronise me, Alison. I'm not entirely senile, you know. I didn't ask you, I asked Sally. Well, Sally, why have you finally come back?'

Stunned to hear her father speak with such clarity, Sally stumbled over her words.

'I . . . I . . . um, I need a safe place. Alison said I could stay here until I find a place of my own.'

He sat forward, looking so much like his younger brother the breath caught in Sally's throat. Most of the time since she'd been here, he'd looked old and frail, but now there was a gleam in his eyes and he seemed to have lost ten years at least.

'And why do you need a safe haven?'

Sally shook her head. 'I've escaped from my husband. He was abusive.'

'I didn't even know you were married. When did that happen? Why were we not invited?'

'You were! We sent you an invitation and then Gordon called you, but you told him you weren't interested in me or my future.'

'That's a lie!'

As he said the words, his face changed. The years seemed to flow back and he aged before her eyes.

'Maggie? Oh, Maggie, I've missed you so much.'

Before she could move, her father grabbed her in a tight embrace. Sally felt the heat of his breath as he rained kisses down on her head. She tried to break away, but he pulled her in even closer. Stunned by the strength in his arms, Sally was unable to move.

'Dad! That's enough. Let her go!'

'Maggie, I love you still, Maggie. Don't leave me again. I'll kill you if you try to leave me.'

Sally felt Alison's arm coming between her and her father. As it did so, she pulled away from him. He staggered backwards and landed on the sofa.

'Go to the kitchen, Sally, while I deal with Dad. Put the kettle on, I think we both need a cup of tea, or maybe even something a bit stronger. It's been a hell of a day so far.'

Sally left the study and crossed the hall to the kitchen. A hell of a day was the understatement of the year. She filled the kettle with water and set it to boil, wondering what Alison had in mind for the 'something stronger' she'd mentioned. Collapsing into a chair, she mulled over her father saying he didn't know she was married. Knowing Gordon as she now did, it was possible, even probable, that he'd lied when he'd said he'd contacted her father after he hadn't replied to the wedding invitation. She remembered all too well the way she'd felt when her father had sent her away after Grandma Fletcher's death. She would have believed anything Gordon said back then.

The kettle had boiled and started to cool long before Alison came down. She sat opposite Sally and sighed.

'I worry so much about Dad's state of mind. I'm scared if he gets any worse I might not be able to manage him.'

Sally stood up and walked over to the kettle, flicking the switch.

'I'm not making it any easier for you, am I?' she said. 'Please be honest – wouldn't it be better if I moved out as soon as possible?'

Alison shook her head. 'Don't you realise, you're the only

127

thing that's keeping me sane. For years I dreamt of having you here. With you I can have normal conversations. With Dad, I never know from one moment to the next which version I'm going to be dealing with. No, it wouldn't be better if you moved out, so please don't mention it again, okay?' she said, giving Sally a lopsided smile.

'Okay, I won't say another word about moving out for a while. But, Alison, can I ask you something?'

'Your voice tells me you don't really want to ask, which sounds ominous, but go ahead. What do you want to know?'

'It's what Peter said. He's holding some sort of threat over you, isn't he?'

'Sally, what went on between Peter and me is something I never want to talk about. I need you to respect that.'

'I do, but—'

'No buts!' Alison yelled.

Sally was horrified to see tears streaming down her sister's face.

'I'm so sorry. I didn't mean to distress you. I seem to be more like my mother than I'd realised, causing upset wherever I go. I just wanted you to know you have a friend in me if you ever want to talk.'

Alison sat down, shaking her head, a deep frown creasing her forehead, clearly unwilling to talk. Desperate to fill the uncomfortable silence, Sally wracked her brains to think of something to discuss other than Peter.

'I can't make up my mind if our father still loves or now hates my mother. What do you think?'

Alison looked confused by the change of topic, but seemed happy enough to answer.

'I'm really not sure,' she said. 'You may have noticed there isn't a photo of you or your mother anywhere in this house, but there are photos of me with my mother during the times that we lived here.'

Sally sat up straighter in her chair. 'Do you know, I hadn't actually spotted that. There's been so much going on since I got here that it hadn't hit me, but you're right. There isn't a single photo of me or my mother to be seen.'

Alison reached across the table and touched Sally's arm. 'I'm sorry, Sally. There used to be family photos all over the house until your mother ran off, then Dad destroyed them all. He wouldn't allow anyone to even mention your mother's name. He told me back then, and remember I was only a teenager myself, that he'd made a vow never to look at her image ever again. Sadly, you *are* the image that he doesn't want to see. I'm not sure what's going on in his head, but he hasn't mentioned Maggie so much for years.'

Sally felt as if she'd been punched in the stomach. It seemed her mother was still destroying her life even though Maggie chose to leave her behind when she left.

'Thank you for telling me, Alison. That couldn't have been easy,' Sally said, hoping her voice didn't betray how devastated she felt. She smiled. 'There's nothing I can do about my looks, so I'll just have to stay out of our father's line of sight as much as I can while I'm here. Tea or coffee?'

Alison stood up and opened the fridge. 'Neither! We're opening this bottle of wine. I'm in need of something to calm my nerves.' She took a corkscrew from the drawer. 'This thing is ancient. I always struggle with it, but never remember to buy a new one.' She glanced at Sally and frowned. 'I have a feeling that Peter is up to something. I think he might be doing something weird with Dad's finances.'

Sally took down two wine glasses and set them on the table. 'What makes you say that?' she asked.

Alison battled with the cork and eventually got it out. 'It was something Dad muttered just before he dozed off. He said we're running out of money, but that's not possible. Dad's business was sold for a huge amount and this house is fully paid for. Dad has investment income and pensions, so how can we be short of money? I wish I could get into Dad's accounts, but even if I could, I doubt I'd understand anything. Peter deals with all of that.'

Sally smiled. 'At last there's something I can help you with. If we can access the accounts online, I'd be able to see exactly what's what with the money. It's what I was trained to do.'

'Brilliant,' Alison said. 'We'll do that over the weekend when there's less chance of Peter dropping in on us. I know he's going to a race meeting on Saturday, so let's play detective then.'

Alison filled the two glasses and lifted one. 'Here's to sisterhood,' she said.

Sally raised her glass. 'I'll drink to that.' She took a sip and placed the glass back on the table. 'Alison, one thing our father said that I know wasn't true was that he didn't know I was married.'

Alison shrugged. 'Why do you think he was lying about that?'

'Because I wrote out the invitation to you and our father. Gordon posted it and followed up with a phone call when we didn't hear back.'

130

'Well, I didn't know you were married until I got your letter saying you were in an abusive relationship and needed a safe haven.'

'Do you think he got the invitation and chose to ignore it?'

'No, I think at the very least he would have sent a reply and a gift, even if he chose not to go. Besides, he would have known that I would have wanted to be there to see my little sister walk up the aisle. He wouldn't have kept that joy from me. In fact, when you got in touch after all those years of silence, I was hurt to think you hadn't wanted me at your wedding.'

Sally shook her head. 'I didn't walk up an aisle. It was a registry office wedding, but I so much wanted you and our father to be there. I'd hoped we could find a way to be a family.'

Chapter Nineteen

Thursday 12th June

S ally woke early the next morning determined to go out for a run. She dressed and put on her running shoes, feeling better about life than she had in quite some time. Knowing what she now did about how Gordon had isolated her from everyone and everything she loved, it was entirely possible, in fact probable, that he'd lied about inviting her family to the wedding, to make her believe they didn't want anything to do with her. Although, that didn't exactly tie in with Alison's revelations the day before. Peter might not want her to be part of the family, but Alison certainly did and that was enough for Sally to feel that she belonged.

She opened her bedroom door as quietly as possible and crept along to the stairs, trying not to wake anyone. Her father was such a light sleeper, unless he'd been sedated, that it was likely the slightest sound would wake him. As for Alison, she seemed to have boundless energy. Sally was constantly amazed at how her sister coped, not just with their father's dementia, but running the home and putting up with their obnoxious uncle.

Tiptoeing down the stairs and across the hall, she was annoyed when she tried to open the kitchen door as gently as possible and a loud creak sounded like thunder in the quiet of the early morning. Sally stood still, listening, but didn't hear any movement from the rooms above. She continued into the kitchen. Rather than open the many locks and chains on the main door, she decided to go out through the kitchen into the garden.

She opened the back door and then slotted the key in the outside, locking it behind her and pocketing the key in her running shorts. Taking a deep breath, she switched on her running light and edged round the side of the house. Without the light she wouldn't have been able to see a thing. With the clouds obscuring the moon and no street lights, it was almost pitch black. Maybe tomorrow she'd run later in the day, but decided to go for a short run anyway now that she was out.

As she reached the end of the drive, she had an overwhelming feeling of being watched. She glanced behind at the house, but although she couldn't see any movement, the feeling persisted. She looked along the drive leading to Mrs Carstairs' house. Someone was up as a light was showing through the curtains downstairs. Just as she was about to turn away and start her run, she saw the curtain twitch. Was the woman watching her? Maybe she'd heard Sally creeping about and was scared it was a burglar. She waved in the direction she'd seen the movement and then turned to begin her run.

She fell into a regular rhythm as she jogged along the track connecting the drive to the road, relying on her running light to show up any potholes or fallen branches. As she relaxed, she thought about her life with Gordon. How had she allowed him to control her as he had? Was it simply because she was so much younger than him? It hadn't been long after her father's rejection that she'd fallen in love. Was it love, or had she been desperate for affection?

She reached the road and turned left, gradually increasing her pace. She felt she'd covered about two kilometres and was getting ready to turn for home when she became aware of a car coming from behind. She veered to the side of the road to give the car room to pass. The engine noise got closer and seemed to speed up. She glanced back. The car had no lights and was coming straight at her! Turning, she tripped and stumbled, falling head first into the ditch.

The car swept past and stopped. It began to reverse, but suddenly took off again with squealing tyres. Sally tried to climb out from the ditch, but her ankle gave way.

'Here, give me your hand,' a male voice said, as a large and very friendly dog jumped down beside her. 'Don't worry about Honey. She won't hurt you.'

Sally tried again to stand, but the pain from her ankle made her cry out.

'Are you badly hurt?' the man asked.

'It's my ankle,' Sally said. 'I think I sprained it when I fell.'

The man dropped down beside her. 'Here, let me hoist you up. Honey, get out of the way. This lady needs my help.'

Sally leaned on the man as he half pulled, half lifted her back onto the road.

'Can you stand?'

She nodded. 'As long as I don't put any weight on it, it's fine.'

'Can you shine your running light down? I'll take a look at that ankle for you.' He laughed. 'This is going to sound corny, but you can trust me. I'm a doctor.'

Sally manoeuvred the light so that it shone on her feet. The man seemed to know what he was doing.

He felt her ankle and then stood up, holding out his hand. 'It doesn't look too bad. Probably just a sprain. Colin Blanchett at your service, and this is Honey, but she's already introduced herself. Are you from around here?'

'I'm staying with my sister and father,' she said. 'The house is on the other side of the water. I hadn't realised how far I'd run.'

'You need to rest that ankle as much as possible. If you can walk the short distance to my house, I'll take you home in my car. I would say to wait here, but I have a horrible feeling that car was aiming for you and might come back. I saw the car reversing, but the driver must have seen me and decided to leave.'

Sally fought to control her shaking limbs. 'I saw that, but thought the driver was coming back to help me.'

Colin shook his head. 'I'd like to think so, but it didn't look like that to me. I wish I'd been able to get the number plate, but I was partially blinded by your running light. I could see it was a dark hatchback, but that's about all I registered before he took off again.'

'He?' Sally asked. 'Could you see the driver?'

'No, sorry. Figure of speech. It could just as easily have been a woman.'

'And it was definitely a hatchback?'

'It was, but I wouldn't be able to say for certain which

135

make. How are you doing now? Ready to set off? My house is not far from here. Honey, get out of that ditch, girl.'

Sally tried putting some weight on her ankle. If she hobbled, she'd be able to walk for a bit.

'Look, please don't think I'm being forward, but if I put my arm round your waist and you lean on me, it might make it easier for you to walk.'

Sally nodded and leaned into him.

'Okay to set off?' Colin asked.

'Yes, let's go,' she said.

'Come on, Honey, let's get this lady home. Sorry, I should have asked your name.'

Sally smiled. 'No, I should have given it. I'm Sally, Sally Watson.'

'Pleased to meet you, Sally. Honey and I don't usually encounter company at this time of the morning. We don't see too many cars either, so it's a great place for a walk.' He hesitated, as if trying to find the right words. 'Look, this isn't any of my business, but you don't seem that surprised that someone tried to knock you down.'

Sally knew she had to say something. She didn't want to go into details with someone she'd only just met, but felt she owed him some sort of explanation.

'I don't want to say too much,' she said, 'but I think I know who might have been driving the car.'

'Really? Well, in that case, I hope you're going to report him or her to the police.'

'I will. Your dog is very well behaved,' Sally said, glancing down at the golden retriever trotting alongside her, grateful to be able to change the subject.

136

'She's a very good girl. She's been with me since she was a pup. You doing okay? Not far to go now.'

Sally hobbled on, answering Colin, but with her mind far from what was being said. Gordon had sworn to come back, but was he crazy enough to try to kill her? Or was he simply trying to force her to stop so that he could grab her? Or maybe it was nothing more than someone who'd forgotten to turn their lights on and got disorientated on seeing the running light. Maybe whoever it was had intended to come back to help, but decided not to as Colin was close at hand. No, that was wishful thinking and she knew it. Deep in her heart she believed it had been Gordon.

She glanced up at her rescuer. Thank goodness he'd been there. She'd have never been able to walk all the way home. If only she'd thought to bring her phone. Next time she would make sure to pick it up.

'Okie dokie, here we are,' Colin said. 'I'll just put Honey indoors and then get you home.' He took out a set of keys and pressed a fob. 'Let me help you into the car. Honey, no! You're not going this time, my girl.'

Sally reached down and stroked the dog. 'You really are a lovely dog. Sorry if I'm taking your place in the car.'

Colin laughed. 'You're not. If she was going as well, she'd be in the back, and she knows it. Right, let's get that injured leg inside.'

Sally slid onto the passenger seat and tried not to wince as he gently lifted her damaged ankle into the car. He shut the door and she watched as man and dog trotted towards the house. It was nowhere as grand as her father's house, built on a much smaller scale, but was far more homely. More of a cottage than a house, it looked as if it might have been built centuries before. A few minutes later, the front door opened and Colin came out carrying what looked like a variety of medical items.

'Sorry to have kept you waiting,' he said as he got into the car, 'but Honey and I are both creatures of habit. She has her food after our morning walk and let me know in no uncertain terms that today would be no different.'

He turned to smile at her as he spoke and Sally had her first chance to see him clearly. Not good-looking in the conventional sense, but his smile was stunning, making him look almost handsome. She felt a strong sense of comradeship with him, which was ridiculous. They'd only just met and she knew nothing about him, but at the same time she felt he was someone she could trust.

'I have an ice pack here, which I'm going to place on your ankle,' he said.

Sally watched as he wrapped a bandage around her foot to hold it in place.

'Are you okay?' he asked. 'Not hurting too much?'

She shook her head. 'No, I'm fine. Thank you.'

He nodded. 'Good. My best medical advice,' he said, smiling, 'is to take some paracetamol when you get home, rest and keep that leg elevated. Okay?'

Sally nodded. 'Yes, doctor.'

He started the engine. 'Okay, Sally, where to? I know you said on the other side of the water, but it's a big area.'

'Anchorage House.'

'Really?' he said.

Sally heard a note of reservation in his voice. 'Do you know it?' she asked. 'It's my father's house. I've only recently moved back. My sister, well, half-sister, has been amazingly kind since I turned up unexpectedly.'

'Are you planning on a long stay?' he asked.

She shrugged. 'I wasn't planning to, but a lot depends on when and where I can get a job. I'd like to move to Oakham. It's such a lovely old town. I've got an interview there next week, but I'm trying not to build my hopes up too much.'

As her words trailed off, she noticed a change in his attitude. Where before he'd been chatty and smiling, he now seemed more reserved. Without the smile, his face looked harsher. She no longer felt as comfortable in his company. Wondering what she'd said or done to cause him to withdraw, she was relieved when the car slowed and turned onto the track leading to the drive. The atmosphere seemed to get frostier the closer they got to the house. Sally desperately searched for something to say to break the silence, but couldn't think of anything.

'Stay there,' he said, as he pulled up outside the house. 'I'll come round and help you out.'

Sally waited until the car door opened and then swung her legs out. As her foot connected with the ground she winced. It wasn't quite as painful as it had been, but it was still too tender to put all her weight on it.

Colin took her arm and helped her hobble to the front door. She reached for the bell, but before she could press it, he was already saying goodbye.

'But won't you come in? I'm sure my sister would love to thank you, as I do.'

He shook his head. 'I have rather a busy day ahead of me.

I'm pleased I was there to help you. You need to get that ankle looked at by a doctor.' He hesitated, as if debating whether to say anything more. Then he nodded. 'Look, Sally, it seems to me that someone was deliberately aiming for you, intent on knocking you down this morning. Here, take my card. If you need a friend, at any time, for any reason, please call me.'

Frowning, he handed her a business card, barely touched her arm, and then turned back to his car.

Sally watched as he drove off, totally bemused. He'd been so friendly. Why the sudden change? She tried to work out what it was she'd said that could have caused the withdrawal. The only thing she could think of was mentioning her wish to live and work in Oakham, but what was there in that to bother him?

Shrugging, she pressed the doorbell and waited. It didn't take long before the door opened. Alison was still in her nightwear, but looked wide awake, as if she'd been up for a while.

'Sally! What's happened? You're covered in mud and leaves.'

Sally looked down and saw Alison was right. She hadn't realised how much muck she'd picked up from the ditch. Thinking of the pristine condition of Colin's car, she wondered if dropping leaves and mud in his car might have been what had caused his change of attitude. No, it couldn't have been that. He must have seen the state she was in when he'd helped her into the car and he'd been friendly after that.

'I had an accident while I was out running,' Sally said. 'I seem to have sprained my ankle.'

Alison held out her arm. 'You poor thing. Let's get you inside and cleaned up. How did you get home? You couldn't have walked. You're barely able to put that foot on the ground.'

'A passer-by took pity on me and brought me home.'

'Ah, I thought I heard a car on the drive, but supposed I must have been mistaken as it was so early.'

Sally took hold of Alison's arm for support and hobbled across the hall to the kitchen, gratefully collapsing into a chair.

Alison put the kettle on and then came and stood in front of Sally. 'Now, what happened?'

'I'm not really sure,' Sally said. 'My good Samaritan was under the impression a car might have driven at me deliberately, but the only person I can think of who'd do that is Gordon. Apparently, it was a dark hatchback and he drives one of those.'

Alison nodded. 'Do you think it could have been him? We might not be able to prove it but, after his recent threats, I definitely think we should call the police and report it. It will add to your reasons for wanting a restraining order against him. Let's face it, it couldn't have been anyone else. Who, apart from someone watching your every move, would know you were out there in the dark?'

'Mrs Carstairs was awake when I left,' Sally said. 'I saw her curtains moving.'

Alison laughed. 'Are you seriously saying it was our next-door neighbour? I know she has good reason to hate your mother, but I don't see her taking revenge on you. Do you?'

Sally shook her head, but wondered if it might have been Mrs Carstairs. She'd definitely been looking out this morning. No, Alison was right, it was a crazy thought. It must have been Gordon.

'Why didn't you invite your good Samaritan in? I would have liked the opportunity to thank him for coming to your aid.'

'I did,' Sally said, watching Alison make a very welcome cup of tea. 'He said he had a busy day ahead of him and had to rush off. He lives on the other side of the water.'

'Did you get his name? It would be nice to send him a thank you.'

Sally felt around for the card in the pocket of her shorts. She pulled the card out and looked at it. 'His name is Colin Blanchett,' she said. 'Oh, he's a psychiatrist! He said he was a doctor. I thought he meant a GP.'

'Who?' Alison said, her voice rising several octaves. 'Did you say Colin Blanchett? No wonder he refused to come in. I'm astounded he had the nerve to come as far as the front door!'

'Why?' Sally asked. 'He seemed nice.'

Alison sat down opposite Sally, tears glinting in her eyes.

'Yes, I know just how nice he can seem. He's a real Jekyll and Hyde character, Sally. I should know, he came close to destroying me.'

Chapter Twenty

'How?' Sally asked, stunned by Alison's distress. Colin had seemed such a nice, caring person. Not at all the kind of man who would want to cause any upset. Then she thought about Gordon, who was the only man she'd ever known since she was a teenager. She'd thought he was the next best thing to a god before they got married and he turned into a monster once the ring was on her finger, so what did she know about men?

'What happened? What did he do?' she asked. 'Not that you need to tell me. You don't have to, especially if it's upsetting.'

Alison grabbed some kitchen paper and wiped her eyes.

'It's all in the past now, but I don't mind telling you.' She sighed. 'To explain properly, I'm going to have to go way back in time. Back to when I was a young girl and Dad hadn't yet decided to swap my mother for yours.'

Sally had picked up her cup to take a sip, but put it back down untouched.

'Colin Blanchett doesn't look old enough to feature in your life back then, or did you know him from childhood?'

Alison shook her head. 'No, his part in the story comes much later. You have to let me tell the story my way. It's difficult for me because a part of me feels I'm being disloyal to my mother.'

Sally didn't want Alison to do anything that made her uncomfortable, but as she was about to say, 'Don't go on if you don't want to,' Alison held up her hand.

'I can see on your face you don't want to upset me, but honestly, I think it's time I told someone who actually cares about what happened to me as a child. I've told my story to loads of people who'd been paid to listen, but none of them were truly interested in me as a person. They let me speak, but didn't try to understand. You'll be doing me a favour by letting me get it all off my chest.'

Sally nodded. 'I won't interrupt again, I promise.'

'I mentioned to you before that my mother was what would now be termed bi-polar. Back when she had me, she suffered from post-partum depression. Apparently, she tried to smother me a few times when I was a baby, but Dad caught her in time.'

Sally gasped and Alison shrugged. 'I don't remember it, obviously, and maybe it's not true because I was told about it by Peter who always has his own agenda, but whether that part is true or not, my mother's moods went from total exhilaration to total black dog depression, sometimes in the space of a few minutes. I never knew which version of her I would be facing at any time.

'When I was five, nearly six, Dad had to have her sectioned.

She was away for close to a year. During that time, because Dad had to go away on business, he hired a live-in nanny to take care of me. I think that year, with my mother away and having Dad all to myself when he was home, was probably the happiest of my life. I was the centre of his world and didn't have to listen to my mother raging and ranting about him all the time.'

She stopped and smiled, seeming to drift into a world of her own remembering. Sally waited, scared to move in case it disturbed her. She looked at peace, but suddenly her expression changed. The soft look of happiness disappeared and her expression hardened.

'Then my mother came home from the asylum. I don't know what they did to her there, but the woman who came home was distant. Oh, she was there to do all the normal stuff like shopping, cooking and looking after the house, but she was incapable of showing emotion. In fact, she actively pushed away anyone who tried to get close to her, including me.'

Alison shrugged. 'I presume she did the same to Dad and that's why he fell into your mother's arms. Maggie was everything my mother wasn't. Everything my mother had never been, even before she went away for that year. Maggie only had to walk into a room and she became the centre of attention. If she smiled at someone that person was a slave for life. I know because that was the effect she had on me. So many people have said you are the image of your mother, Sally, but please don't think I'm being unkind when I say you are only the candle to her sun. Yes, you look like her, but you don't have her charm and charisma. Well, you do, but at a much lower level.'

Rather than being upset, Sally was glad to hear she wasn't like her mother in character. If she lacked her mother's charisma, good! She didn't want to seduce anyone in the way her mother clearly had.

'Did you like her?' Sally asked. 'It sounds as if you did.'

'Like her? No, not at all, but I worshipped her. I was bedazzled and would have been her slave if she had shown me any affection, but she wasn't capable of it. I honestly believe that none of the men constantly falling at her feet touched her heart. My mother was damaged for sure, but yours was self-centred and cold. She set out to damage others and succeeded. Even Peter, who later came to hate her, was under her spell for a short time until he realised all her charms were just a tool to manipulate men into doing what she wanted. Once she saw she couldn't bring him to heel like other men, she turned on him like a vicious viper and tried to convince Dad to stop him coming to the house.'

Sally found she couldn't disagree with her mother on that aspect. She would ban Peter from ever being allowed near the house if it was down to her, but no way would she say that to Alison, who clearly had her own issues with the man.

'To continue. Your mother and our father became an item and she fell pregnant with you. Divorce and remarriage were soon on the cards. My mother and I were packed off to a house in Peterborough and your mother took up residence here.' Alison sighed again, much deeper this time as if whatever she had to say next was going to be painful.

'I'm so sorry,' Sally said.

Alison laughed, but not in a way that brought joy into the room. 'What are you sorry about? You didn't do anything.'

146

'I know,' Sally said, 'but my mother did. My being born pushed you out of your home.'

'Yes, it did, but more than that, it pushed my mother over the edge again. She was in and out of psychiatric care for years after that. Every time she was institutionalised, I was dumped on your mother. To be fair to her, she never refused to have me here, but she also didn't take any interest in me. As I said, a kind word and I would have walked on broken glass for her, but that kind word never came.'

Alison smiled. 'Anyway, moving on through the years, your mother ran off with David Carstairs so that was the end of her taking care of me when my own mother went off the rails. Dad, once he recovered from the shock of losing his wife and of you almost dying after falling down the stairs, decided that I should live mainly with my loopy mother but that I should stay here with various nannies during the periods she was hospitalised.'

She shrugged. 'You, of course, were sent to live with your grandmother, which I'm sure was a much more secure upbringing compared to the erratic one I had. As I got older, I understood more about my mother's illness and realised she couldn't help the way she was. I started taking an interest in her psychiatric care, going to support her when she had appointments, learning how to care for her. All of which was how I came into the orbit of Colin Blanchett. At one time he was my mother's psychiatrist.'

'But he isn't any longer?' Sally asked.

Alison stood up, clearly agitated. 'No, he is not! In fact, he's lucky to still be in practice. I reported him to the General Medical Council for serious misconduct, but he managed to worm his way out of trouble. He got his receptionist to lie for him. She's an old motherly figure who adores him. I believe she has been with him since he first set up his own practice, so her loyalty was to him, but she should have told the truth.'

Sally tried to sort out the confusion in her mind. What on earth could Colin have done to make Alison so angry?

'Did he mistreat your mother? Is that why you reported him?'

Alison snorted. 'No! My mother worshipped him. Probably still does, but he refused to treat her after I reported him. Said it was in her interest to move to another psychiatrist. My mother was furious with me. She wanted to stay with him, but I did what I had to do after he attacked me.'

'He attacked you? What, physically?'

'You could say that. He sexually assaulted me.'

'When? How? I mean . . . I don't know what I mean, to be honest. He didn't seem that type of person.'

'I know,' Alison said. 'That's why I trusted him. He'd asked me to his office to discuss my mother's state of mind. He knew I was her primary carer at that time and said he wanted to talk about various options for her ongoing care. Of course, I agreed and went to his office.'

She strode up and down the kitchen, clearly beside herself. Sally wished there was something she could do to calm her. Eventually, she stopped moving and sat down again.

'You need to understand just how charming he'd always been. Up to that day he'd flirted a little, but I didn't really take too much notice. It all seemed very harmless and so when he said to come in without my mother, I didn't think anything of it. We chatted about her ongoing care for a few minutes and then he said he wanted to show me the results of a recent test my mother had taken. He claimed he was delighted with her progress and said to come round to his side of the desk to read the report. I did and as soon as I was standing next to him he put his hand on my leg and began stroking it. I was horrified, but in such a state of shock I didn't immediately move. The next thing I knew, his receptionist came into the room without even knocking! I told her what he'd done and she said to come outside and tell her all about it. Clearly, it wasn't the first time she'd had to deal with something like that. She tried to make light of it, but could see how distressed I was.'

'And then you reported him?' Sally said.

Alison nodded. 'As soon as I got home. I assumed, wrongly, that his receptionist would back me up, but instead she lied for him and said I'd come on to him! She claimed that he'd called for her to come into the room, but I swear he never made a sound. All I achieved was for him to stop looking after my mother, for which she has never forgiven me, even after I told her what he'd done. I haven't seen him since that time, but I'm sure now you understand why he wouldn't come inside. He would have been too ashamed to face me.'

Chapter Twenty-one

Friday 13th June

Sally has just turned off her bedside light. She doesn't like it when Mummy and Daddy go out. Sometimes she wakes up in the night, scared to be on her own in the dark, but Daddy said she mustn't be scared because Alison will look after her.

Mummy was cross tonight. She didn't want to go out with Daddy. Sally heard her shouting at Daddy, saying she didn't like the people they were going to meet, but Daddy said we have to go, it's important. Daddy was also cross, but not with Sally. When he came in to say goodnight to her, he sat on the bed and read The Very Hungry Caterpillar before kissing her cheek and saying goodnight.

Mummy came in after that. She smelled nice, but she had that look on her face. It wasn't a good idea to talk to Mummy when she looked like that. Mummy shouted a lot. She shouted at Alison all the time. She shouted at Daddy when he wasn't away on business. She said he goes away too much. Mummy also shouted at Sally if Sally didn't do what Mummy wanted, but sometimes Sally didn't know what Mummy wanted and did the wrong thing. When she did the wrong thing Mummy shouted even louder and made her go to her room to think about what she'd done wrong, but she never knew what she'd done wrong, so when Mummy asked if she'd thought about it, Sally would lie and say yes.

Sally pulled the cover up over her head. She didn't like thinking about Mummy shouting. It made her tummy hurt. Mummy told her not to go to the boathouse because it was dirty, but Mummy sometimes went and spent lots of time in there. Sally saw her once when she came out and Mummy shouted at her for sneaking around, but she hadn't been sneaking around. She'd woken up and was scared because she couldn't find Mummy so she'd gone to look for her.

She squeezed her eyes shut. She wasn't going to think about Mummy saying she'd be sent away if she ever told Daddy Mummy had been in the boathouse.

Daddy said Alison would look after her tonight, but Alison was too big to go to bed when Sally did. She stayed up and watched television downstairs. That meant Sally was upstairs all alone in the dark.

Sally wanted to go to sleep, but it was scary. She reached over and turned her light on again. Mummy would be cross, but she wasn't here.

The bedroom door slowly opened. It must be the monster coming in.

And then Peter was in the room . . .

Sally woke drenched in sweat. She tried to control the tremors coursing through her, but couldn't stop shaking. What the hell was that dream all about? Was her mother really that unkind, or was it just a warped series of memories tangled in a dream? Dream? It was a nightmare.

She reached for the bedside light and fumbled with the switch, struggling to control her shaking hand. Finally managing to turn it on, Sally was relieved to find her breathing had eased.

She took a tissue from the box and wiped her forehead. Looking at her phone, she saw it was just past three in the morning.

The thought of going back to sleep made her feel ill. Had she really been that helpless little girl, or was it a figment of an overactive imagination? But why would she dream anything so hurtful? There must be an element of truth in it.

If the dream was a childhood memory returning, then her father had been the loving parent and her mother . . . what had her mother been? Certainly Sally couldn't remember any moments of closeness with her. She'd always looked amazing, but had she ever got down on the floor and played with her? Sally vaguely remembered her father doing so, but he had been away so much, it couldn't have happened very often.

There was no way she'd be able to get back to sleep now, so Sally reached for the book Alison had suggested she read. It was a psychological thriller she'd started just before dropping off. She read the blurb on the back. The storyline was all about child neglect, absent parents and a killer on the loose. No wonder she'd dreamt about her parents.

Sally put the book back on the bedside locker. No way was she going to read any more of that if it was going to bring on nightmares. She opened her phone instead. Playing spider solitaire might send her off to sleep dreaming of cards moving of their own accord, but that would be far preferable to drifting back into the nightmare brought on by the novel.

Sally woke sitting up with an ache in her neck. She looked for her phone, but it wasn't on the covers. Looking down, she saw it was on the floor. She must have fallen asleep playing the game and the phone had slipped off the bed. She reached down for it to check the time, relieved to find it was no longer the middle of the night. It was time to get up.

She swung her legs out of bed and put her feet on the floor. As she stood up and put weight on her swollen ankle, she cried out, falling back onto the bed. The doctor Alison had taken her to yesterday had said nothing was broken. Ice and compression apparently were the answers, but the pain made her realise it would be a few days yet before she could even think about running again.

Sally hobbled across the room to the door, hoping to get to the bathroom without disturbing Alison. She needed some time to think about her dream, but also what Alison had revealed about Colin Blanchett. Sally had liked him. He'd been kind to her, but was that his stock-in-trade for seduction? Did he use his friendly smile to draw women in and then take advantage of them? She wished she knew more about men, but her only experience of love had been Gordon.

She closed the bathroom door and headed for the shower, putting all thoughts of Colin from her mind. As she washed, she thought again about her dream, casting her mind back to see if she could bring any elements of it to her mind as genuine memories, but nothing came.

By the time she'd dried herself and hobbled back to the bedroom to get dressed, Sally felt more at peace. A dream was just a dream.

Sally slipped a sock over her injured ankle, but didn't try to put on a shoe. There was no point in adding to her discomfort. She was just wondering how she'd manage the stairs when there was a knock on the door and Alison came in.

'Good morning. I heard you up and about and thought I'd come to offer a big sister's arm to negotiate the stairs.'

Sally grinned. 'Perfect timing. I was planning to go down on my backside rather than risking falling.' She shrugged. 'You know, it's funny, but I don't remember anything about the day I fell and banged my head, ending up in a coma. In fact, I remember very little of my life before that fall.'

Alison sat on the armchair next to the dressing table. 'Really? How much *do* you remember?'

'Odd bits and pieces flash through my head, but nothing that makes sense. Everything is blurry and confused. I get a feeling that something important is hovering just out of reach, but don't know how to grasp it, or even why it might be important.'

Alison frowned. 'That must be so frustrating for you.'

'It is,' Sally said. 'Apparently, it's quite normal to have long-lasting memory loss after being in a coma. Some people regain their memories after a time, sometimes even years later, others don't ever get the lost memories back. I must be in that category because my mind is as blank as it ever was.'

'Maybe that's just as well,' Alison said. 'It was the day your mother left, so that's not a trauma you want to remember. Shall we go down and get some breakfast?'

She gave Sally her arm to lean on, but even with her support Sally found the stairs tricky. She hadn't been quite truthful when she said the images floating in her head didn't make sense, but they were so brief and out of context, could they really count as memories? She knew she'd been frightened that day, but not why.

They reached the bottom of the stairs and made their way across the hall.

'Talking of remembering things,' Sally said. 'I think some memories are trying to break through in my dreams.'

'Really? What sort of things?'

'Last night, for example, I dreamt about being a child here.'

'Before or after your fall?' Alison said. 'Oh, stupid me. It must have been before because you never returned to live here after you were discharged from the hospital. What did you remember in your dream? Anything you want to share?'

'That's just it,' Sally said. She stopped walking and turned to face Alison. 'I don't know if it was a memory or wishful thinking. In my dream, Dad was loving and kind. Completely the opposite to how he is now.'

'Just that and then you woke up?' Alison asked. 'It could be your mind wanting to see life differently from how it turned out.'

'Yes, but there was more. I think I was scared a monster would come into my bedroom. I was holding myself so still that my stomach hurt. It was while you were babysitting me because my parents were out and—'

Before she had chance to finish, the front door opened and Peter came in.

'Sally, will you never learn Alison is not someone you should be close to? Where is my brother? Still upstairs in a sedated stupor? You really need to hold off on the injections, Alison. Anyone would think you were using them to keep John out for the count. Is that what you're doing? Making it easier for you to manage what goes on here?'

Alison let go of Sally's arm and took a step towards Peter. Sally was convinced Alison was going to attack their uncle, but she stopped mid stride.

155

'You know I wouldn't do that to Dad.'

Peter shrugged. 'I don't know anything of the sort, but you do seem to have an endless supply of sedatives. Have you got a tame doctor under your control? Don't bother answering. I've already worked out where you get your extra supplies. After all, I do the accounts.' He turned to Sally. 'Don't you ever wonder why your father is comatose most of the day? Or don't you care? Why should you? His being out of it means you can take advantage and freeload off him without his knowledge. Anyway, speaking of that, our household accounts need my attention. I'll be on the laptop for an hour or so and then I'll be out of your hair.'

'For God's sake, Peter, why don't you buy a computer of your own? There really is no need for you to keep coming over.'

'In point of fact, I have my own computer at home, but it's easier to look after John's accounts over here. Don't let me keep you from your breakfast,' he said, striding towards the study.

Sally hobbled into the kitchen and sat down. Alison followed her in looking angrier than Sally had ever seen her.

'That bloody man,' she said. 'I don't usually allow him to get under my skin like that, but he managed it today. Tea or coffee with breakfast?'

'Tea for me, please,' Sally said. 'He seems determined to make people dislike him. Has he always been that way?'

Alison didn't answer immediately. Sally watched as she filled and switched on the kettle and began to gather together the plates and cutlery for breakfast. Eventually, she turned to face Sally.

'Believe it or not, when I was growing up, he used to be great fun to be around. He had the same wit as he has now, but back then it lacked the spite. I can remember always being overjoyed whenever he came to visit. He even used to visit me at my mother's house until . . .'

She shrugged and turned away.

Sally wondered what Alison had been about to say, but the look on her sister's face told her whatever it was had been a painful memory. Poor Alison. She seemed to have had so little love in her life. Even now their father was distant towards her. Not that he was unkind to her, but he definitely never showed her any affection either, at least not when Sally was around.

Once the table was laid, Alison began preparing scrambled eggs for breakfast. 'I'm going to take Dad's up to him on a tray. Do you want to have yours now, or wait until I come down?'

'I'll wait for you.'

'Good, and then you can finish telling me your dream.'

Sally nodded, but decided she wouldn't say anything more about it until after Peter had left. The last thing she wanted was for him to come in and make fun of her while she was explaining it to Alison.

Her sister had no sooner left the room with the tray than the door opened again and Peter came in.

'All alone, Sally? I shall have to keep you company until Alison returns, unless you'd prefer to hobble back upstairs and pack up whatever belongings you have. I'll take you in my car and drop you at the nearest station.'

As always, Sally struggled to find the right words to answer him, resorting to shrugging to indicate she wasn't prepared to go down that road yet again, but it didn't seem to fool Peter.

'Lost your tongue, Sally? Never mind, if you're not prepared to do the right thing and leave then I'll talk for both of us. Alison says you don't remember your early years here, but I find that very strange. Surely you must have some memories. No?'

Sally shrugged again. 'I remember bits and pieces from back then, but nothing very clear.'

'You know, I feel almost insulted that you don't remember me.'

'You look so much like my father that maybe I do vaguely remember you, but I confuse memories of you with him. Why does it matter?'

He sat down opposite her. 'I didn't say it mattered. I just wonder if maybe you're playing a game with us and you actually remember far more than you're letting on.'

'What are you on about, Peter?' Alison said from the doorway. She came in and walked over to the work surface.

Peter stood up. 'Just trying to jog Sally's memory. There are things she should know.'

A look of fear flashed across Alison's face so quickly that Sally almost thought she had imagined it.

'Have you considered the possibility that remembering might be too painful for Sally? There is nothing she needs to know.'

Peter shrugged and headed for the door. 'At least I can comfort myself with the knowledge that I tried,' he said and left.

Sally waited until she heard the front door close before speaking. 'What was that all about? What is it that I should remember?'

Alison sat down. 'Probably that I wasn't always kind to

158

you when you were young. I felt pushed out and resented you. Peter wants you to dislike me because of how I was back then.'

'He is the nastiest person I've ever known,' Sally said.

'Even worse than your husband?' Alison asked.

Sally felt her face flush with heat. 'No, of course not. It was a figure of speech, that's all. So that's why he was asking me about my memory, which is odd considering the dream I started telling you about. I don't know if that was my subconscious running amok, or it was actual memories surfacing.'

Alison sat down. 'The eggs can wait. We're not going anywhere today. Tell me more about your dream. You'd got to the part where you were scared to go to sleep because your tummy would hurt during the night.'

Sally took a deep breath. 'That's where you came into my dream,' she said.

'Was it me you were scared of? If that's the case, I'm truly sorry, Sally. You were so young and I was already a teenager. There was too big a gap between us for friendship, unlike now.'

Sally shook her head. 'No, I wasn't scared of you. You were babysitting me because my parents were out for the evening. In my dream I was convinced a monster was coming in. Then, suddenly, Peter was there.'

'That did happen!' Alison said.

'Really? When?'

'Your mother and our father had gone out for the night and I was babysitting. Peter came over to be with me. He said he heard you cry out and so went into your room to comfort you, but you confused him with a monster and starting screaming. I heard the commotion and rushed upstairs. I told him to leave you to me. Like all men, he thought he knew best, so I had to shout at him to get out so that I could calm you down.'

'When did this happen? How old was I?'

'You hadn't long turned seven. I remember it well because it was only two weeks before your mother left and I found you at the foot of the stairs with your head cut open.'

Chapter Twenty-two

S ally spent the rest of the day mulling things over.

If only her ankle wasn't so sore, she'd get out of the house and go for a walk around Rutland Water. Thinking of the water reminded her of Colin Blanchett. She had thought that he was a decent person, which just went to show how skewed her judgement was when it came to men. She realised she'd left her phone in the kitchen after lunch, so got up from the sofa in the drawing room to fetch it. She'd told the employment agency about her accident and they had said they would try to rearrange her interview for a week later to give her time to heal. She needed to see if she'd received anything new from them.

As she hobbled across the hall, she wondered how it would have felt to be raised in a home this size. Even though she'd spent the first seven years of her life here, she couldn't imagine what her life would have been like had she grown up in such luxurious surroundings. The hall was vast, almost as big as the downstairs area of the house she'd shared with Gordon. They'd used her inheritance from Grandma Fletcher as a deposit when they were first married and had never lived anywhere else. Gordon had often complained that they couldn't afford to move anywhere better, but Sally hadn't minded as it was the first place where she'd felt she belonged.

Grandma Fletcher's house had been large, but not on this scale. She'd been quite old when Sally first went to live with her. She'd had Maggie, her only child, quite late in life. Sally knew she'd been loved, but her time with Grandma Fletcher hadn't been easy as her grandmother's health had meant she'd needed to live very quietly. Consequently, Sally hadn't been able to bring school friends home or take part in many of the activities her classmates had considered normal. She hadn't been allowed to go out in the evenings and had spent most weekends reading or making a fourth at bridge with Grandma Fletcher's elderly friends.

As she crossed the hall, the doorbell sounded. Oh no! Was that Gordon again? She crept forward and peered through the spyhole, relieved to see it was no one more threatening than a delivery man holding a small package. She opened the door.

'Good morning, madam,' he said, holding out the box for Sally to take. 'Would you please sign here?'

'This isn't for me,' Sally said. 'Don't you need my sister's signature?'

'Not me, madam. I don't care who signs it as long as someone from the household does, so, if you wouldn't mind, please put your full name and then sign where I've put the cross.'

Sally did as she was instructed and then handed back his pen.

'That's the ticket,' he said. 'See you again next week.'

Sally smiled and waved as he strolled back to his van. At least someone was cheerful this morning. The package was very light, almost as if there was nothing inside but some packing materials. She wondered what it was that Alison had delivered, seemingly on a weekly basis, if the delivery man's words were anything to go by. A memory of Peter's words about Alison over-sedating their father flashed into her head, but she pushed it to one side. No way was she going to allow Peter to poison her mind against Alison.

She reached the kitchen, put the small box on the table and retrieved her phone. Alison was upstairs sitting with their father. Sally had offered to go with her, but Alison had felt he was too agitated today and seeing Sally might upset him even more.

Sally flopped down at the table and opened her phone. No message yet from the agency. Bored to tears at having nothing to do, she decided to make a cup of tea. Not because she was thirsty, just for something to do. She'd just sat down and placed the tea on the table when she heard the front door open.

She could tell by the sound of his footsteps that it was Peter back yet again. Earlier this morning she'd felt he'd been fishing to see if she had any childhood memories. He seemed to imply she remembered more than she was letting on.

Sally got up and limped to the kitchen door. Peter was already halfway across the hall, heading for the study.

'Peter, do you have a moment?' she asked, wondering how on earth she would be able to bring up the subject of her dream without stammering over every word.

'I'm sure I can make time in my busy schedule. What can I do for you?'

'Perhaps we could talk in the kitchen?' she suggested.

'Oh, sounds ominous. Or have you finally decided to take my advice and leave? My offer still stands.'

Sally turned and limped back into the kitchen. She sat down and waited for Peter to arrive.

'Close the door, please,' she said as he came in.

'Oh, so we're going to talk secrets,' he asked, flicking the door closed with his hand. 'Have you remembered something?'

'Sit down, please,' Sally asked, trying to frame the right words in her mind. If she didn't come straight to the point, she knew Peter would wriggle out of admitting anything.

He pulled out a chair and sat down, grinning at Sally as if he was in the middle of a particularly entertaining game, then he pointed to the box on the table.

'I see Alison has received another of her regular supplies. Shall we open the box so that you can see how right I am about your precious sister?'

He reached forward, but Sally snatched the box away and put it on the chair beside her.

'If Alison wants either of us to know what's in this parcel then I'm sure she'll tell us. That's not why I asked you to come in. Look, Peter, I'm not quite sure how to put this, but I need to ask you about something that might have happened when I was a child while I lived here with my mother and father.'

The look of amusement left his face. 'I was hardly ever here when you were growing up. I don't think I'm the one to answer questions about that time of your life. Why don't you ask Alison?' He stood up so quickly, the chair fell backwards. 'Damn,' he said, reaching down to right the fallen chair. 'I have things to do, places to go, can't stop here to talk about events I wasn't ever party to.'

'Please, Peter, I need to know—'

'Need to know what? There's nothing that happened when you were a child that had anything to do with me, regardless of what Alison might have said. She's not well, you know that,

164

right? She's been unstable since she was a child. She has a screw loose. Always has had, just like her crazy mother. Did you know she was institutionalised?'

Sally nodded. 'Yes, Alison has told me about her mother.'

Peter snorted. 'Her mother? I'm not talking about her. I'm talking about Alison. She was institutionalised for nearly a year the first time she was put away. She went completely loopy and John had to pack her off to the nuthouse. That was while you were in hospital in a coma. Poor old John. He hasn't had the best of luck, has he? First he married Constance whose whole family has a nutty streak, then he married your mother and we all know the type of woman she was.'

Sally struggled to her feet. 'I just wanted to know what you remembered about me and my mother when I was a child. Alison says my mother—'

'Alison says, Alison says. You want to be very careful listening to what Alison says.'

'Why? I want to know the truth.'

Peter laughed. 'Well, you can't rely on Alison for that. She hated your mother.'

'Are you saying she would lie to me?'

He shook his head. 'Not at all, Sally. I am simply saying, don't believe everything Alison spouts. Your sister is far more like *her* mother than she wants you or anyone else to know. Whatever she says is likely to be a distortion of the truth, although, to be fair, she'll probably believe every word herself. You really should pack your bags and get out of this nuthouse.'

He opened the kitchen door to leave and Sally was shocked to see Alison standing outside the door. How much had she heard? Sally wondered. She soon found out.

165

'How dare you?' Alison raged, stepping forward to confront Peter.

Peter slid past her and then turned back. 'I dare, Alison, because I know what I can say and what I can't. Now, if you'll excuse me, I have work to carry out. Your father's investments seem to have taken a dive and need my urgent attention.'

As he strode away, Alison came into the kitchen and flopped onto the chair Peter had just picked up.

'What was that all about?' she asked Sally.

Feeling guilty at subjecting Alison to Peter's spite, Sally wasn't sure where to start. She hesitated and Alison held up a hand.

'Don't bother trying to explain. I understand Peter only too well and know how he twists whatever you say to him to suit his needs, but you might as well know that some of what he said was true. I was institutionalised for a few months. It was the same year you had your fall. That time is difficult for me to talk about.'

'You don't have to tell me anything,' Sally said, wanting to smooth away the look of anguish on Alison's face.

Alison stood up and walked over to the work surface. 'Tea?' she asked, waving the kettle at Sally.

'Yes, please. I need another one after listening to Peter leading me down a rabbit hole.'

'That's exactly what he does,' Alison said. 'He's like an eel, wriggling around, only telling half-truths and filling in the gaps with malicious titbits. I told you about my years growing up with my mother dumping me here and then demanding I go back to her whenever she came out of hospital. What I didn't mention was the toll that took on my own mental health. After your fall, it was only natural that Dad would concentrate totally on your recovery. You were in a coma for such a long time and there was a point when it looked like you weren't going to make it.'

The kettle boiled and Sally watched as Alison made the tea. Her hands were shaking and the liquid spilled over.

'Here,' Sally said, standing up and moving over to Alison. 'Why don't I finish doing this and you sit down for a change?'

Alison shrugged, but moved back to the table and went to sit down.

'When did this arrive?' she asked, holding up the small box Sally had put on the chair.

'It was delivered a little while ago. Peter wanted to open it, but I wouldn't let him.'

Alison scowled. 'There's nothing in here important enough to bother Peter, but he likes to cause trouble whenever he can.' She stood up and walked over to the pantry, placing the box on one of the shelves. Then she went back and sat down.

Sally couldn't help but wonder if there were sedatives in the box, it was light enough for that, but she had no intention of asking. If Alison wanted her to know, she'd tell her. She took the cups over one by one as she wasn't sure she'd be able to manage both while limping.

'Thank you,' Alison said, lifting her cup in a gesture of salute. 'To get back to our earlier conversation, I couldn't cope with everything that was happening back then and tried to end my life.' She put the cup down and pulled up her sleeve, showing Sally the scars across her wrist. 'Dad had me sectioned. I think today I'd have received better care. I certainly hope so, but back then suicide attempts were not treated with the kindness I believe they are today.'

'I don't know what to say,' Sally said. 'Except that I wish we'd had chance to get to know each other sooner than this. I wish I could have been there for you.'

Alison smiled. 'That's a nice thing to say, but to be honest, I'm not sure how much good you could have done. You were only young and in a coma for months. Besides, as I said, I resented the hell out of you back then.'

Sally reached across and touched Alison's arm. 'I might not have been old enough then, but afterwards, while I was growing up, safe with Grandma Fletcher, you were going through so much trauma. I could have been a friend to you.'

'Well, you're being that now,' Alison said. 'You will never know how pleased I am that you're here.'

Sally smiled and drank her tea, glad Alison felt that way, although she felt bad about what had happened today. If she hadn't accosted Peter, Alison's trauma needn't have come up. He'd been only too ready to try to drive a wedge between them. What was he hoping to achieve? There was definitely something he believed Sally needed to know, but at the same time, he seemed fearful that she might remember something he didn't want her to recall.

Sally thought about how hard he had tried to get her to leave with him today. Why? It couldn't be for any altruistic motive. He didn't seem to have a decent bone in his body. Was he the one who'd tried to run her over? Was he so scared about what she might remember that he'd kill her before she could tell anyone?

What could she possibly have seen as a child that he was worried she might recall? Or was it something to do with Alison and he *wanted* Sally to remember it? She had a sudden vision of Alison's horrified face over some of his comments. And then there was the evidence Alison had over Peter. Her sister claimed she hadn't said it, but Sally knew what she'd heard. Alison had threatened Peter with evidence, but evidence of what?

Chapter Twenty-three

Saturday 14th June

'Why are you packing, Mummy? Where are we going?'
Mummy had on her cross face. Sally wished she'd stayed in her bedroom as Mummy had told her she should do, but she was bored and lonely in there with no one to talk to.

Sally wanted to ask again about the suitcases, but Mummy didn't like it if she didn't shut up.

There was a loud thumpity-thump on the door downstairs and Mummy looked up. There was another thumpity-thump and Mummy looked even crosser than before.

'Go to your room. I'll call when I'm ready for you.'

Sally didn't move fast enough, so Mummy pushed her out of the room.

'Go!' she said. 'I need to see who's at the door, although whoever it is needs to learn some manners, making all that racket.'

Sally went towards her bedroom as Mummy headed downstairs to open the door. Wondering who it was who'd made Mummy so angry, Sally stopped and crouched down to peer through the balustrade. She saw Mummy stride across the hall and wrench open the door.

'What the hell do you want?' Mummy asked.

Alison's mummy pushed her way inside, dragging Alison along by her arm. 'Where's John? Where is he? I can't cope!'

'He's away in France for the whole of next week. He left this morning.'

Alison's mummy began to cry. 'I need him. I can't deal with Alison. I have to go away for a rest.'

Sally saw Alison look at her mummy. She didn't look happy. Was Alison going to stay again? She hadn't been here for ages. Not since Sally's birthday.

'He isn't here and I'm going away myself today so you can't leave Alison. You'll have to take her somewhere else.'

'I can't!' Alison's mummy screamed. 'I can't cope. I might kill her if I have to put up with her much longer. You'll have to look after her until I'm better.'

'I've just told you, I can't. I'm going to my mother's for a while. There must be someone else.'

Oh, goody, Sally thought, bouncing up and down with excitement. We're going to Grandma Fletcher's. Sally's mummy looked up and scowled.

'Sally! What are you doing there? I told you to get to your room. Go now and stay there until I call you. Go on, go!'

Mummy was really cross now, thought Sally, but she didn't care because they were going to Grandma Fletcher's. She would make a fuss of Sally and make her feel happy. She stood up to go to her bedroom, glancing back down as Alison's mummy started crying and screaming. Mummy looked as if she wanted to hit her. She was yelling at Alison's mummy to stop making so much noise, but Mummy was almost making more noise.

Sally really wanted to stay and see what happened, but if Mummy spotted her again she'd be in big trouble. She carried on to her bedroom and lay down on the bed. Maybe if she fell asleep, when she woke up it would be time to go to visit Grandma Fletcher. Sally closed her eyes and thought about all the nice times she'd had with her grandmother. Ice cream, cuddles and hot chocolate, even when Mummy said she couldn't have any. She hoped they'd stay there for ever and ever. She felt herself drifting away on a big fluffy cloud.

Suddenly Sally woke up. Had she heard Mummy scream? She scrambled to her bedroom door, pulling it open, but couldn't hear anything. Should she go to find Mummy, or should she go back to bed? Mummy would be so cross if she didn't do as she'd been told, but maybe Mummy needed her. Sally crept along the hallway to Mummy's bedroom. Maybe she could peek in without Mummy seeing her.

Mummy's bedroom door was half open. Sally peered through the gap. Mummy wasn't there. There were noises from downstairs. Maybe she was in the kitchen. Sally crept down the stairs, holding on to the banister. She heard voices and stopped moving. She wanted to run back upstairs, but she needed to know where Mummy was.

Sally reached the kitchen door, heart pounding so hard she felt sick. The kitchen door was open.

All she could see was red and there was a funny smell. She stepped inside to see if Mummy was there, but there was a man in the way, standing with his back to her. He had a knife in his hand. Blood was dripping from the blade. Sally gasped. She turned and ran back up the stairs . . .

Sally sat bolt upright, heart thumping and drenched in sweat. She reached for the glass of water on the bedside table, desperate for a drink, but her hands were shaking so badly she spilled most of it before she could take a sip.

What had she just dreamt? Was any of it true? Who was the man? Was it Peter? Could he have murdered her mother? But that didn't make sense. Her mother had been alive for years after leaving this house. Surely, the cards and money she'd received twice a year had proved that.

Was she remembering something that had really happened or was her mind creating nightmares because she disliked Peter so much? Could her mother be dead? Is that why she'd disappeared? Then who had sent the birthday and Christmas cards?

Sally forced herself to stay in bed when all she really wanted to do was get up and run as far away from the house as it was possible to get. Had she just dreamt about the day she fell down the stairs? Is that what had happened? Was it her mother's blood she'd seen? Had she run upstairs with the man holding the knife chasing her?

As the images from the dream faded, Sally struggled to recall the exact sequence of events. Alison's mother had been raging, but what had taken place after Sally had been sent to her room and fallen asleep? Had anything happened? Alison had been there that day. Maybe she would be able to tell Sally if any of what she'd dreamt was even partially true, or was it all a figment of an overactive imagination?

Putting the empty glass back on the bedside table, Sally picked up her phone to check the time. It was just after half three. She'd need to wait until morning to talk to Alison about her dream. She lay back down and closed her eyes, not expecting to be able to go back to sleep.

The next thing Sally knew, the sun was shining through her bedroom curtains. She reached for her phone. It was gone ten! Throwing back the duvet, she cautiously climbed out of bed, testing her sore ankle. She'd expected to feel more pain, but realised it was no longer anywhere near as bad as it had been. She might not be able to run, but a walk later should be possible. She wondered if Alison might like to go with her. Maybe a stroll around Rutland Water would be a better place to discuss last night's dream than here in the house where the events may, or may not, have taken place.

She went to the bathroom and showered, feeling immediately better as the water cascaded over her. That was the second disturbing dream she'd had since arriving here. The first had revealed something her subconscious had clearly kept hidden for all these years.

As she dressed, she thought about the horrible life Alison had endured growing up. She'd been shunted from pillar to post between her parents and had to put up with Sally's mother, who had clearly shown she hadn't wanted her predecessor's child. It was no wonder she'd tried to take her own life. Not that Sally had any intention of asking Alison any questions about that.

She finished getting dressed and went downstairs, ready to apologise for arriving so late for breakfast. No way would she allow Alison to make one of her fabulous cooked breakfasts this morning. A bowl of cornflakes and a cup of coffee would be just fine.

As she came down the stairs, Sally heard her father's voice coming from the drawing room. She couldn't make out exactly what he was saying, but she heard her mother's name over and over. Then she heard Alison's soothing tones. Their father must have responded because he was no longer shouting.

Sally stopped in the hall, debating whether to head for the kitchen or the drawing room. Should she go to help Alison, or would the sight of her set him off again? He'd been shouting Maggie's name. Usually when that happened, just seeing Sally made him worse.

She walked to the centre of the hall and peered into the drawing room. Alison was facing the door, standing in front of their father's armchair. As his back was to her, unless he stood up and looked round, he wouldn't be able to see Sally.

Her sister looked up, so Sally did a mime asking if she should come in. The way Alison shook her head and waved Sally away answered the unspoken question. It would be better if she made herself scarce for a while.

'Who are you waving at?' their father yelled. 'Is it Maggie? Has she come back?'

He stood up and turned, spotting Sally. 'Maggie! My darling, come here.'

Sally stood rooted to the spot, not knowing whether to turn away or go to him. Before she could decide, his expression changed from one of love to one of hatred.

'I thought you were dead, you bitch!'

Alison waved her arms frantically and Sally didn't wait. When he went into one of these rants it was easier for Alison if Sally wasn't around. She turned towards the kitchen, went in and grabbed the back door key. She needed to get out.

Sally walked slowly along the drive and onto the track

leading to the road, aware of her ankle, but not feeling too much pain. As she turned onto the road, she spotted a familiar golden shape up ahead. Honey was walking towards her, closely followed by Colin Blanchett. Sally didn't know which way to turn – go back to avoid him, or walk towards him and simply nod her head in greeting?

Remembering his kindness when he'd helped her, she couldn't turn her back on him, so headed in his direction. A few strides brought them face to face.

'Hello,' he said as the dog's tail wagged furiously. 'Looks like Honey remembers you.'

Sally reached down and stroked the dog's back. 'I remember her, too.' She looked up, feeling shy and awkward. 'You didn't give me chance to thank you properly the other morning.'

Colin shrugged. 'No thanks required. Honey and I are always on the lookout for damsels in distress. Are you going my way? We're heading around the water towards home, or is your ankle still too sore?'

Sally shook her head. 'I can hardly feel it now.'

He raised an eyebrow. 'Good. I'm pleased to hear that. Would you like to keep us company? I'm sure Honey would like that, wouldn't you, girl?'

'I can't . . . That is, I'd like to . . . but I don't think that's a good idea.'

Hearing a car coming along the narrow road, Sally stepped to the side. As the hatchback passed and turned from the road onto the track, she saw Peter staring in her direction. Praying he wouldn't mention seeing her with Colin to Alison, she smiled and gave a rueful shrug.

'I'd best head home,' she said.

'Did Alison give you her version of what happened in my office when she was my patient?'

Sally shook her head. 'Her mother was your patient. Not Alison.'

'I have never met her mother, Sally. What Alison claimed happened didn't occur. I never made any kind of advance. I would never do that. When she came around to my side of the desk and stood too close to me, I pressed the panic button under the desk to call in my secretary.'

'Please don't say any more,' Sally said. 'I won't be disloyal to Alison. Besides, if Alison really was your patient, then I don't think you should be telling me this. Wouldn't that be a breach of patient–doctor confidentiality?'

'It would be if I told you anything that was discussed,' Colin said. 'Look, I can understand you would feel awkward fraternising with the enemy, but please believe me when I say, if you ever need a friend, a sounding board, or a safe harbour, you have my card. Call me.'

Sally felt her eyes fill with tears. He sounded so sincere, but what he'd done to Alison wasn't something she could ignore, and to add to his sin, he'd lied about it to try to make himself look better. To be friends with him would mean being disloyal to her sister. And after everything Alison had done for her, there was no way she would stab her in the back by befriending someone who had abused her.

Unable to put her thoughts into words, she nodded. Colin smiled and called Honey to heel.

'I'd hoped to see you again, Sally. I think the time will come when you'll need a friend. Remember, if you need help, call me.'

She watched him walk away, wanting to call him back just for some company, but that would mean betraying Alison. She turned to walk back along the track until she reached the drive. With every step she took, it felt as if someone's eyes were boring into her. Was Mrs Carstairs peering through the curtains again? Resisting the urge to look towards the house and wave, Sally kept her focus straight ahead.

Chapter Twenty-four

Gordon lowered the binoculars. So that was her fancy man. She must know him really well judging by the fuss the dog had made of her. How long had this been going on? Was he the reason she came to live here? No, she came here because of that bitch sister of hers. That cow must have decided to find a new man for Sally.

He'd teach her not to interfere. He'd deal with them all. Sally's new lover would be first, then her sister, and after her the two old men he'd seen around the big fancy house where Sally was living. One of them must be her father. The other looked like a younger version. The family resemblance between them was very strong, but Sally didn't look like any of them. She must take after her mother.

Thanks to Sally reporting him, he was reduced to watching her from a distance. It was the only way he could keep an eye on her. Ever since the police had warned him off, he'd kept far enough away so that he couldn't be seen, but not for much longer. Sally was his and she was coming home with him. He just needed to bide his time and wait for the right moment.

He kicked the rear tyre of his car. After all he did to stop Sally from getting in touch with her family, it wasn't fair that she'd found her way back to them. He thought he'd convinced her they didn't want anything to do with her – even down to saying her father had refused an invitation to the wedding. He'd never even contacted the man, but Sally was so gullible she'd believed her father didn't want any part in the ceremony, that he had refused to walk her down the aisle. Not that there'd been an aisle to walk down; the registry office had done just fine.

He would have preferred to deal with the sister first, but it would be easier to take out Sally's new lover. He'd be an easy target early in the morning while walking with that dog. It was a shame having to hurt the animal, but sometimes sacrifices had to be made.

Chapter Twenty-five

Sally went back into the house, convinced someone had watched her all the way to the door. Was it Gordon? Who else could it be? Maybe she'd just imagined it. Even so, she shivered as she entered through the back door and made for the kettle. She'd make a pot of tea and then find Alison. She was just being paranoid. No one had been watching her.

Any hope she'd had that Peter wouldn't mention seeing her with Colin disappeared the moment she heard the door slam open against the wall behind her.

'How could you, Sally?'

She whirled round on hearing Alison's voice and didn't try to pretend she didn't know what her sister meant. Even if she had wanted to do so, the look of satisfaction on Peter's face would have told her not to bother trying.

'I went for a walk and bumped into him at the end of our drive. It was impossible to avoid him.'

'That's not what it looked like to me,' Peter said. 'The pair of you were having a great conversation while you petted his dog.'

Rage such as she'd never known filled Sally's entire body.

'And you couldn't wait to get in here to tell Alison, could you? I've only known you five minutes, *Uncle* Peter, but it's clear you take delight in stirring up hornets' nests.'

'If you'd left when I first told you to, I wouldn't have had the opportunity. Maybe now Alison will add her voice to mine. Come on, Alison. You need to let her go. You don't need her here.'

Sally turned to her sister who looked furious. 'Alison, I hardly spoke to Colin, other than to tell him my loyalty lies with you.'

'So, you discussed me with him?'

'No! Yes! Not really.'

Alison banged her hand on the dining table. 'Well, which is it? Did you or did you not discuss me with Colin Blanchett?'

'He asked me to walk with him around Rutland Water and I said no. He then asked if it was because of what had happened between you and I said—'

'He had the nerve to ask you that?' Alison hissed. 'The man's a pig. Look, Sally, I'm sorry, but I don't want you to fraternise with him while you're living here.'

'She should leave,' said Peter. 'There's been no peace since she arrived. Poor old John doesn't know if she's his daughter or his wife, and isn't happy either way.' He frowned at Sally. 'I told you the day you arrived that you don't belong and should leave.'

'That's enough, Peter,' Alison said. 'Of course she belongs here. I won't have you saying otherwise. Do I make myself clear?'

Sally put her hand out towards Alison. 'I'm really sorry. I didn't intend to meet up with Colin. It happened by chance. I definitely won't see him again. The last thing I want to do is to upset you.'

'Or lose a roof over your head,' Peter said.

Sally turned to him. 'If Alison wants me to leave then I will, but not because of your goading. I'm staying here until I have a job and enough money to pay my way in the world. When that happens, I'll move out. Not a second sooner.'

Alison took hold of Sally's hand. 'I want you to stay. Ignore Peter. I should have known better than to believe him when he said you were making up to Colin Blanchett. I know you wouldn't do anything to cause me pain, and you getting friendly with that man would destroy me.'

'Very touching, ladies,' Peter said, moving towards the door. 'I'm going to work on John's accounts before this sisterly love-in makes me vomit.'

As the door closed behind him, Sally looked at Alison and held out her hands. 'Why does he hate me so much that he can't bear for me to be here?'

Alison shrugged. 'Who knows what goes on in that man's head. Look, I'm sorry I jumped at you like that, but the way Peter described it. Oh hell, I fell for his twisted lies yet again. Sit down, Sally. Tell me what was actually said so that we can put it behind us.'

Sally pulled out a chair and sat down, relieved that Peter had left the room, but also that Alison seemed to have accepted she hadn't deliberately done anything to hurt her.

'It's as I said,' Sally began. 'I got to the end of the lane just as Colin and Honey, his dog, arrived. As he'd helped me after I fell in the ditch, I didn't feel I could just turn my back on him. When he suggested I walk around the water with him my face must have told its own story because he immediately guessed I was going to say no and why. Then I came home.'

'So when did Peter see the two of you together?'

'He turned onto the track from the road seconds before I parted from Colin.' Sally hesitated. 'One thing Colin Blanchett said that threw me was that *you* were his patient and he's never met your mother.'

Alison laughed. 'Now, why would he say that? It doesn't make sense to tell such an outright lie. He must know you'd tell me.'

'I wondered that,' Sally said, 'and what I came up with doesn't redound to his credit. I think he was trying to undermine your version of events by making out you were his patient and therefore unstable.'

'You could be right,' Alison said. 'We'll never know, as you will never see him again. Are you hungry? I made breakfast earlier for Dad and he's gone up to his room to rest for a few hours. We could have a nice brunch.'

'I'd love that,' Sally said, 'but please let me help you.'

Alison shook her head. 'Not a chance. I'm only happy when I'm queen of the kitchen.'

Sally laughed. 'And I can't even be a lowly scullery maid?'

'No, you can be a much-loved sister and enjoy being pampered.' She sighed. 'I suppose I'd better go and offer Peter some food, although I'd be happy if he choked on it. I'll be back in a bit.'

She left the kitchen and Sally heard her footsteps crossing the hall. Looking down at the way she was dressed, she decided to go upstairs and get changed out of her running gear into something a bit smarter.

As she crossed the hall, she heard voices coming from the study. Alison and Peter both sounded angry.

'How many times do I have to tell you you're on dangerous ground, Peter? Stop trying to get Sally to leave. If you say anything else to her about moving out, I might have to—'

'You'll have to do what? That ship has sailed, Alison. If you were going to do anything with it, you'd have done it by now.'

Feeling like an eavesdropper, Sally moved quickly to the stairs. Why was Peter so opposed to her being here? But in a way he was right, ever since she'd arrived the household had been upset in so many ways. First there was her father who, she had to admit, was upset just by the sight of her. Sally was sure Alison was sedating him so that he spent more time in his room and didn't have to come into contact with her. Is that what was in the box she'd signed for? More sedatives? Then there was Gordon's arrival at the front door and the need to call the police. Alison had enough on her plate without Sally adding to it.

She was glad she'd been able to rearrange the interview in Oakham. Fortunately, the company had been understanding when she'd called to explain why she'd had to put it off for a week. As soon as she got a job she would find somewhere to live, but close enough so that she could be on hand if ever Alison needed her.

By the time Sally had changed and gone back to the kitchen, all was quiet. Only Alison was in there, busy at the Aga.

'I take it Peter didn't want to stay for brunch?' Sally said.

Alison looked round and scowled. 'I think he picked up that I would rather poison him than feed him at the moment. He's gone back to his own place on the other side of the water.'

She picked up a serving dish and placed it in the centre of the table.

'Help yourself to whatever you fancy,' she said, lifting the lid.

The fabulous aromas of sausages, bacon, eggs and mushrooms wafted up, making Sally's mouth water.

'Toast?' Alison asked.

Sally shook her head and Alison sat down opposite her at the table. 'Listen, don't take anything Peter says to heart. I couldn't bear it if you left.'

'I don't want to leave,' Sally said and laughed. 'I couldn't even if I wanted to as I don't have enough money to move in anywhere else. Can I ask you something?'

Alison smiled. 'Of course you can.'

'Peter keeps on about me leaving, but he takes even more delight in upsetting you. I've seen how strong you are. I saw how you handled Gordon, but Peter needles you day after day and you let him get away with it.'

Alison picked up her cup and took a sip of tea.

'Apart from helping with Dad, there is another reason I can't bring myself to forbid Peter from coming to the house. I don't want to go into why, but there's something I did when I was a teenager that I'm not proud of. In fact, I'm deeply ashamed of it. Somehow Peter found out. Dad doesn't know and I'd be mortified if he did. Peter likes to hold the threat of exposing me over my head. Please don't ask me for details. I can't bear to talk about it.' Alison reached for her cup and took another sip of tea. 'I know he gets under your skin, but if we both ignore his jibes, he'll stop eventually.'

'Has he been goading you for all these years?'

Alison banged her fist on the table. 'For God's sake, Sally! Let it go. Peter and I have come to a standoff. I don't tell anyone what I know about him and he keeps quiet about my teenage misdemeanour.'

'I'm sorry,' Sally said, instinctively cowering away from Alison's sudden show of anger. Her sister must have seen how she'd reacted because she reached out and grabbed Sally's hand.

'There's no need to be sorry. Let's not talk about Peter,' Alison said.

Sally knew it would be hard to let go of some of the things Peter had said, but if Alison was prepared to put up with him then she had to find a way to do the same.

'I'd rather talk about anything other than Peter,' Sally said. 'I won't let him upset me any more. You don't need to worry.'

Alison frowned. 'I'm actually more concerned about your health, to be honest. You're looking very peaky. It's not because of what's happened this morning, I hope?'

Sally sighed. 'No. I didn't sleep well last night. I had a nightmare that really upset me.'

'Do you want to talk about it?'

'I don't know, to be honest,' Sally said. 'I'm not sure if it was a dream or a memory, or a mix of both. It started with my mother packing a suitcase and me thinking we were going to Grandma Fletcher's house, but it all went wrong from that point onwards.'

'How old did you think you were in the dream? Sometimes you did go with your mother to visit your grandmother.'

'Did I?' Sally said. 'I can't remember anything clearly from my early years, which is why I'm not sure if the dream is a memory or something else entirely.'

'It might help if you tell me all about it and we can try to make sense of whatever it is your subconscious is trying to tell you.'

Remembering the way the dream had ended, Sally shuddered and pushed her plate to one side.

'It must have been bad if it put you off your food,' Alison said.

Sally nodded. 'It was.' She reached for her cup to give herself some thinking time. Alison would think she was mad if she said she thought it might have been a memory of the day she fell down the stairs, because that was the same day her mother left, so the part with the knife couldn't have happened. Unless the blood wasn't her mother's but someone else's – but whose?

Alison reached across the table and squeezed Sally's hand. 'Don't tell me if you'd rather not. I don't want to pry into something that you'd rather keep to yourself. Once we've cleaned up here, I'm going to do some gardening. If you like, you can come out and give me a hand.'

Once again overwhelmed by Alison's kindness, Sally realised she owed her sister an honest answer.

'I don't know why, but in the dream, it felt like it was the last time I saw my mother. She was angry with me, but I think she was often angry, not just with me, but with everyone. She was packing a suitcase and then people came. She sent me to my room, but I didn't go. I was peering through the balustrade. She saw me and shouted. I ran to my room and fell asleep. When I woke up it was quiet, but then I heard my mother scream. I got up and went downstairs.'

Sally realised she was shaking so badly she'd spilt tea over the table. Hand trembling, she put the cup down.

'I'm sorry, I've made a mess,' she said, getting up to fetch some kitchen paper, but Alison beat her to it.

'Sit back down,' she said. 'I'll clean this up. You're shivering. What happened next in the dream?'

Sally opened her mouth, but no words came out. She could feel her throat closing. She couldn't breathe. As she gasped for air, Alison came round and shook her.

'Breathe in, Sally, breathe out!'

Shuddering, Sally drew in gulps of air.

Eventually, she felt herself beginning to relax.

'Sorry,' she whispered. 'I didn't react like that when I woke up, so I have no idea why talking about the dream had that effect on me.'

'Let's leave it for now,' Alison said.

But Sally knew if she didn't put it into words now, she never would.

'There was a man in the kitchen – this kitchen – holding a knife that was dripping with blood. I turned and ran back upstairs. Then I woke up. I keep thinking, wondering, is that what happened to my mother? Did our father kill her? Or did Peter kill her?'

'Wow! No wonder you're so distressed.' Alison was frowning. 'Okay, let's try and put everything into perspective. Your mother sent you cards and money twice a year until you moved from Cornwall, isn't that right?'

Sally nodded.

'Okay, so we know she was alive at least until then. In addition, if your dream was about the day you fell, then that was also the day your mother left. I was here and saw she was alive and well. She argued with my mother and Mrs Carstairs.

There were no men here until after you fell. Dad was in France and Peter was at home until he arrived to find me in hysterics and you at the foot of the stairs.'

'Where were you when my mother left the house?'

'I was outside in the garden for a while. I came back in through the kitchen and I can promise you there was no blood, no knife and absolutely no dead body. I heard you call for your mother to come back and then a harrowing scream. I knew straightaway that you'd hurt yourself badly by the noises you made as you fell.' Alison shuddered. 'I had nightmares about those sounds for years afterwards. The bad dreams only stopped once I was in regular therapy.'

'Alison, why do you think I dreamt about a man with a bloodied knife?' Sally asked, tears dripping from her face and making damp spots on her jeans.

'I'm no psychiatrist, but I wonder if it's because being here has reminded you of how it really was back then. Maybe your subconscious mind would prefer to believe your mother was dead than knowing she walked out and left you behind.'

Alison grabbed Sally's hand. 'I'd promised myself I would never tell you this, but I think you have a right to know. I came running from the kitchen after I heard you scream. As I reached you lying in a heap in the hall, I heard the door slam and the car pull away.'

Sally felt as if she'd been hit by a freight train. If Alison had heard her as she fell, then surely her mother must have done so as well – and yet she'd left. She'd been so keen to go off with her lover she hadn't even stopped to see if her daughter had been badly injured.

She looked up at Alison and caught a fleeting expression of

relief on her face. But why was she relieved? Was it because she had finally told Sally what really happened that day, or was it because something she'd said wasn't true and she was relieved that Sally had believed her?

Chapter Twenty-six

Sally swallowed hard. She had to know the truth.

'You're keeping something from me,' she said, watching Alison's face. If there was worse to come, then she needed to hear it.

'What makes you say that?' Alison asked.

'I don't know. It was something in your expression that made me think you know more than you're telling me. What is it?'

'Let's have another cup of tea,' Alison said. 'I don't think we should be raking up what's best left in the past on such a lovely day. In fact, let's go into the garden and have tea there. We can do some weeding afterwards.'

'Alison! Please, whatever it is, I need to know.'

'No matter what?'

Sally nodded. 'No matter what.'

Alison stood and paced up and down the kitchen.

'I don't feel comfortable telling you this, but your mother wasn't good to you.'

Sally shrugged. 'I guessed as much. I don't think she wanted to be a mother.'

'It went deeper than that,' Alison said. 'She was actively unkind to you. It was bad enough that she pushed me away, I could understand that, even though I would have done anything to make her like me.'

'But she also pushed me away?' Sally said, the lump in her throat making it hard to get the words out.

'If only that were all,' Alison said. 'She used to treat you appallingly when Dad was away on business. She would lock you up in the airing cupboard or in the boathouse if you did the slightest thing wrong. I often used to rescue you, but I wasn't here all the time, so who knows what happened when it was just the two of you.'

'Why don't I remember any of this?' Sally asked.

Alison shrugged. 'I don't know. It seems as if you don't remember much from your childhood. Maybe it's your mind's way of protecting you from being hurt.'

Sally stood up, wrapping her arms around herself and wishing she hadn't pushed Alison to tell the truth.

'Do you think I dream about something bad happening to my mother because I hated her? Maybe I wanted her to die.'

Alison rushed over and put her arm around Sally. 'No! I don't think that at all. You loved her. We all did. She held everyone under her spell, but what we wanted from her we couldn't get. We needed her to love us.'

Sally felt tears running down her face. 'But she didn't love us. She didn't love me.'

'I'm sorry, Sally. I shouldn't have told you.'

Sally pulled a tissue from her pocket and wiped her eyes. 'No, it's better for me to know. Maybe now I can stop hoping against hope that one day she'll come back into my life.'

Alison patted Sally's arm. 'I think that's very unlikely. She left without looking back. Let her go, Sally. Don't let her hurt you more than she already has. Let's go outside and get some fresh air. I want to show you what I call my secret garden. It's beautiful at this time of year.'

Alison kept up a flow of gentle chatter that Sally found soothing as she followed her sister into the garden. She'd been aware of the expanse of lawn, but hadn't previously taken notice of the abundance of flower beds that created separate areas. If this was all Alison's work then Sally was in awe. She'd always struggled even to keep houseplants alive. As for their postage-stamp stretch of back garden, Gordon had insisted that it be used solely to grow vegetables. This garden couldn't have been more of a contrast. It was a riot of colours.

Suddenly realising that Alison had called her name, Sally looked over at her sister.

'Sorry, Alison, I was miles away admiring the garden. It's almost like a park the way the various beds and trees have been planted to provide different walks.'

Alison beamed with pleasure. 'I'm so pleased you like it. The garden has been my own project since before you were born. As a small child Dad encouraged me to take an interest and it sort of grew from there. Once I moved back home permanently, I landscaped the garden to create exactly what you said: a feeling of being in a park. Come, I want to show you my pride and joy.'

She turned and walked past a laburnum tree with a fabulous display of drooping yellow flowers, through an arch covered in honeysuckle that was so heavily fragranced it made Sally feel light-headed for a moment.

Walking through the arch, she came into a part of the garden she had never seen before. No wonder Alison was so proud of her work here.

'This is absolutely gorgeous, Alison.'

Alison smiled. 'As a child I was captivated by *The Secret Garden* by Frances Hodgson Burnett. Have you ever read it?'

Sally shook her head.

'It's a fabulous book and was later made into a film, but anyway, from the time I read the book I wanted a secret garden of my own and this is it! It's taken me years to get it to the way it is today.'

Sally breathed in the mixed fragrance of masses of rose bushes.

'I had no idea there were so many different types of roses,' she said, looking around in wonder. 'There must be thirty or forty different colours spread across all these beds. Have you got one of every variety?'

Alison laughed. 'I wish! There are over thirty thousand varieties, so I only have a small selection, but I'm particularly proud of this part of the garden. I started planning it when I was eight and first moved away with my mother after your mother moved in. I used to draw designs for how it would all be laid out. Each time my mother dumped me back here I would come down to this section and try to put my ideas into practice. When Dad was home, he used to help me by digging the beds. Of course, once I was strong enough to do it myself, I no longer needed his input.'

'This is amazing. What's going in there?' Sally asked, pointing to a bed against the hedge with a framed arch over it, that was bare of plants.

'Every year I try to add one new variety. That bed is intended for a climbing rose called Golden Opportunity. Last year's planting was that one,' she said, pointing to a rose with dark, velvety red blooms. 'Isn't it fabulous? It's called Dark Knight.'

'Is there anything I can do to help you?' Sally asked, praying the answer would be no. With her non-green fingers, she would probably kill Alison's precious roses.

'You could fetch a kneeling pad from the boathouse and the hand tools that are on the shelf at the far end, if you would.'

'Is that all?' Sally said. 'Surely there's more I can do?'

Alison smiled. 'There's a fold-up chair in there as well. Bring that out and you can sit and chat to me while I do a bit of weeding.'

Sally nodded and headed back through the fragrant arch towards the boathouse. From the doorway she looked back. You wouldn't even know that part of the garden was there, she thought, gazing on the artfully placed hedges and shrubs. It was more sheltered there, as well. She hadn't been aware of the breeze until she passed back through the arch to this part of the garden, she realised, swiping the hair from her face for the second time.

As she opened the boathouse door, she once again experienced such a feeling of dread that it was all she could do to go in. One foot raised, she hesitated, but forced herself to enter. Alison was waiting for the tools and kneeling pad. She'd run in, grab them, and then get out as fast as she could.

Heart pounding, she ran to the far end of the boathouse and reached up towards the shelf. As she did so, the door slammed shut behind her.

196

Sally felt her throat close up in fear. She couldn't breathe, couldn't scream. She was trapped in here again, with the rats and the snakes. She stumbled back towards the door, praying it wouldn't be locked, like it had been when she was a child.

She forced it open and staggered out, collapsing in a heap on the lawn. This time she'd escaped. She hadn't had to wait for her mother to let her out.

The wind was stronger now. Sally could see the branches of the laburnum bending in the breeze. The door must have blown shut when the wind caught it, but why had she panicked? What were those memories of being locked in all about?

'Sally! Are you okay?'

Alison's voice seemed to come from a long way off. Sally forced herself to concentrate. She looked up to see Alison running towards her from the direction of the arch.

'What happened? Did you fall?'

Sally dragged herself upright, clinging to the boathouse wall for support.

'I'm so sorry, Alison, I didn't get the things you needed.'

'Never mind that,' she said. 'What happened to you?'

'I had a panic attack in the boathouse. The wind must have blown the door shut and I felt trapped. So many memories came rushing back: fear of rats and snakes while I was locked in. I also remembered my mother opening the door so that I could get out.'

Alison frowned. She opened her mouth to speak, but shook her head instead.

'What?' Sally asked. 'You were going to say something. What was it?'

197

'Nothing,' Alison said. 'Let's go back inside. The wind is really picking up now.'

Sally grabbed Alison's arm and shook it. 'Please, if you know something, tell me! I was close to collapse in there. I was terrified, but not because of what happened today. I think I had a flashback to something from when I was very young.'

'Do you really not remember?'

Sally shook her head. 'No. All I know is that I was frightened almost to the point of a heart attack. Is it because of what you said? That my mother used to lock me in there? Is there something else? Alison, you have to tell me! I need to know!'

Alison shrugged. 'Okay, but I'm not happy doing this. Come with me,' she said, taking Sally's hand and leading her around the side of the boathouse to the back of the building.

Sally was amazed to see a tiny headstone.

'Dad had this made for you, but he insisted the puppy had to be buried behind the boathouse so that you wouldn't see it all the time. This is Rolo's grave, the puppy you got for your seventh birthday.'

Sally had a vague memory of holding a tiny warm creature in her arms.

'I remember I called him Rolo because he had dark chocolate fur with light brown patches, just like a Rolo chocolate, my favourite.'

Sally felt herself drift off into the past. She could almost feel the warmth of his small body in her arms.

'I used to love stroking his soft silky fur.'

'I know,' Alison said. 'You were forever being told off for picking him up.'

Sally felt tears come to her eyes. 'I remember my mother telling me to put him down. She said puppies didn't want to be held all the time, but I wouldn't listen to her.'

'Do you remember what Rolo used to do when you picked him up?' Alison asked.

Sally nodded. 'Yes, he used to wriggle and jump down out of my arms. I couldn't understand why he didn't like it.'

'I told you that Maggie used to lock you in the boathouse as a punishment. I think you might have remembered the time she locked you in after Rolo died.'

'But why would she punish me because my pet had died?'

Alison looked away. 'Let's go inside. Your mother wasn't a nice person. Can we just leave it at that?'

Sally held out her hands, pleading with Alison. 'Please, don't cover it up. What happened to Rolo? Why was I punished? Did I do something bad to him?'

'You did, but not on purpose. You loved the puppy so much you wouldn't put him down. Your mother kept telling you to leave him alone, but you were too young to understand that it wasn't good for him to be picked up all the time.'

'And then?' Sally asked when Alison stopped talking. 'Clearly I did something wrong. What was it?'

'Rolo tried to wriggle away from you, but you wouldn't let him go. You accidently broke his neck trying to stop him from jumping out of your arms.'

Sally remembered the feeling of Rolo's tiny body. She remembered him wriggling, desperate to get back on the ground. She remembered squeezing him, but not that he had died because of her.

'I'm sorry, Sally. I shouldn't have told you. That was why

your mother put you in the boathouse. She said you had to be punished.'

Sally sank to the ground, weeping. She'd killed her own puppy. She'd deserved her mother's punishment.

Chapter Twenty-seven

As he clicked through the options on the computer, Gordon's mood improved. Who'd have thought buying chloroform would be so easy? At first he'd been frustrated, as all the results that had come up for his search had been American companies, but once he'd refined the search for UK only, he'd been able to find what he wanted. The company he decided to use not only had a great delivery service, but they also allowed customers to collect from one of their various locations.

He'd need to do some more research into how much of the stuff to use. He only wanted to knock Sally out. From what he'd read so far, there was a fine line between the right amount and what could cause serious health issues, maybe even death. Sally deserved to be punished, but not until he had her safely back under his control.

She would never want to leave him again once he showed her how much she'd hurt him.

He placed his order and chose to have the chloroform delivered. He decided against going to collect it in person. Best to keep it as anonymous as possible, although he'd had to use his bank card details to fulfil the order.

All he had to do once the stuff arrived was to wait for Sally to go out for a walk. She never seemed to have anyone with her, so it should be fairly easy to grab her, use the chloroform to make sure she didn't scream, put her in the car and take her home.

He sat back with a satisfied sigh. Soon life would return to normal and he'd never have to worry about Sally ever again. She would give up work and stay home to look after him. She wouldn't even need to go shopping. He would take care of everything. In fact, once she came home, she'd never leave the house ever again.

Chapter Twenty-eight

Sunday 15th June

'But why does Mrs Carstairs want us to go to her house for tea this afternoon?' Sally asked. 'She doesn't even know me and has every reason to hate my mother.'

Alison shrugged. 'I don't know what's on Mrs Carstairs' mind, but when she phoned this morning she took me so much by surprise I didn't have time to come up with a valid reason not to go.' She laughed. 'Don't look so downcast. It will only be for an hour and then we can make our escape. She's probably just being nosey, wanting to know why you're here and for how long.'

'Why would she care?' Sally asked.

'I have no idea,' Alison said. 'We're not exactly on friendly terms. We're fine as neighbours, but don't socialise. Dad said it was years before he was able to break the ice after Maggie ran off with Mr Carstairs. Apparently, she wouldn't talk to Dad for a long time and then only if they met at a social event and she couldn't avoid him.'

Sally smiled. 'Sounds like all the more reason not to go. After all, it wasn't our father's fault that Mr Carstairs ran off.'

'I agree, but she made it clear she thought it was Maggie's fault.'

'Yes, but why take it out on our father? That seems illogical. He'd also suffered.'

'Mrs Carstairs is often illogical in the way she thinks. Dad believed she blamed him for not keeping control of Maggie, but then Mrs Carstairs didn't exactly keep control of her husband either.'

'Do we really have to go?' Sally asked.

'Look, she's very prominent in the area on lots of local committees and I would rather not upset her. The invitation was for both of us, and it will look bad if I go on my own. So, will you come with me? Please? For me?'

Sally thought about all she owed to Alison, and this was obviously important to her. Putting up with Mrs Carstairs for an hour was a small way to pay her sister back for taking her in and providing a safe haven from Gordon.

At three in the afternoon, Sally went upstairs to change. She had half an hour to get ready. As she had never before been to an afternoon tea, she hadn't known what to put on, but Alison had suggested wearing something reasonably smart, but not formal. Looking through her still meagre wardrobe choices, Sally decided to go for the pencil skirt and blouse she'd bought to wear for her interview on Wednesday.

Thinking about that brought a smile to her face. If she got the job, she'd be able to start making a contribution to the household, which would at least stop Peter from making so many digs about the finances being in a state, implying it was her fault.

She had done some online research, so knew that to move into a new place she would need a month's rent as deposit, plus the first month's rent up front. As soon as she had enough money, even if all she could afford was a bedsit, she would move to Oakham. It would be a wrench because Alison wanted her to stay but it didn't make sense to live so far from where she would be working. Until she moved, it would mean needing to use Alison as a taxi service to get to and from work. Apart from not wanting to put her sister to so much trouble, Sally wasn't sure her nerves could survive Alison's erratic driving morning and night every day from Monday to Friday.

Realising she'd been daydreaming, Sally shook herself. If she didn't get a move on, she'd be late.

She slipped on her new work clothes and freshened her make-up, thankful she didn't have to worry about covering up any new bruises. That side of her life was over forever. Giving herself a satisfied look in the mirror, she headed out to join Alison.

Her sister was waiting for her in the hall. She looked annoyed.

'Sorry,' Sally said, 'have I kept you waiting?'

'No, not at all. We still have a few minutes before we need to leave. Mrs Carstairs has just sent me a text asking for some laburnum seeds. Her tree is nearing the end of its life and she wants to try growing one to replace it.'

'Did you grow the one in the garden from seed? It's fabulous.'

Alison smiled. 'I did, and that's why I'm looking so cross. Mrs Carstairs knows I harvest seeds from most of my plants and trees, but I have very few laburnum seeds. Unfortunately, even though I only want to give her a couple, I'm going to have to give her all my stock. She'll need to plant several as most of the seeds won't take and few of the seedlings will survive.'

'Do you need your seeds? Your tree looks very healthy.'

'I was planning to cultivate another for the front garden. Never mind, I can harvest more seeds in September. She can have whatever I've got.' She smiled. 'Shall we go?'

Feeling as if she was about to face her old headmistress, Sally followed Alison to the door.

'What about Dad?' she asked as they headed down the drive.

'He's sleeping,' Alison answered. 'I was going to ask Peter to come over, but it didn't seem worth it just for an hour, so I gave Dad a mild sedative. He'll nap until we get back.'

Sally couldn't help thinking that her father spent more time sedated now than he had when she'd first arrived. Was Alison protecting him from seeing Sally, given it brought on such disturbing memories for him of Maggie? She couldn't get the words of the delivery man out of her head when he'd dropped off the box of sedatives. He'd been delivering weekly since before Sally had come to live in the house. Alison did seem to sedate their father at least once a day. Was that normal with dementia patients?

As they reached the end of the drive Sally looked along the track towards the road. She didn't know whether to be glad or sad that she had found out the truth about Colin. He'd seemed

206

like a knight in shining armour before she'd found out what he'd done to Alison. And yet, he'd been so kind to her. *But not to Alison*, the other part of her brain reminded her. Also, what did he mean when he'd said to call him if she needed help. Who did he think she might need rescuing from? It seemed that since she'd left Gordon there were more people worried about her well-being than there ever were when she had really needed someone's help to escape from his abuse.

Mrs Carstairs' drive almost met the end of her father's, running off at ninety-degree angles to each other. The Carstairs home was much closer to the road. The front of the house could clearly be seen as they turned onto the drive. Sally remembered seeing the curtain twitch the morning she'd nearly been knocked down. That seemed almost a lifetime ago, but it had been only a few days. She could have been forced into the car and made to return home with Gordon, she thought, relieved that Colin had been there to prevent Gordon reversing back to grab her.

'Penny for them,' Alison said as they approached the house.

'Sorry?'

'A penny for your thoughts,' Alison repeated. 'You were miles away.'

'Sorry. I was thinking about Gordon trying to run me down.'

'If I hadn't already had the pleasure of meeting your husband I'm not sure I would've believed you, but I can see why you might've thought it was deliberate and he'd been driving the car,' Alison said. 'I don't have many good words to say about Colin Blanchett, as you know, but I'm very glad he was there for you that morning.'

As she spoke, the door opened. 'I heard you mention poor Colin's name,' Mrs Carstairs said. 'Isn't it terrible? No one is safe these days the way people drive along our narrow roads, as I've pointed out to you many times, Alison. Do come in. Tea is almost ready. Please come through to the conservatory. I thought that would be the nicest place for our high tea.'

Sally followed Alison and Mrs Carstairs, wondering if she had misheard. As they reached the conservatory she decided to ask.

'I'm sorry, did you say something has happened to Colin Blanchett?'

Mrs Carstairs threw up her hands. 'So you didn't know? I'd assumed you were speaking about it when I opened the door. I must have misheard. Colin was involved in a dreadful hit and run accident early yesterday morning while he was out with Honey. He's in hospital in intensive care. Honey is being cared for by the chairman of our residents' association. Sebastian called me this morning to tell me what had happened. Apparently, a witness reported seeing a dark hatchback driving away.'

'He's in intensive care?' Sally asked. 'That sounds as if he was badly injured.'

'I agree. It doesn't sound good,' Mrs Carstairs said. 'Would you like to sit down? You seem to have lost all colour in your face. I had no idea you knew Colin so well.'

Sally sank gratefully onto the chair, feeling as if her legs would have given way if she hadn't. Was it Gordon? Did he see her talking to Colin and decide to take him out? Was he really that twisted? Remembering the threats he'd made against such innocent young men as the supermarket checkout attendant, in her heart she knew the truth. It could have been her fault that Colin was lying badly injured in intensive care.

'I'm fine,' Sally said. 'I barely knew Colin, but it's frightening to think such an accident could happen so close to home.'

'I agree,' Alison said, giving Sally a look as if to tell her not to say anything else. 'We all need to be careful. By the way, Mrs Carstairs, here are the seeds you wanted.'

'Thank you, my dear. I think my laburnum may last another couple of years, so this will give me time to grow a new one from seed. Such a satisfying way to garden, don't you think?'

Sally started when she realised the last remark had been addressed to her. 'Oh, I'm not a gardener at all. You and Alison are talking a foreign language as far as I'm concerned.'

'Really? Oh well, make yourselves comfortable for a while. I just have a few things to finish up in the kitchen.'

Sally waited until she was sure Mrs Carstairs was out of earshot before whispering to Alison. 'Do you think it could have been Gordon who knocked Colin down? Mrs Carstairs said a witness spotted a dark hatchback and that's the same type of car that almost ran me over. Gordon drives a car like that.'

Alison nodded. 'I know. You said that before. That seems too much of a coincidence.'

'Do you think we should tell the police?'

'I think we should, but they might not believe us, considering Gordon didn't even know the man.'

Sally felt the tension intensify in her body. 'You're right. I'll have to think of a way to convince them. I often get the sense someone is watching me. I'll tell the police that.'

'Are you sisters talking secrets?' Mrs Carstairs said, coming into the conservatory with a laden tray. 'Alison, I wonder if you would do me a favour and look at my roses,' she said as she unloaded cups, saucers and tiny plates from the tray.

'Are you concerned about them?' Alison asked.

Mrs Carstairs nodded. 'I think they might have a fungal infection, although my gardener says I'm imagining things. He's getting old, like me,' she said, laughing, 'but I think his eyesight is failing. I don't have the heart to fire him. I tried to pension him off, but he begged me to keep him on. Please, would you take a look, just to put my mind at rest?'

'Yes, of course,' Alison said, getting up. 'I'll go now.'

'Thank you, my dear,' she said, opening the conservatory door to let Alison out and then closing it behind her.

She turned and smiled at Sally. 'Now we can have a comfortable chat while we wait for Alison to come back.'

Sally smiled, unsure how to answer her. She couldn't imagine what they would have to talk about, but she soon found out.

'When did you last see your mother, my dear?'

'I'm sorry?'

Mrs Carstairs sat in the chair next to Sally. She reached across and patted Sally's knee.

'I haven't seen my husband since he left to be with your mother. I've always wondered about him. You would be doing me a tremendous kindness if you could tell me where he is and how he's getting on.'

'But I don't know,' Sally said. 'I haven't seen my mother since the day she left. I didn't know until Alison told me that she'd run off with your husband. I'm really sorry, but that's the truth. You haven't heard from him since that day?'

'I haven't,' she said, 'but what about your mother? Surely she must have contacted you.'

Sally shrugged. 'Not in person.'

'Never?'

Sally shook her head, fighting back the tears she could feel forming. If only Alison would come back to put a stop to this interrogation.

'But you knew where she was?' Mrs Carstairs insisted.

Sally sighed. 'As I said, I never saw her and had no idea where she was from that day to this. My only contact with her was through the cards she sent me for my birthday and at Christmas.'

'Did they have a return address or maybe airmail stickers on them?'

Sally shook her head again. 'I'm sorry, I don't remember.'

'Not to worry,' Mrs Carstairs said. 'The envelopes will have marks showing where they were posted. Perhaps you would be kind enough to look at them and let me know?'

'I would if I still had them, but my husband threw them away when we moved from Cornwall to Nottingham. He didn't want me to have any contact with my family.'

Mrs Carstairs shook her head. 'How very odd of him.'

'He is very controlling.'

'Most men are unless they are dealt with firmly by their wives. You probably allowed him to browbeat you. Did you know your mother and my husband ran off together on the same day you fell down the stairs?'

Sally felt as if she was being interrogated and had a sudden vision of Mrs Carstairs shining bright lights into her eyes to press her to tell the truth. She swallowed back her resentment and forced herself to smile.

'Yes, but I only found that out when Alison filled me in. Didn't your husband tell you he was going to leave?'

'He did, but not in person. David was unkind enough to leave a note for me to find, rather than have the courage and the decency to tell me face to face. He took his passport, you know, and your mother's car was found abandoned in the long-term parking at Heathrow airport. David took his car as well, but that was never found. I suppose he must have sold it. When I searched his wardrobe and bathroom, I discovered his toiletries and some clothes were missing, so they must have planned their escapade long in advance.'

Mrs Carstairs paused, looking pensive. 'You know, my heart almost stopped when I bumped into you that day in Peterborough. I thought I'd lost my mind because for a moment it really seemed as if it was Maggie standing in front of me. I automatically looked around for David, but then realised you had to be her daughter. I've always thought of her as a witch, but even she couldn't turn back time.'

Sally shifted in her seat, desperate for Alison to return. She had no idea what to say, but it seemed she didn't need to speak because Mrs Carstairs continued.

'I wonder sometimes if they're still together, or if she dumped him for a new man soon after he went off with her. I hope she did. It would serve him right for leaving me like that. I was a good wife to that man, Sally, and he repaid me by humiliating me in front of our friends and neighbours.'

She looked across at Sally and smiled.

'I always allowed him to be seen as the big-shot business

owner. I'm quite sure that even your mother as his PA didn't know I held the purse strings. I let him take over Daddy's business without anyone knowing he hadn't a penny of his own.'

Feeling she had to say something to stop the flow, Sally looked out across the garden. 'Do you think we should call Alison?'

'No, my dear. Alison is fine where she is. Once David ran off, I made sure he had no chance to call on any of our bank accounts. Your mother probably expected David to take over from John and keep her in luxury. Hah! I fixed that.'

Sally felt overwhelmed by what she was hearing. If only Alison would come back, but there was still no sign of her.

'When I saw you, I did wonder what you were doing back in Rutland. And with Alison of all people. Considering your mother was responsible for sending Alison's mother into an asylum, I'm amazed she took you in, but then Alison has always been far too ready to give up her own life for others.'

Mrs Carstairs patted Sally's knee again and it was all she could do not to swipe the woman's hand away.

'I hope you don't mind my discussing this with you, Sally. I was certain you would know where David's currently living, but it seems I was wrong. You look very much like your mother, but I think you're probably a nicer person, so I do hope you aren't going to prove me wrong by keeping things from me. What do you recall about the day your mother and my husband absconded?'

'I don't remember anything, Mrs Carstairs. I fell down the stairs and ended up in hospital. That's all I know.'

Mrs Carstairs nodded. 'I called for the ambulance, you

know. I'd found David's note and went over to your house to see if your father knew where they had gone. I don't know why, but I thought your mother might have told him. As you probably know, your father wasn't even there. He'd left for France that morning.' She sighed. 'I can't say what I expected to discover, but it certainly wasn't you lying in a heap at the foot of those lethal marble stairs. Alison was having hysterics and your uncle was clueless. I had to take charge. I brought Alison back here and looked after her until your uncle returned from the hospital to say you were in a coma.'

Sally didn't know what to say. She tried to steer the conversation in a different direction.

'It must have been very difficult for Alison,' Sally said. 'She was only fourteen. Speaking of Alison, I wonder if I should go and see if she has found anything wrong with your roses.'

Mrs Carstairs waved away the suggestion.

'She'll come back in her own time, my dear. I had really hoped you would be able to give me a hint as to what happened, but it seems you know as little as I do.'

'Mrs Carstairs, I wish I knew where they went. I've spent most of my life wondering why my mother deserted me. Until recently I hadn't known that she walked out knowing that I'd fallen down the stairs. That came as a shock, and hurt me more than I can put into words. I'm sorry for what my mother did and the distress she caused you, but I really don't want to talk about her any more. It's upsetting for me to keep hearing about the type of person she was.'

Mrs Carstairs stood up. 'I quite understand, my dear. I'm sorry if I've distressed you. I'll go and see if the cake is ready. I know Alison isn't keen on seed cake, so I also made a Victoria

214

sponge for her, but I hope you will at least try a piece of my special cake.'

Sally sat thinking over what Mrs Carstairs had told her. If her husband had taken his passport, it seemed likely that her mother had moved abroad with him, which would make it easier for them to hide away. That would explain the complete lack of direct contact. She wondered if her mother had been in touch with Grandma Fletcher other than via the cards. But why would her grandmother not tell her if that was the case? Probably to stop her from being hurt even more, if her mother had made it clear she wasn't interested in seeing her only child.

Sally resolved to stop thinking about Maggie. It was clear the woman had been spiteful, selfish and thought only of her own needs. She was still deep in thought when the door opened and Alison came back from the garden.

'I couldn't see a thing wrong with the roses,' she said as Sally looked up.

Sally shook her head and whispered, 'I think it was just an excuse to get you out of the way. She's been asking me questions about my mother and her husband.'

'Really?' Alison whispered back. 'What did she want to know?'

'She seemed to believe I knew where they were. Even when I told her I haven't seen my mother since the day she left, she clearly didn't believe me.'

Sally stopped whispering when she heard Mrs Carstairs' footsteps in the hall. She glanced at Alison and was surprised to see a look almost of anger on Alison's face.

'Here you are, my dears,' Mrs Carstairs said, placing a tray on the table.

To Sally it looked like enough food for three times the number of people. There were minuscule sandwiches and miniature savoury pastries, which explained the tiny plates. In addition, there was a beautifully decorated sponge placed alongside a delicious-looking seed cake.

'I think your gardener is right, Mrs Carstairs. I couldn't see anything amiss with the roses.'

'Thank you for looking, Alison. I feel you probably know more than my gardener, so you have put my mind at rest. Please, help yourselves to the savouries. As you can see, Alison, I have made a Victoria sponge especially for you.'

Sally found the next hour both boring and painful. The conversation ranged across various local issues that she knew nothing about. None of the names mentioned meant anything to her. As time wore on, she became more convinced than ever that she had only been invited so that Mrs Carstairs could quiz her about her mother and Mr Carstairs.

The only good thing about the afternoon had been the seed cake. So when Mrs Carstairs suggested they take it home with them, Sally was disappointed that Alison demurred saying it was bad for her father's digestion.

'What about you, Sally? You seem to like my seed cake. Wouldn't you like to take some home with you?'

'Thank you, that would be lovely,' she said, then wished she hadn't when she saw the look of triumph Mrs Carstairs flashed at Alison.

Chapter Twenty-nine

'I hope you didn't mind me accepting the cake, Alison,' Sally said as they walked back along their drive. 'Mrs Carstairs looked so much like the cat that got the cream when I said yes that I immediately wished I hadn't.'

'She likes to get her own way. You agreeing to take the cake home is no problem at all. You clearly enjoyed it, so why not have more? The only thing is, we'll have to make sure Dad doesn't see it. He also loves seed cake, but even a small piece wrecks his digestion for days afterwards.'

'Maybe we should just throw it in the bin,' Sally suggested.

'Don't be silly. I'll hide it in the pantry. He never goes in there, but it does mean you'll only be able to eat it when he's upstairs.'

As they arrived at the front door, Sally turned to Alison.

'I'm convinced it was Gordon who knocked Colin Blanchett down. That's just what he's like. If he's been watching me and seen us talking then he'd jump to the conclusion that there was something going on between us.'

Alison opened the front door, then looked back at Sally, frowning.

'But when would he have seen you? I thought the two of you had only met twice?'

'We did. Once when he brought me home after my near miss and then when I bumped into him at the end of the track leading to the road.'

'Well, your husband wouldn't have seen him in the dark the morning you were almost run down, even if he'd been the driver, as you said Colin came up to rescue you from the ditch after the car had gone. Are you saying Colin might have seen the driver?'

Sally shrugged as they headed for the kitchen. 'No, he said it was too dark to make out who was driving, but that doesn't mean that Gordon, if it *was* him, didn't see Colin.'

'Let's say he did see him, why would that make Gordon think the two of you were an item? I'm not doubting you, just trying to see how the police might view it.'

'If a man so much as looked at me when we were out of the house, Gordon would become convinced I was leading the man on. I agree, he might not have seen Colin that morning, but if he's been watching me since then he might have spotted the two of us when we met at the end of the drive.'

'Did you see Gordon?'

'No, I didn't see him, but that doesn't mean he wasn't hiding somewhere.'

'I thought you and Colin barely spoke to each other on that day? If you were only talking for such a short space of time, how could Gordon read anything into that?'

Sally thought about the many times she'd received a

beating for nothing more than thanking someone for holding the door open for her. Hours later Gordon would ambush her with the information that he'd seen her smile at a man. She would never know when he was watching, but if she couldn't convince Alison, then would she be able to get the police to understand that level of obsession?

'You're probably right, but I still feel maybe we should tell the police Gordon is a possible suspect.'

'Sally, unless we have something tangible to offer regarding Colin Blanchett, I doubt the police will do anything. Gordon and Colin have never met. You've barely interacted with him, so as far as the police are concerned, what would be the motive for your husband to try to kill him?'

'When you put it like that, it does sound ridiculous.'

'It is. Now, hand over that cake so that I can hide it before Dad wakes up and comes down looking for a snack. I'd better go up and make sure he's okay. I know we were only gone for just over an hour, but I always worry about leaving him on his own. Do you want to put the kettle on, or have you had enough tea?'

'I'd love a cup of normal tea! I must be a total pleb because I can't stand Earl Grey. It's too perfumed for me. Did you notice I only had the one cup?'

Alison grinned. 'I did. It's an acquired taste. I like it, but will make sure never to offer you a cup. However, there are a few lovely herbal teas you should try. I think you might enjoy some of them.'

Sally touched her sister's arm and smiled.

'I'll sort things out down here while you go up. Should I make anything for our father?'

Alison had reached the kitchen door, but stopped and looked back.

'You never say "Dad". I don't blame you, considering you barely know each other, but it would please me if you did.'

Sally shrugged. 'I haven't tried to analyse how I feel about him, but you're right. I never got to know him as a proper dad. Grandma Fletcher always said your *father* is coming, or your *father* wants us to meet him somewhere. He was never "Dad" to me.'

Alison put her head on one side, as if weighing up what to say.

'That's sad, but maybe in time you and Dad can find enough common ground to get to know each other properly. It's such a shame that Dad has this dreadful disease, but when he's lucid it might be possible to bring the two of you together.'

Alison left to go upstairs and Sally filled the kettle. She would have loved to have a proper relationship with her father, but he had always been so distant on the few occasions she'd seen him while growing up and now he'd made it very clear he blamed her for not keeping in contact. She hoped Alison was right and there was still a way to forge some sort of relationship, but it seemed doubtful to Sally.

Alison came back down on her own. 'Dad wants to stay upstairs to read, but says he would love a cup of tea and something to eat. I'll make a sandwich if you could sort out the tea for him.'

'Yes, of course,' Sally said. 'Alison, I've decided it's better if I don't go out walking or running on my own until we're certain it wasn't Gordon who tried to run me down, even if he had nothing to do with what happened to Colin.'

She hesitated, not sure how what she had to say next would be taken.

'I know you won't like this, but I want to visit Colin Blanchett in hospital. I need to ask him if he saw the person who was driving the car. I'm sorry, I know how you feel about Colin and I understand why you have every reason to be angry with him, but he might be able to tell me whether or not it was Gordon.'

Alison slowly put down the knife she'd been using to butter the bread. Sally could see the tension in her sister's neck and wished she hadn't said anything, but if she didn't ask Colin if it had been Gordon who ran him down, she would never feel safe.

'I'll call to find out if he's receiving visitors,' Alison said. 'If he is, I'll take you to the hospital, but don't expect me to be in the same room as that man. I'm going to finish making this sandwich for Dad and take his tray upstairs. When I come back down, I'll phone the hospital.'

The icy tone made Sally shrink back.

'Alison, please don't be angry with me. I don't want to see Colin for any reason other than to know if it was Gordon driving the car, you do understand that, don't you?'

Alison nodded and turned back to finish the sandwich. Sally watched, feeling her eyes filling with tears. She had hurt Alison who had done nothing but welcome her into her home. She sat, misery flooding her body, as Alison picked up the tray and left the kitchen without uttering another word.

Sally heard Alison come back down the stairs and then her voice, but couldn't make out the words. Alison must have been making a call from the drawing room. Then there was a moment of silence before Sally picked up the sound of Alison's footsteps crossing the hall.

'I've spoken to the hospital,' Alison said. 'Colin Blanchett is in intensive care and is not allowed visitors.'

The coldness in Alison's voice made Sally jump up from her chair.

'Alison, I'm sorry for upsetting you.'

'Sally, you will never know how much you asking me to make that call has hurt me. If you don't mind, I'm going to pass on the tea for now. I need to lie down for a while.'

As Alison left the room tears fell unchecked down Sally's face. She'd put her own feelings above Alison's. She must be more like her mother than she'd realised.

Chapter Thirty

Monday 16th June

After a miserable night during which she had tossed and turned, unable to get over Alison's unhappy face, Sally got up and went directly to Alison's room. She knocked on the door.

'Alison, it's me. May I come in?'

'Sure.'

Opening the door, Sally saw Alison sitting at her dressing table. She was overwhelmed with relief when her sister smiled and held out a welcoming hand.

'I'm sorry for being so mean to you yesterday,' Alison said. 'Let's not mention that man's name again. I understand why you're scared of your husband, but you don't need to be. You're safe here with your family. We won't let him hurt you.'

Sally took Alison's hand. 'I'm the one who should apologise, not you.'

Alison laughed. 'Good. Now we've both apologised, we can forget all about it. Let's go down for breakfast.'

'Give me a few minutes to get dressed and I'll be there,' Sally said.

She returned to her room with conflicting emotions. There was no way she would ask Alison to take her to the hospital, but once Colin was out of intensive care, she had every intention of talking to him. Alison didn't understand how Gordon's mind worked. Until she was certain he had nothing to do with Colin's accident she would not be able to relax.

She dressed in jeans and a tee-shirt, slipped on her trainers and was about to leave her bedroom when she heard a strident voice. It sounded like a woman – a very angry one at that.

Sally opened the bedroom door and walked along the corridor to lean over the balustrade. The woman yelling was below in the hall with Alison attempting to calm her down. Sally realised it was Alison's mother, but why on earth was she so angry?

'Where is he, Alison? Don't tell me he isn't here. He never leaves the house unless he's with you.'

'Mum, will you please calm down and tell me what's wrong.'

'What's wrong? What's wrong? I haven't received my allowance, that's what's wrong. Am I supposed to live on fresh air?'

As she spoke she looked up and must have spotted Sally because her expression changed from one of anger to one of pure venom.

'Oh, I see that bitch is back. Is that why my allowance was stopped? Am I going without because the woman who destroyed my marriage has crawled back home?'

Alison looked up. 'Mum! That's not Maggie. That's Sally, Maggie's daughter. Will you please calm down and explain what you mean about your allowance? Dad hasn't stopped it. I doubt he would know how to do it. Peter deals with all Dad's finances. He has for years. I'll call him and find out what's happened, but you have to calm down first.'

'Not Maggie?' Alison's mother said, ignoring the rest of her words. 'She looks so much like her. What's she doing here? I thought you didn't know where she was living?'

Sally watched as Alison took her mother's arm and led her into the kitchen. 'I didn't know her address. It's a long story, but Sally is staying here for the time being.'

As the two women disappeared from view, Sally turned to go back to her bedroom. No way was she going down there to upset Alison's mother even more. She wondered what was going on with the finances, though. Peter had made quite a few comments about there being a shortage of money. Alison had said it was just Peter wanting to get a rise out of her, but what if it was true? What if money was that tight and she was adding to the problem?

In her bedroom Sally grabbed her handbag and turned out her purse to see how much money she had left. The cash she'd taken from Gordon and the money she'd borrowed from Alison had gone on her new clothes and the other things that had seemed essential at the time. After paying Alison back she would only have a few hundred pounds. She'd be able to stay in a B&B for a couple of nights, but it was nowhere near enough for her to be able to rent an apartment. Even if she could afford one in the cheapest area, she couldn't drive, so wouldn't be able to get to work once she had a job.

The interview on Wednesday suddenly became a matter of urgency. She had to get the job so that she could contribute to the household finances. After she'd been working for a few months, she'd be able to look at finding a place of her own.

Even that plan wasn't without its problems. Until she could afford driving lessons and earned enough money to buy a cheap car, she would be dependent on Alison taking her to work each morning and picking her up again in the evenings.

Sally slumped onto the bed. It felt as if she had an impossible mountain to climb. Then she thought about her life with Gordon. If she could survive that then she could cope with anything. She sat up. First things first – pay Alison back the moment the bank card arrived. Go to the interview on Wednesday. Get the job. She could worry about what happened after that when the time came.

Feeling more positive, she began to put everything back in her bag. The last thing left on the bed was Colin Blanchett's card. She could call him and ask if he'd seen who had been driving the car that knocked him down. That way she wouldn't have to ask Alison to get involved.

Picking up the card, she tapped out his mobile number on her phone. It went immediately to voice mail. Of course, he was in intensive care and probably not able to use his phone at the moment, she thought. Sally ended the call without leaving a voice message.

Maybe if she sent a text then he'd see it when he was able to use his phone.

Colin, this is Sally. I was sorry to hear about your accident. Did you see who was driving the car? I am worried it might have been my ex-husband. Please, when you are feeling better, could you call to let me know what you remember? Or send a text if you would rather not call.

226

Pleased that she had been able to do something constructive that didn't put Alison in an impossible position, Sally pressed send. She had just put her phone in the back pocket of her jeans when Alison knocked on her door and then came in.

'I'm sorry, Sally. I hope my mother didn't upset you.'

'It's okay. She wasn't expecting to see me here, but I couldn't help but overhear what she said about money. Alison, when my bank card arrives, I'll pay you what I owe you and you can also have however much is left after that for the household bills. Peter is always on about the finances being in a dire state and I know he blames me for it.'

Alison waved her hands in a gesture of refusal. 'Rubbish! No way am I taking your money. I don't know what Peter is on about, but clearly something has gone wrong with my mother's allowance. I know when Dad sold the business there was loads of money invested in various places. Even if some of those have gone down, there shouldn't be any reason to worry. I wish Dad had given me power of attorney over his finances. As it is, I don't even know how to access any of his accounts.'

'I could do that for you if we found the passwords,' Sally said.

Alison looked stunned. 'Really? Peter always makes out as if it was such a complicated process.'

Sally laughed. 'I looked after several accounts in my last job. Most financial institutions are straightforward. Let's go and see if we can find details of the accounts and the all-important passwords.'

As they went downstairs, Sally was happy finally to be able to do something positive for Alison. In the study, she began to go through the drawers of the desk. She didn't find any

227

financial documents or information relating to her father's accounts. However, the bottom drawer on the right-hand side of the desk was locked.

'Any idea where the key is for this drawer?' she asked Alison who was busy leafing through a pile of papers she'd found on one of the bookshelves.

'I didn't even know the drawer was locked,' Alison said, shaking her head.

'I haven't been able to find anything to do with the accounts so far, which makes me think that drawer might have the information we need. Let's see if we can find the key.'

Half an hour later, having searched every conceivable nook and cranny, Alison suggested they give up looking.

'I'll call Peter today and get him to come over,' she said. 'He must have the key. Isn't there something we can do in the meantime?'

Sally had been staring at the laptop screen, but looked up and shook her head. 'I can't even see any banking apps. I'm wondering if Peter has hidden them, but why would he do that if he's the only one with access to them?'

'I'll ask him when he gets here,' Alison said. 'But right now, I am dying for a cup of tea and something sweet to eat. Would you like a piece of Mrs Carstairs' seed cake? You seemed to love it yesterday.'

Sally smiled. 'I did! I didn't like Mrs Carstairs or her horrible tea – the whole visit was difficult – but I really loved her seed cake.' She hesitated, then shrugged. 'Before we leave the study, I think we should talk about what happens when I get a job. I can't drive and I don't want you to feel you have to act as my taxi once I start working.'

Alison held up a hand. 'Let's stop right there if you're going to start on again about moving out. This is your home for as long as you want to live here, which I hope is for a very long time. I love having my long-lost sister in the house and I'm delighted we're finally getting to know each other properly. That is my final word on the matter. Now, come on. That cake is calling you and I happen to know a packet of chocolate digestives has my name on it. I can hear the biscuits whispering to me.'

In the kitchen Sally put the kettle on while Alison called Peter. She could only hear one side of the conversation, but it didn't sound as if Peter was in any hurry to do as Alison was asking.

'What do you mean you're too busy to come over today? . . . Of course it's not urgent. . . . No, I'm not being unreasonable. . . . Fine. Suit yourself. Come tomorrow!'

Alison ended the call and scowled. 'I swear if I'd told him not to come over today because it was inconvenient for me, he'd have been here like a shot. It seems he can only spare some time tomorrow.'

Sally was surprised. Since she'd been in the house, she seemed to be falling over Peter every five minutes. Maybe Alison was right. He was only saying he couldn't come to make Alison's life difficult.

Chapter Thirty-one

Tuesday 17th June

Sally clutched her stomach and hoped she wasn't going to throw up again. Three times during the night she'd had to make a dash to the bathroom. As another gripe shot across her abdomen, she swore she'd never have another piece of seed cake as long as she lived. She'd been fine after the first piece yesterday, but she deserved everything she was going through because she hadn't stopped at one. Encouraged by Alison, she had devoured three slices and then suffered the consequences throughout the night.

Sally reached out for her phone. It was just after seven. Time to get up, but that was the last thing she felt like doing. She closed her eyes and prayed for the discomfort to ease.

She must have fallen asleep again because the next thing she knew Alison was knocking on the door before coming in.

'Hi, are you okay? I thought I heard you up during the night.'

'I think I overdid the seed cake. I feel dreadful,' Sally said.

'You should probably stay in bed for a while. You look ill. I'll bring you up a cup of herbal tea to settle your stomach.'

Sally sat up. 'What time is it?'

'Half past nine.'

'I should get up.'

'No, you stay there. Peter will be here in half an hour. I'm going to tackle him about my mother's allowance to find out why it wasn't paid. I'm also going to make him hand over the key to that drawer. I'll tell him that he can't keep making vague comments about our finances. I want to know what's going on.'

'Would it help if I were there with you?'

Alison shook her head. 'No, this is a conversation I need to have with Peter on my own. He might not be as open if you're in the room, but if we're really short of money then I have to know. I'll be back in a bit with your tea.'

Sally lay back down. Just sitting up for that brief time had been a struggle. She closed her eyes. When she opened them again, it was to find a cold cup of tea on her bedside table. Alison must have come in with it, seen she was asleep and decided not to wake her. Once again, the kindness Alison showed her made Sally determined not to do anything that would add to her sister's responsibilities.

The sleep must have done the trick because Sally felt able to get out of bed. She'd get dressed, then go downstairs to see if there was anything she could do to help Alison, even if it was just weeding one of the flower beds.

She went to the bathroom, feeling even better once she'd showered and got dressed. Definitely no more cake for her!

As she started down the staircase, she heard raised voices coming from the study. Peter must still be here, she thought, hesitating between continuing down to the kitchen and going back to her bedroom. Then she heard her name and decided to see what it was Peter was saying about her.

She crept down and stood in the hall, ready to defend herself if Peter was giving Alison a hard time, which he was.

'Why should I allow Sally access to the accounts? She has no place here. You know full well, she shouldn't even be here, far less in *your* company. I know what you're planning and I'm not going to stand by this time and do nothing!'

'Peter, let's leave my intentions out of this. I want to know what's going on with the finances. My mother's allowance has been stopped. You keep telling me that we're spending too much, but you don't go into detail.'

'I have no intention of discussing the finances with you or with Sally. Your father gave me power of attorney regarding his finances, not you. And why was that? Because you have no idea how to manage investments.'

'No, but Sally says she does.'

'You know as well as I do that she shouldn't be here. She needs to leave.'

'She's staying,' Alison said. 'If you do or say anything that makes her move out, I swear I will use everything in my power to—'

'To what, Alison? I am so sick to death of your threats. Do your worst. I've had enough.'

'Don't tempt me. You know what I have on you!'

'Go to hell!' Peter yelled as he came out of the study. 'As for you,' he said, seeing Sally, 'why are you always hanging around eavesdropping? You need to be careful, or you might hear something you don't want to know.'

'Leave her alone, Peter. I told you, Sally is staying here.'

Peter came and stood directly in front of Sally. She instinctively stepped back.

'Can't you get it into your thick head that you're not wanted?'

'I want her here, Peter,' Alison said, grabbing his arm and pulling him away from Sally.

'Don't worry, I'm going.' He turned for the door, but then looked back. 'Do you really not remember your childhood? Or are you pretending not to know what happened the day you nearly died, Sally?'

Sally shook her head. 'No, what should I remember? Are you talking about when I fell? The day my mother left?'

Peter looked as if he was about to speak, but then he shrugged. 'You'd be wise to pack your things and leave. This is not your home, and you shouldn't be here. Don't stand there looking at me as if I've gone mad. Go on, get your stuff together and go!'

'Sally, ignore him,' Alison said, pushing Peter towards the door. 'If anyone needs to get out, it's you, Peter. I've waited years for Sally to be here, and now she is I'm not going to let you ruin everything.'

'What's going on?'

Sally whirled round in surprise as she heard her father's voice behind her.

'Dad, you shouldn't be out of bed. Let's get you back upstairs.'

'No, Alison, I know I have issues, but right now I want an answer.' He glanced at Sally as he spoke and for the first time he smiled at her. 'Sally! I'm pleased you're here, even though it's unforgiveable that you shunned us for so long,' he said in the most lucid voice Sally had heard him use.

233

Tears starting to fill her eyes, the pain she felt at hearing him say those words without his usual ranting was more than she could bear.

'But it was you who turned me away,' she said, but before he could reply Alison cut in.

'Peter says we're short of money, Dad,' Alison said, 'but won't allow me or Sally access to the accounts. Sally worked in finance, so she understands more than I do. She probably understands even more than Peter does.'

'Is this right?' he asked, glaring at Peter. 'Since when?'

Peter looked as if he wanted to be anywhere other than facing his brother.

'Well, I . . . er, that is—'

'I think we should all go into the study. Peter, bring up the accounts. Sally, come and tell me what you see.'

'John, can we have a word in private, please?' Peter said. 'I have things I need to explain.'

'It sounds as if you have. Sally, Alison, I'll come to speak to both of you once Peter and I are done.'

Sally was finishing her second cup of tea when the kitchen door opened and her father came in. He no longer looked as sharp as he had half an hour earlier. And Sally felt sorry for him. He looked broken, but still more in control of his mind than he had been since she'd arrived.

'Peter has shown me the state of our finances. It seems many of our investments were hit in the last financial crash. We're not on the verge of destitution, but we're nowhere near as comfortable as I would have hoped.'

234

Alison pulled out a chair. 'Sit down, Dad. You look all in.'

He slumped onto the chair. 'I feel it,' he said. 'It seems we're going to have to make some adjustments.'

'In what way?' Alison asked. 'I thought it was just Peter wanting to get under my skin.'

He smiled. 'Nothing major, but we need to cut back on our heating bill and such like.'

'But what did he actually say, Dad?' Alison asked. 'What's happened to the money? We can't suddenly be in a hand to mouth situation. Your business was sold for a major amount, plus you already had a large investment portfolio.'

'Alison, I told you! Peter explained it all to me. Please don't ask for exact details because I can't remember them. It seems there have been several bad setbacks and Peter is doing his best to deal with them.'

Alison looked as if she wanted to question her father more, but she must have realised it would be futile, because she sighed and sat down.

'I'll look closely at our household accounts,' Alison said. 'I don't think I've been particularly extravagant, but I might be able to cut back here and there. Did Peter say how serious the situation was?'

He nodded. 'It's pretty dire, I believe.'

'Not so bad that we'd need to sell the house?' Alison asked, horror in her voice.

'No, not as bad as that. At least, I don't think so. You'd better speak to Peter tomorrow. I told him he has to confide fully in you. He's looking into ways of increasing our investment income and believes we'll soon be in a more positive position.'

'I'm hoping to get a job tomorrow,' Sally said. 'Anything I earn can go into the household accounts.'

Her father smiled at her. 'Things have not yet come to the state where we would need to take your earnings, but thank you for the offer.'

He turned to Alison. 'You need to deal better with Peter.'

Alison shook her head, but before she could speak, he jumped up and stared at Sally.

She watched in horror as the look on his face changed to one of rage. She could see he'd lost touch with the present and drifted back into the past. Instead of wanting to hold her, as he usually did when he thought she was her mother, he looked as if he wanted to hurt her.

'What the hell are you doing here? Why have you come back? Maggie, where did you go? You left me for another man.'

As he said the words he stood up and lunged at Sally. She tried to get out of his way, but she wasn't quick enough to avoid a stinging slap as his hand connected with the side of her face.

'Dad!' Alison shouted. 'That's not Maggie. It's Sally. Your daughter.'

Sally managed to get up off the chair and scramble away from the table. Her father came after her and she was terrified to see he'd picked up a knife from the table. It was a blunt butter knife, but he was wielding it as if he wanted to stab her.

'How could you leave me? I loved you! I'd rather see you dead than with another man.'

'Dad, put the knife down,' Alison said, speaking in a calm tone that Sally could only envy. She was incapable of saying anything at all.

He turned to Alison. 'She left me, Alison. She left me,' he cried.

Sally was distressed to see tears running down his face, but knew there was nothing she could do to comfort him. She was the cause of his misery. Rather, her mother was, but her resemblance to Maggie was the reason her father was falling to pieces in front of her.

'Let's go upstairs, Dad,' Alison said. 'I'll bring you up a nice cup of tea and a chocolate digestive. You'd like that, wouldn't you?'

He nodded. 'I would, but I'm very tired. I think I'd like to have a nap first.'

'Come on then, Dad. Let's get you upstairs to bed. I'll bring your tea and biscuits up in an hour or so.'

As they left the kitchen, Sally slumped onto a chair, shaken and scared. What if it had been a sharp knife and Alison hadn't been there to calm him down? Would he have attacked her with it, believing he was dealing with his wife?

By the time Alison came back down Sally had managed to calm her breathing, but her heart was still pumping faster than it should have, making her feel nauseous.

'Well, that was quite an episode,' Alison said as she came into the kitchen. 'I don't know about you, Sally, but I think I need a cup of tea with a little slug of something in it. Don't you think that would be a good idea?'

Sally could only nod in agreement, still unable to gather her thoughts enough to answer Alison.

When Alison placed a cup of tea in front of Sally, together with an open brandy bottle, Sally finally felt able to speak.

'He wanted to kill me,' she said. 'My father wanted to stab me.'

Alison smiled. 'Not exactly, Sally. He wanted to stab your mother. Whether or not he wanted to kill her we will never know. Would you like a biscuit to go with your tea?'

'Are you not distressed by what happened?' Sally asked. 'He could have killed me.'

Alison laughed. 'With the butter knife? I hardly think so.'

'No, I realise he wouldn't have been able to kill me with that,' Sally said, 'but what if it had been a sharper knife? What then?'

'Sally, you're making too much of what happened. I know it was distressing, but it's really nothing to get worked up over.' She sat down opposite Sally and picked up the brandy bottle, pouring a good slug into her cup. 'For you, it's a major incident, but you have to remember that for me it's nothing I haven't had to deal with many times before.'

She pointed at the brandy bottle. 'Now, I suggest you dose yourself up with a drop of brandy and put the whole thing out of your mind. You're making a mountain out of a molehill.'

Sally picked up her cup and swallowed a few sips. As she glanced across at Alison, she was stunned to see a look of glee on her face. It disappeared almost immediately, leaving Sally bemused. Why had Alison looked as if she'd just won the lottery?

Chapter Thirty-two

Wednesday 18th June

Sally woke Wednesday morning exhausted from the drama of the day before. For a few minutes she had seen the person her father used to be before his illness struck, but then he had reverted to the man she had become accustomed to since her return to Rutland. No, that wasn't true. He had been far more violent and intent on injuring her mother than he had been up to that point. Regardless of what Alison said, Sally felt unsafe and would take care never to be alone with her father.

She went through to the bathroom, wondering how she would be able to face Peter when he arrived to be with his brother while Alison took Sally to Oakham for her job interview. She just hoped he wouldn't try once again to make her leave. She felt like a parasite as it was, without his venom adding to her discomfort.

On the plus side, since she'd made Alison throw away the rest of the seed cake her stomach upset seemed to have cleared up.

She applied her make-up carefully, wanting to achieve a cross between looking well groomed and natural. Alison had said Sally didn't need make-up, having been born beautiful, a comment that had reminded Sally all too much of her mother and the distress she had caused in this house.

Once she was dressed in the pencil skirt and white shirt she'd worn to go to Mrs Carstairs' on Sunday, she gave a final glance in the mirror. Whatever she looked like, she knew she didn't have to worry about her work ability. She'd get the job if success was based solely on aptitude. Fortunately, she was armed with a fabulous reference letter from her previous company. Brenda from HR had included it with her bank card, which she intended to draw on while in Oakham to repay Alison.

As she went downstairs to find Alison, Sally felt like singing. She was dressed in new clothes, trying for a new job to pay for her new life. A life without Gordon in it.

'Wow! Look at you,' Alison said. 'A successful job applicant if ever I saw one.'

'Thank you,' Sally said. 'I feel great. What time is Peter due to arrive? I'd rather wait in the kitchen if you don't mind. I don't want him to upset my mood. I need to feel confident today and he seems to have the knack of making me feel like I'm . . . I don't know what he makes me feel like, to be honest, but whatever it is, I don't like it.'

'No problem,' Alison said. 'You wait in there. I'll deal with him when he arrives. You won't need to see him at all as Dad wants him to go straight upstairs when he gets here. Dad's in one of his lucid periods and seems quite determined to have something out with Peter.'

Sally heard a car pulling up on the drive. 'That sounds like him now. Let me know when you're ready to leave,' she said, heading for the kitchen.

As Alison overtook yet another car on the narrow road, Sally gave an involuntary gasp. Even if she got the job, would her heart survive this kind of car journey every weekday for the next few months? Clutching the door's armrest, she realised she had no choice. She'd spent time online yesterday going through all the possible ways of getting from Oakham to any point on Rutland Water and found it was impossible. There were buses, but they ran so infrequently it was pointless even considering them. No, she would just have to find a way to cope with Alison's manic driving style.

'Okay, here we are,' Alison said, slowing the car down and pulling over to the side of the road. 'Station Approach Industrial Estate. Which part do you need?'

Sally looked on her phone at the address the agency had given her. It was a little further along, but she kept that to herself.

'Here is perfect! Thank you, Alison.'

'Great,' Alison said. 'Send me a text when the interview is over, and I'll pick you up here. Good luck!'

Sally got out of the car on legs that weren't quite steady. She hadn't mentioned it to her sister, but she was still feeling the after-effects of overindulging on the seed cake. Struggling to control the combination of a queasy stomach and interview nerves, Sally walked along until she spotted Oakham Financial Solutions. She took a deep breath, lifted her head high, and went in.

★

Half an hour later, stomach still churning, Sally left the building. The company had other applicants to see, but she felt the interview had gone well. She'd only find out on Friday if she'd been successful. She pulled her phone from her bag and sent a text to Alison and then crossed the road to wait for her.

A few minutes later she heard a screech and looked up to see a dark hatchback hurtling along the road. Why Alison couldn't drive at a slower pace was beyond Sally, but she was grateful to her sister, regardless of how she drove.

But it wasn't Alison who jumped out of the car as soon as it came to a stop.

'Sally, you are coming home with me. I've had enough of this nonsense. We belong together!' Gordon said, running round to the pavement and pulling Sally into his arms.

She tried to push him away, but he was too strong for her.

'I can't live without you. Please, I know I haven't always been good to you, but I can change. I'll do whatever you want.'

'Gordon, let me go. You're suffocating me.'

He loosened his grip, but still held her so that she couldn't break away.

'How did you know I would be here today?' Sally asked.

'You don't need to know that. All that matters is we're together and I'll never let you leave me ever again. You're coming home with me.'

'No, we're over, Gordon. I can't go back to living like that.'

'Is it because our house is so much smaller than that mansion you've been living in? We can have a house as big as that if you want. You can have all the money your grandmother left you. I won't keep it from you any longer.'

Leaning away from him as much as she could, Sally looked up into his face.

'What do you mean? What money? You said it had all gone years ago.'

'I know I did, but that was only because I thought you might leave me if you knew how rich you were. I haven't spent any of it, Sally. I kept it for you.'

She tried again to push him away.

'Let me go! I don't want to come with you.'

'You have to. I can't live without you! You're getting in the car!'

'No! Let me go!'

'Listen to me, you bitch. You've led me on a fine bloody chase but it's over now. You're coming home,' he said, dragging Sally towards the passenger side of the car.

She was vaguely aware of people looking from across the road, but no one seemed to be coming to her rescue.

'Leave me alone. I'm not going with you,' she yelled, just as another car pulled up behind Gordon's and her sister leapt out.

'Let her go!' Alison shouted.

'Fuck off, bitch!' Gordon said, turning to face Alison and receiving a full blast of pepper spray in his eyes.

'Fuck! Shit! You've blinded me, you fucking cow! I'll get you for this! I'll get you all! Every fucking one of your fucked-up family is getting what they deserve. You hear me, Sally?' Gordon yelled as he staggered around rubbing at his eyes.

Alison grabbed Sally's arm. 'Come on, let's go. We don't need to listen to this.'

They ran to Alison's car and climbed in.

As she buckled her seatbelt tears flooded Sally's eyes.

'How did he find me? How could he have known where I was?'

Alison pulled away and for once Sally was happy to hear the tyres squealing.

'I don't know,' Alison said. 'Maybe you're right and he's watching you from a distance. He might have seen me drop you off and waited for you to come out again. You have to report this to the police. You know that, don't you?'

'Should I also tell them I think he tried to knock me down that morning and that he might have run over Colin Blanchett?'

Alison nodded. 'Yes, absolutely. They need to know exactly what you're having to deal with. We'll go to the police station and then go home. It seems almost mundane to ask, but how did the interview go?'

'I think it went well,' Sally said, 'but that's not the most important thing I have to tell you. Gordon said I'm rich. He said Grandma Fletcher's money isn't gone as he'd told me. We need to get some legal advice. If I have money from my grandmother, I'll be able to pay my way.'

Chapter Thirty-three

Thursday 19th June – morning

'I'm coming! I'm coming!' Gordon yelled as he came downstairs to open the front door. 'There's no need to make that bloody racket.'

He yanked open the door, stunned to see two uniformed police officers.

'Gordon Watson? I'm PS Stubbs and my colleague is PC Constant. Could we come in to have a word?' the taller of the two said.

'What about?' Gordon asked.

'I think it would be better if we discussed it inside,' PS Stubbs said. 'It's in connection with your wife.'

'Has something happened to Sally? Is she hurt? Where is she?'

'As I say, sir, it would be better if we could come in.'

Gordon stood back to let them pass. 'Go into the room on the right,' he said.

He followed them into the lounge.

'Well, what's happened to Sally?' he demanded.

'As you should know, your wife was granted a temporary restraining order.'

'Only because that stupid bitch sister of hers made her do it.'

'Regardless of the reasons or motivating factors, the order was granted and it requires you to refrain from contacting her in any way until such time as the case has been fully investigated and the order is either declined or granted.'

'I know all that,' Gordon said. 'Waste of time and money, if you ask me. Are you going to tell me what's happened to my wife or not?'

'Sir, we are here to tell you we are aware that yesterday you breached the temporary order. We have been tasked with reminding you that breaching a protective order is an offence. The maximum sentence is five years' custody.'

Both police officers glared at Gordon. 'Your wife reported your harassment of her yesterday. We are not here to arrest you, but should you breach the order again we will do so and pass the matter to the Crown Prosecution Service to be dealt with in the criminal court. Am I making myself clear, sir?'

Gordon swallowed the retort that was burning his brain. How could Sally do this to him? She'd pay for this humiliation.

'Yes, officer. It was a mistake. It won't happen again.'

'Make sure it doesn't,' PS Stubbs said. 'Only cowards beat up women and we don't like cowards on our patch. Good day to you, sir. We will see ourselves out.'

Gordon followed them from the room, wanting more than anything to shove his fist in the man's face, but managing to hold back and even smile as he reached round them to open the door.

Fuck that bloody cow, Gordon fumed as he slammed the door closed. *How dare she report me? I'm her husband. She belongs to me!*

Gordon spent the next hour going over all the things he should have said to the jumped-up busybody trying to tell him how he should treat his own wife. None of the words that came to mind did justice to how angry he was. Suddenly, the doorbell rang again, but not as persistently as earlier when the police had called. Gordon stormed into the hall and wrenched the door open.

His words of anger disappeared when he saw the delivery driver's uniform.

'Gordon Watson?' the man asked.

Gordon nodded.

'Sign here,' the man said, offering Gordon a clipboard and pen.

Gordon signed the top page, took the package from the man, and closed the door. He carried the small parcel to the kitchen and pulled a steak knife from the cutlery drawer. Carefully cutting through the tape, he eased off the outer wrapping, giving a sigh of satisfaction when the contents were revealed.

At last! Now that he had the chloroform, he'd easily be able to subdue Sally.

Chapter Thirty-four

'Do you think the police have given Gordon the warning they promised?' Sally asked, sipping herbal tea in the kitchen.

'The officer we spoke to yesterday said they would pass on the information to the station nearest to where you used to live, so I would imagine Gordon will have received a visit by now.'

'I hope so,' Sally said, 'but there's not much more we can do about him. I'd far rather spend some time finding out about my inheritance from Grandma Fletcher. Any ideas on how to go about it?'

'Can you remember the name of your grandmother's solicitor?' Alison asked.

Sally shook her head. 'I didn't have much to do with him. I gave Gordon power of attorney and he travelled to Cornwall to sign all the papers on my behalf. I'm not sure he ever told me the solicitor's name.'

'But yesterday Gordon definitely said there was money belonging to you?'

Sally nodded. 'Yes, but what I don't understand is why he didn't use it. It sounded as though he couldn't touch it, but that can't be right as I gave power of attorney to him.'

'Well,' said Alison, 'that's one thing I do know a little about. It depends on how the power of attorney was worded. It's possible you only gave him permission to deal with the probate of your grandmother's estate, but it didn't give him full access to the funds once probate was finalised. Our first job has to be to find who dealt with it back then.'

'We could search online to find a list of solicitors who practise in the area,' Sally said. 'Then I could call each of them.'

'You could do that,' Alison agreed, 'but they probably won't tell you anything over the phone. Why don't we see if there's a way to find out who dealt with probate on her estate. I'm sure there must be a record of it. Let's look online.'

Sally put down her cup and followed Alison to the study, wishing she could shake off the queasiness she'd been experiencing for the last few days. The herbal tea was lovely, but it wasn't giving her the relief Alison had said it would.

Alison sat at the laptop and fired it up.

'I'll put in a search to see who might have handled probate of the estate.'

Sally sat on the armchair nearest to the desk. 'Good idea. As you say, there must be a record.'

'And so there is!' said Alison. 'Look at this. It's a government website. We can order a copy of the probate report for the grand sum of £1.50.'

'That sounds almost too easy.'

Alison laughed. 'I know, but let's see what comes back. Okay, there are some basic questions such as name of your grandmother and the year of her death. I take it you know the answer to those?'

'I do,' Sally said.

As Alison worked through the questions on the form, Sally gave her the answers she needed to complete it.

'It says we have access to the documents for thirty-one days. We need to create an account. I'll just go and get my purse for my card to pay the fee.'

Sally put out her hand to stop her. 'No! I can do that now I have my bank card.'

She got up but had to clutch the wall for support. 'Wow! I felt really light-headed for a moment there.'

'Sit down,' Alison said. 'We can use my card.'

Sally shook her head. 'I feel fine now. I'll be back in a moment.'

She left the room feeling less steady than she'd claimed. Alison did so much for her, surely she'd be able to get upstairs, grab her bag and come back down again. As she climbed the stairs, she felt less able with every step. She reached her bedroom, went in and grabbed her bag and went slowly back down to the study, relieved at being able to sit down again.

'You took ages,' Alison said. 'I was about to come looking for you.'

'I'm sorry. I wasn't feeling very well. I'm fine now, though,' she lied, passing Alison her bank card.

'This is like being a private detective,' Alison said. 'Okay, that's all set up. The report should start printing now.'

Sally forced herself to stand, trying to ignore the feeling of nausea that seemed to be a constant companion nowadays, and went to the printer.

'There are already some papers in the printer tray,' she said. 'They must be from when Peter was last in here.'

Alison held out her hand. 'What are they?'

Sally passed the papers to Alison and then turned back to collect the probate report.

'Sally!' Alison said. 'Just look at this. It's a statement of some sort of . . . an online gambling account? It shows that Peter has lost thousands.'

'No wonder he's always so nasty,' Sally said, 'if he's losing like that.'

'You don't understand,' Alison said. 'Peter doesn't have that kind of money. He's always been dependent on Dad financially. If he's lost this amount then there's only one place he could have got the money and that's from Dad's accounts. No wonder we're no longer well off. We need to dig a bit deeper. I wonder if this is Peter's only account.'

'We should try to get into that drawer that he keeps locked,' Sally said.

Alison jumped up and ran from the study. She returned a few minutes later with a large screwdriver. 'This is fairly hefty. We might be able to lever the drawer open.'

Sally watched as Alison put the tip of the screwdriver into the top of the desk drawer and applied force. After a few attempts, the wood splintered, and the drawer flew open.

'There's a file and all sorts of papers in here,' she said. 'Here, Sally, you look through those and I'll deal with these.'

Silence reigned for a few minutes before Sally was shocked to hear Alison swear. It sounded odd coming from her sister, but if the papers Alison was looking at were similar to the ones Sally had just read, she could understand why Alison had let rip.

'The bastard has taken Dad to the cleaners,' Alison said.

'It looks that way,' Sally said. 'He has several gambling accounts, each one linked to our father's finances for payment.'

'I'm going to call him,' Alison said, 'and get him to come over. I won't mention any of this until he gets here. I'll pretend we need to go into Peterborough, and I want him to sit with Dad.'

An hour later, Sally was resting in the drawing room when she heard the front door open. She'd agreed with Alison that it would be better if she stayed out of the way while her sister confronted Peter. The fraud had clearly been going on for months. He'd been blaming the additional cost of housing her and the collapse of institutions for the shortage in their finances when all along he'd been stealing from his own brother.

'Alison, where are you?' Peter called out. 'It's not convenient for me to drop everything whenever you want to go gallivanting.'

'I'm in the study, Peter. Come through.'

Sally heard his footsteps cross the hall and then silence when he reached the study door.

'Don't stand there, Peter. Come inside and close the door.'

Sally would have loved to be a fly on the wall and was tempted to try listening at the door, but she had to leave it to Alison to deal with Peter. She could hear voices raised in anger, but not make out any of the words.

Suddenly, the study door flew open.

'Threaten me with whatever you want, Alison,' Peter shouted. 'I've had enough. It's time the truth came out and I'm going to make sure it does. I'm ready to face the consequences. Are you?'

He stormed to the front door and yanked it open, slamming it behind him.

Sally stood up, but she had to sit down again as the room seemed to spin.

'Are you okay?' Alison asked, appearing in the doorway.

'I got a bit light-headed again when I stood up. I haven't been feeling well for a couple of days, not since I made a pig of myself with that cake. Once I started eating it, I just couldn't stop.'

'You need to get some rest. All this drama isn't good for you. First Gordon and now Peter.'

'What happened with him?' Sally asked, grateful that Alison had come in and sat down instead of making Sally move.

'Peter has been syphoning money from Dad ever since the dementia first hit and he was given power of attorney,' Alison said. 'I told him we know what he's been doing, and I threatened him with court action. You heard his response.'

'Did he admit to anything?' Sally asked.

Alison nodded. 'He admitted he has a gambling addiction. I need to get in touch with our solicitor to see if I can get the power of attorney overturned. I'm sure I can, considering what we've found out.'

'Peter sounded as if he *wanted* the truth to come out. Maybe he's been feeling guilty and that's why he was always so nasty to everyone. He knew what he was doing was wrong.'

Sally closed her eyes as a wave of nausea washed over her.

'You could be right. Are you okay? You really don't look well at all,' Alison said.

'I'm not feeling good.' Sally stood up, clutching the arm of the sofa as she felt herself sway. 'I think I need to lie down and rest.'

'Why not sit on the terrace?' Alison suggested. 'A spot of sunshine will do you wonders.'

She held out her arm. Sally took it and leaned on her for support. Her legs felt like jelly. She could barely walk.

'I need to see a doctor,' Sally said. 'I can barely think straight.'

'If you're not any better tomorrow then I'll take you to the doctor's,' Alison said, putting her arm around Sally's waist.

'Who will stay with our father while we're out? You won't want to call on Peter.'

'Dad will just have to come in the car with us. It's time he had an outing. If he chooses to stay here, I'll simply have to sedate him.'

There was something in the way Alison talked about sedating her father that felt wrong to Sally, but her mind was too fuzzy to work out what it was. Then it came to her! Sedation, that was it.

'Peter says you sedate our father too much.'

'Since when do you care about what Peter says?'

Sally knew there was a thread to follow, but she couldn't quite grasp it. It was something else Peter had said. What was it?

Alison held Sally up as they walked through the drawing

254

room and out through the conservatory to the rear terrace. Sally sank onto one of the padded loungers, thankful to be able to close her eyes.

'Can I get you anything?' Alison asked. 'Something to eat or drink?'

'Nothing to eat,' Sally said. 'I still have an upset stomach from that cake, but a cup of tea would be wonderful.'

Alison went back inside leaving Sally to close her eyes and enjoy the summer sun. A few minutes later, her eyes shot open. She was being watched. She could feel someone's eyes on her. Could Gordon be hiding somewhere? She scanned every inch of the garden that she could see, but there was no sign of him. Her line of vision settled on the boathouse. Could he be in there?

When Alison came out with the tea, Sally told her about the sensation of being under scrutiny.

'Could he be in the boathouse?' Sally asked.

'I'll go and check,' Alison said. 'If he is in there then you'll hear me scream. If that happens, call the police.'

Sally watched as Alison made her way across the vast expanse of lawn. She reached the boathouse, opened the door and peered inside. Then she looked back and gave Sally a double thumbs up.

There was something she needed to remember about the boathouse. What was it? It was to do with her mother and someone else, but who? Why did she feel it was so important to grasp a memory that was just out of reach? What was it about?

Sally thought about poor Rolo buried behind the boat-house who she'd literally loved to death. But had she? How could she have been strong enough? She'd only been seven. She wished she could clear her head and think properly. Something wasn't right with Alison's account of what happened to Rolo, but what was it? Had Alison lied to cover up something even worse?

Chapter Thirty-five

Gordon threw down the binoculars in frustration. He'd been watching the drive for nearly the entire day and Sally hadn't set foot outside. He had everything ready, the chloroform, a blanket to cover her on the back seat so that she wouldn't be seen if anyone looked through the car window, some gaffer tape for her mouth and cable ties for her wrists and ankles so that she wouldn't be able to make a run for it if she woke up before he was ready for her.

Was the bitch sister keeping her inside? What a fucked-up family that seemed to be. The whole lot of them needed to be put away so that Sally didn't have anyone to fall back on.

He thought he'd managed to sort out that problem twenty years ago, but he'd made a mistake. It wasn't a mistake he'd make again. This time he'd tie up all the loose ends so that Sally would have no one to turn to and nowhere to run.

Fuck Sally! He'd even told her about her grandmother's money and she hadn't come with him. He could have kept quiet about it, but no, he'd done the right thing and let her know she was rich. Maybe that was another mistake. Now she knew she had money, she thought she didn't need him to take care of her.

Well, he would take great pleasure in showing her how wrong she was, but first he had to get her home.

Gordon went through his options, but quickly came to the conclusion that the only way to get her was to go into the house and take her. It would be a risk, but one he was prepared to take.

Tomorrow night he'd wait until dark and then sneak in around the side of the house. There must be a back way in. He'd chloroform Sally and take her away without anyone ever knowing he'd been there.

He'd train her not to disobey him again. It wasn't how he would have wanted their life back together to start, but it had to be done. Sally would thank him for it one day.

Chapter Thirty-six

Friday 20th June

'Sally, did you go in the boathouse?'
  'No, Mummy.'
'Don't lie to me!'
'I'm not lying, Mummy.'
'What did I tell you?'
'I mustn't go there.'

Sally shifted from foot to foot. She wanted to tell her mummy the truth, but then she would be in even more trouble. What if Mummy saw her? But her mummy hadn't looked up, only the man . . . Sally tried not to think about what she'd seen when she opened the boathouse door. Mummy and the man were wriggling on the mattress. She'd shut the door and run back to Alison and Alison had been cross because Sally hadn't brought the rake that Alison had asked her to fetch from the boathouse.

'Sally,' Mummy shouted, 'I'll ask you again, but this time don't lie. Did you go to the boathouse this morning?'

And then, suddenly Mummy wasn't there any more. Sally was

standing outside the kitchen. She looked in and everything was red and there was a funny smell. Where was Mummy? Then she saw the man. He had his back to her. She could see a knife in his hand, blood dripping from it forming pools at his feet.

Then Mummy was back and she was even angrier than before. She was covered in blood, hands stretched out.

'Who did you see? Sally, you must remember. Who did you see?'

Sally's eyes flew open and she sat up, gasping for breath. What the hell had that dream been about? Who was the man with her mother in the boathouse? It must have been David Carstairs. Who else could it have been? Was she remembering things that had happened, or was her mind trying to deal with all she'd discovered since she'd come back to this house?

That was the second time she'd dreamt about a man with his back to her holding a knife dripping with blood. Had she actually seen that? Could her father have murdered her mother and only pretended she'd run away? But Alison said their father had already left for France that morning, so who was the man in her dream? Or had her father only pretended to leave? Had he hidden somewhere, stabbed his wife and then left?

Or had it been Peter? Had he killed her mother? But why? What reason would he have to do that? If she was dead, it would explain why Maggie had never bothered to get in touch directly with her since she'd disappeared. But what about the birthday and Christmas cards she'd received every year until her grandmother had died. Had Grandma Fletcher sent them, pretending they were from Maggie?

Sally thought about her grandmother. In fact, that was exactly the kind of thing she would have done, thinking it would be kinder for Sally to believe her mother sent the occasional message, rather than being totally ignored.

She hadn't lied to Mrs Carstairs about the envelopes. She didn't have even one left from that time showing where the cards had been posted. Gordon had made sure of that. She had no idea where David Carstairs and her mother had gone. Besides, Maggie might have dumped Mr Carstairs if she thought she'd found someone better.

Unless she'd been murdered by Peter or her father. What about David Carstairs? If it had been him she'd seen in her dream, had he later killed her mother in the boathouse and fled? But what had he done with the body? Where would he have hidden it?

Sally was vaguely aware that her thoughts were going round in circles. She tried to tie actual memories with what she could recall from the dream, but the details kept slipping away from her. If only she didn't feel so confused all the time. Added to that, she was constantly nauseous.

She climbed out of bed and had to clutch the wall to stay upright. She must have some kind of illness. She'd thought at first it was the cake, but the queasiness had gone on too long for that to be the cause. She would ask Alison to take her to the doctor's. She might need an antibiotic, or something to settle her stomach at the very least.

There was a tap on the door and Alison came in.

'I thought I'd come and see how you're doing, but I can tell just by looking at you that you're not well at all.'

Sally felt so weak she sank back onto the bed.

'I'm not! I need to see a doctor. I must have a stomach bug or something. I feel as if I'm constantly about to throw up.'

Alison helped Sally get settled in the bed, plumping up her pillows so that she could partially sit up.

'I have to go out this morning, but I can take you to the doctor's later if you don't feel any better. You stay right here until I get back. I'll only be an hour or so. Dad had a bad night, so I've given him a sedative. He'll be asleep for most of the morning. You just rest and take care of yourself.'

She turned to go, but Sally called her back.

'Alison, our father isn't the only one who had a disturbed night. I had a weird dream.'

'Another one?'

Sally nodded. 'It was to do with my mother and the boat-house. Well, that's how it started, but then it sort of morphed into something completely different.'

She stopped, wondering how to ask Alison the question that was burning her brain.

'You look as if you're bursting to ask something,' Alison said. 'What is it?'

Sally told Alison about seeing her mother with a man on the mattress in the boathouse.

'No wonder you're upset. That can't have been pleasant.'

Sally shook her head. 'It wasn't, but that wasn't the worst part. I had the dream again where there was a man holding a knife with blood dripping from it. Alison, do you think it's possible that Mr Carstairs or Peter murdered my mother?'

Alison sat on the bed. 'What made you think either of them killed her? Didn't you say you'd received cards every year from Maggie?'

Sally nodded. 'I did, but they might not have been from her.'

She told Alison her theory that Grandma Fletcher might have sent the cards and money.

'But you're forgetting, Sally, I heard your mother's car driving away.'

'I know you did, but what if my mother wasn't the one driving it? What if she was dead and whoever killed her took her body away in the car? Isn't that a possibility?'

Alison nodded. 'It is. I simply assumed it was Maggie. I know she'd called Peter over to be with me, but he only arrived after she'd gone.'

'As far as you know,' said Sally. 'What if he came earlier and had a fight with my mother over something? He could have killed her, taken her body away, and then come back as if nothing had happened.'

Alison looked stunned for a moment but then smiled. 'Don't you think I would have noticed pools of blood on the kitchen floor?'

'You're right,' Sally said, 'but there's another thing. Remember when I told you about the dream of the monster coming into my room?' Alison nodded. 'Could it have been Peter who I was scared of?'

Alison didn't answer, she turned her head away and her shoulders began to shake. When she finally looked back, Sally was stunned to see tears streaming down her sister's face.

'Alison, why are you crying? Is it because of what I asked? I'm so sorry, I would never upset you intentionally.'

Alison pulled a tissue from her pocket and dried her tears. 'It's not you who's upset me, Sally. It's the painful memories from when I was very, very young.'

'What is it?' Sally asked, but already guessed the answer.

'It *was* Peter who came to your room. I knew why he was there, so I came in and made him leave. I had to save you from him.'

The tears started up again and Sally passed Alison a tissue from the box on her bedside table to replace the sodden mass in Alison's hand.

'Peter would have molested you if I hadn't stopped him. It's possible your mother realised that and threatened to tell Dad. I don't know, but it is possible.'

Sally thought for a moment. 'No, that can't be right. If my mother suspected Peter was a paedophile, she wouldn't have called for him to come over to be with you, especially if she knew she was going to walk out and leave me behind. I know she was selfish and self-centred, but I can't believe she would have left either of us with someone she knew, or even suspected, was a paedophile.'

Alison stood up and walked across the room. She threw the tissues in the bin and then turned back to face Sally.

'Maybe your mother didn't know, but I'm going to tell you something I have never told anyone, not even the therapist I saw while I was institutionalised. Peter abused me throughout my early years. That's how I knew when he tried to get to you, and I also knew I had to protect you. Because of my mother's illness and Dad being away on business so much, there hadn't been anyone to protect me. It's because of the years of abuse I suffered with Peter that I was institutionalised. I eventually snapped.'

She sat down next to Sally. 'I am so lucky you're here. I've never felt able to trust anyone enough to tell the truth, but I trust you, Sally.'

Chapter Thirty-seven

Later the same afternoon, Sally had managed to get out of bed and downstairs to the drawing room by the time Alison came back home. Her head was swimming even more than it had been earlier in the day and the nausea was almost unbearable. She wasn't sure she could endure it for much longer.

'I hope you're feeling better now, Sally,' Alison said, sticking her head round the door. 'I just need to go upstairs to check on Dad and then I'll be back to take care of you.'

Sally must have dozed off again because she had no idea how much time had passed before Alison came back downstairs. She looked up as her sister came into the drawing room.

'How are you feeling?' Alison asked. 'You don't look any better. I think you should rest there on the sofa for the rest of today. If you're still feeling sick by morning, I'll see if I can get an appointment for you at the doctor's.'

Sally wanted to argue and beg Alison to take her to the emergency centre, but she lacked the energy. 'Alison, I'm sorry to be a pain, but I'm so thirsty. I finished the tea you made me earlier, but my mouth is now so dry. Could you please bring me a glass of water?'

'Yes, of course,' Alison said. 'But maybe another cup of tea would be better. How about some toast to go with it?'

'No, thank you,' Sally said, wishing Alison would call the doctor. It wasn't like her sister not to do all she could to take care of her.

'Okay, if you change your mind, just yell.'

As she spoke, the doorbell rang.

'I'd best see who that is first,' Alison said, 'and then I'll make the tea.'

Sally heard the door being opened followed by Alison's gasp of surprise.

'Are you here about my brother-in-law?'

'No, ma'am. Would it be possible to come in? We have some difficult news to give you.'

Sally sat up straighter as Alison came back to the drawing room, closely followed by two uniformed police officers.

'Please sit down,' Alison said. 'I was just about to make some tea. Would you like a cup?'

The two officers remained standing. 'Nothing for us, thank you. I'm sorry we have some bad news to report. Your uncle, Peter Marshall, was found dead earlier today. A neighbour heard a commotion and went to investigate. I'm sorry to say he was stabbed to death in his back garden.'

Sally sat up straighter. 'Did the neighbour see who did it?'

'No, by the time she got to Mr Marshall's house he was already dead. The side gate into the garden was open. She called out and, when there was no answer, she went inside. She later recalled that a dark car had passed her as she was on her way to your uncle's house.'

'Gordon!' Alison said.

'But why would he attack Peter?' Sally said. 'That doesn't make any sense. Gordon didn't even know him.'

The officer looked over at her, notebook in his hand. 'I'm sorry, and you are?'

'I'm Sally Watson, also Peter's niece.'

He turned back to Alison. 'You seemed to feel you know who might have done this?'

She nodded. 'It must have been my brother-in-law, Gordon Watson.'

'And why would you think that, Miss Marshall?'

'My sister's husband has been threatening her entire family since she took refuge here with us. She has registered complaints about his behaviour with the police and currently has a temporary restraining order against him.'

'I see. Could you give me his address?'

'I don't know it,' Alison said, looking over at Sally.

Sally gave it and the officer went out into the hall. She could hear his voice, but not make out the words. She shook her head again, trying to dislodge the cotton-wool feeling. If only she could concentrate!

'I've arranged for officers in the area to interview him and take him into custody, if it proves necessary,' the officer said as he came back into the drawing room.

Sally wanted to feel sorry that Peter was dead, but after what she'd found out about what he'd done to Alison, it was impossible to feel anything other than that he'd got what he deserved. She just wished that Gordon hadn't been the one to mete out the justice. But why had he killed Peter? Something wasn't right about this. If only she could think straight!

'Sorry to do this, I can see you're not well, but we have a few more questions.'

Sally managed a smile. 'It's fine. What do you need to know?'

The next fifteen minutes were spent filling in the officers with every detail Sally could think of, from Gordon's date of birth to what she could recall of his medical record. They were interested in the threats he'd made, but said there would be other lines of enquiry should Gordon have an alibi for the time of the murder.

Eventually the questions ceased, by which time Sally could barely keep her eyes open. The officers were about to leave when the older of the two's phone rang.

'Please excuse me while I take this,' he said.

He went into the hall for a few minutes, but came back in looking very grave.

'It seems your husband left home early this morning. One of your neighbours saw him leave. He had a backpack with him, so it's possible he's planning a trip somewhere. However, if he should show up here, please call this number,' he said, handing his card to Alison. 'I will ensure someone comes out immediately if a call is received.'

Alison went to the door with the officers to see them out. When she came back to the drawing room, she looked stunned.

'Peter dead!' she said.

Sally tried to stand, but fell back again before she'd even got halfway up.

'Do you believe Gordon did it?' Alison asked, putting a

cushion behind Sally's head and lifting her legs onto the sofa. 'The police seem convinced to me.'

'I don't know,' Sally said, wishing her thoughts weren't so sluggish. 'I'm not sure.'

'Of course the police will arrest Gordon for it. Who else could it be?'

Sally tried once again to gather her thoughts. But she couldn't. Her brain just wouldn't cooperate. Everything was muddled. She felt sleepy, so sleepy. Why couldn't she keep her eyes open? What had been in the tea she'd had earlier? Her mouth was as dry as dust. For some reason sedatives kept coming to mind, but why was she thinking about those? What had sedatives to do with Peter's murder? Something about Alison and sedatives. Something Peter had said. The temptation to close her eyes was too strong. When she opened them again, she didn't know how much time had passed. A minute? An hour? No, Alison was still there.

'Why do you sedate our father so much?' she asked, struggling to stay awake.

'He gets aggressive. You've seen that.'

'I have, but . . .' again her mind drifted. Alison's words brought her back to the present.

'But what? Do you think you know better than me how to deal with him? You've only been here five minutes.'

'No, of course not.' Finally something clicked in her brain. Peter had said the doctor wouldn't have prescribed the number of doses Alison dished out. She remembered the delivery man's words. 'See you next week!'

'You're buying extra supplies. I've seen them being delivered.'

Alison laughed. 'Of course I am! His idiot of a doctor refuses to prescribe the dosage he needs, the dosage *I* need so that I'm not constantly at his beck and call. It's easy enough to buy most drugs on the internet, so that's what I do.'

Sally again tried to stand up, but fell backwards. 'That's why he sleeps so much. You keep him drugged!'

'Well done, Sally! Ten out of ten for observation, although it's taken you long enough.' She smiled. 'You haven't drunk the tea I made while you were sleeping. You need to drink it now.'

Sally tried to focus on Alison's face. She looked different. Harsher. She tried to picture Gordon stabbing Peter, but the image refused to hold. He would attack Sally but in all the years of their marriage he'd never shown the violent side of his nature towards a man. Alison had been right when she'd said Gordon was a coward. He didn't have the courage to attack someone who could fight back.

'Alison, I'm not . . . convinced . . . Gordon did . . . it,' she said, fighting to keep her eyes open.

There was something different about her sister. She looked irritated, as if Sally had said something stupid.

'Who else would want Peter dead?' Alison asked.

Scraps of overheard conversation drifted in and out of Sally's mind. Peter had threatened Alison. Or had she threatened him? Why couldn't she *think*!

'Where . . . did you . . . go . . . today?' Sally slurred, once again losing the battle to stay awake.

Chapter Thirty-eight

Sally slowly opened her eyes. Why did she feel so weak? What was wrong with her? She tried to sit up, but it was too much of an effort.

Peter was dead and it seemed Gordon had murdered him. But why? What if he came after Alison and her father? Even though she didn't have much of a relationship with her father, she wouldn't want anything bad to happen to him. Alison was all she'd ever wanted from a family. Someone who loved her and cared about her. Gordon wanted to destroy that. He'd already made sure she wasn't able to keep in touch with her sister by lying to her about the wedding invitation all those years ago. What he was doing now was even worse. But still, why kill Peter who was no threat to him?

'Ah, you're awake,' Alison said, coming into the room with a cup in her hand. 'I've brought you some more herbal tea. Can you sit up?' she asked, putting the cup on the side table next to the sofa.

Sally struggled into a semi-upright position and reached for the tea. She was so thirsty she swallowed half of it in one go. She put the cup back on the table and looked over at Alison.

'I can't see why Gordon would want to murder Peter. I wish I could think properly! My mind feels like I'm wading through treacle.'

What had she been thinking about before she fell asleep? Something to do with Alison going out that hadn't seemed right. Then it hit her. Alison had left without arranging for Peter to come over to sit with their father.

'Did you sedate our father today?'

Alison's eyes seemed to glitter in the light from the window. 'I had to,' she said, 'knowing Peter wouldn't be available.'

'How did you know that?' Sally asked, fighting against the nausea that threatened to overwhelm her.

'How did I know what?'

'That Peter couldn't come. You didn't know he was dead until the police told us.'

Alison smiled. 'You're tiring yourself with all these questions. Drink some more tea and rest.'

Sally remembered the question she'd asked before dropping off to sleep earlier. 'Where did you go today?'

Alison grinned, but didn't answer.

Sally felt her eyes beginning to close. She fought to keep them open. It was so hard, but something at the back of her mind refused to let her rest. Of course! That was it! Her eyes flew open.

'How would Gordon know where Peter lived?'

Alison shrugged. 'He could have followed him home.'

'That doesn't make sense,' Sally said. 'Gordon had no reason to kill Peter. He was no threat to him.'

She tried again to sit up, but it was impossible to move. The idea forming in her mind was too horrible to put into words, but she had to.

'He threatened *you*,' Sally said. 'He was going to spill the family secrets.' She paused, but knew she had to go on. 'Alison, where did you go today?'

Alison smiled. 'Why do you want to know?'

'I . . . I am . . . no, I must be wrong,' Sally stammered.

'About what, Sally? I agree with you that Gordon had no reason to kill Peter.'

'So why did you tell the police you thought it was Gordon who'd done it?'

Alison smiled again. 'It suited my plans.'

'What plans?'

'You're asking too many questions, Sally. Why don't you close your eyes for a while?'

Sally fought against the urge to sleep. There was something different about Alison. Something Sally needed to question.

'Peter is a paedophile, so maybe one of his victims attacked him,' Sally said, trying to make sense of things in her muddled mind.

Alison laughed. 'You are really so gullible, Sally. Peter was annoying in many different ways, but he wasn't a paedophile. He never touched me. He didn't come into your room to molest you that night you dreamt about. He came to save you. He never tried to molest me or anyone else. Your mind created the scenario. I just fleshed it out with a few creative details.'

Chapter Thirty-nine

'But why? Why did you say it if it wasn't true? My head is all over the place. I'm struggling to understand what you're saying. If only I could make my brain work!'

Alison sat down on the armchair facing the couch. 'Don't try to think. There's no point. You'll get it all wrong. You always do. You even believed me when I said your mother shut you in the boathouse.'

'But she did! I remember her letting me out. She was so angry.'

Alison laughed. 'I know she was. She came to find me and swore she'd tell Dad what I did to you when no one was looking. She threatened to have me locked up like my mother. I hated Maggie with every fibre of my being, but she was smarter than I'd given her credit for. She'd started watching me and so she knew I'd locked you in the boathouse. She came to let you out.'

'But why did you do that?' Sally asked, feeling as if she'd woken up in a horror film.

'Because I hated you,' Alison said with such a lack of emotion in her voice that Sally shivered.

She tried once again to sit up, but she couldn't move. Her arms and legs were too heavy.

'But that was when we were children,' Sally said. 'All siblings go through periods of hating each other.'

'I've never stopped hating you. I tried to kill you when your mother first brought you home,' Alison said, her dreamy tone even more frightening than the words. 'Peter caught me putting a pillow over your face. You'd have died if it wasn't for him. That was the first time he saved you. I've never forgiven him for stopping me. He thought I wanted to hurt you just because I felt pushed out. What an idiot! He was so convinced he understood me, he went out of his way to make me feel special.'

'But you just said he never touched you,' Sally said, trying to make sense of Alison's words.

'He didn't,' Alison said. 'He was very boringly kind and sweet and useless. He didn't understand the first thing about me.'

She stood up and stamped her foot. 'The only person who ever understood me turned on me when I needed him the most.' She spun round as Sally gasped.

'Colin Blanchett was telling the truth. *You* were his patient, not your mother.'

'That's right! Your precious Colin Blanchett *was* my therapist. He was telling the truth when he said he'd never even met my mother. I adored him and I told him everything. Well, nearly everything. I kept the best bits to myself. I never told him how much I hated you, or that I'd tried to kill you as a baby — I kept that all to myself.'

Sally felt as if nothing made sense any longer. The one person she'd believed cared about her had hated her all her life.

'I wanted so badly to hurt you, but had no idea where you were. And then, almost like a gift from heaven, you sent me that letter saying you needed somewhere to hide from your husband.'

Alison laughed so hard Sally hoped she would choke.

'It had never occurred to me that you'd meet Colin Blanchett before I got rid of you, but fate had other ideas. I was stunned when I found out he was the one who'd brought you home that morning. I couldn't have the two of you getting all friendly. He knew too much about me. I had to do something. And very satisfying it was until I had to drive off before I'd finished the job.'

'So it was *you* who ran him over?'

Alison laughed. 'Of course it was me. I couldn't have him befriending you, now could I?'

Sally realised that was exactly what Colin had tried to do. He'd known Alison was disturbed and had offered Sally a hand of friendship should she need it, but even he couldn't have known how Alison felt about her sister. She'd hidden her hatred of Sally from everyone, apart from Peter, who Sally now realised had been trying to save her by driving her from the house.

'So was it you who tried to run me over that morning?'

Alison nodded.

'You thought it was your husband, didn't you? It was me. Why are you so bloody hard to kill?'

'Alison, you need therapy, someone to talk to about how

276

you feel. I want to get you the help you need. I can be there for you.'

Alison moved to stand next to Sally. 'You haven't finished your special tea when I went to so much trouble to make it for you. Come on now, drink it all up.'

Sally gripped her lips together as Alison picked up the cup and tried to pour the liquid into her mouth.

'Open up,' she said, pinching Sally's nostrils closed until she was forced to open her lips to breathe. 'You have to finish your tea, Sally.'

Sally tried to cough the liquid away from her throat, but found herself swallowing as much as she spat out.

'I couldn't believe my luck when Mrs Carstairs gave you the rest of the cake to bring home. You loved it so much I thought it would be an easy way to get rid of you, but no, you had to be selfish and stop eating it. I'd pushed the last of my dried laburnum seeds into it. Such a waste. I would have made an infusion of them for your tea instead if I'd known you wouldn't finish the cake. As it was, I had to search for an alternative. The one I came up with is much better.'

Sally spluttered as Alison poured the last of the tea down her throat.

'It's your own fault you're choking. You wouldn't have had to drink this if you'd just eaten the seed cake.'

Alison put the cup on the side table and sat facing Sally.

'You were starting to remember too much, so I've had to rethink my schedule on getting rid of you. Those dreams of yours were too close to the truth. I did think about putting all the blame on Peter, but if you'd remembered any more that would have pointed your attention too much in my direction.'

Sally's vision was blurring, but she forced herself to concentrate so that she could focus on Alison.

'My dream about the man with the knife. Was that real? Did it happen?'

'Oh yes,' Alison said. 'The man was Peter. The blood was your mother's.'

Chapter Forty

'**M**y mother is dead?'

Alison laughed. 'She's been dead for decades.'

'Did Peter kill her? Is that what I saw?'

'Peter hasn't the guts to kill anyone. Sorry, I should say *hadn't* the guts to do it. He didn't even have the guts to stand up to me for all these years.'

'I don't understand. What do you mean?'

'*What do you mean?*' Alison squeaked, parodying Sally's voice. 'I mean I've kept Peter at my beck and call for decades in fear of being blamed for your mother's murder.'

'But you said he didn't kill her.'

'That's right, Sally, he didn't. *I* did. I stabbed her to death in the kitchen.'

The feeling of living in a horror film deepened. Sally knew she had to get away, but when she tried to move her limbs, they refused to budge.

'What was in the tea you've been giving me?'

'Just a little concoction of my own devising that's semi-paralysing. It's not permanent, but right now I need you to be immobilised. I don't want you getting up and running away.'

Sally strained every muscle, but couldn't move.

'You might just as well give up, Sally. You're not going anywhere until I take you to your final resting place. I have a lovely spot picked out for you. I thought about pushing you down the stairs again, but decided that would look a bit too suspicious.'

As she said the words, Sally had a flashback to Alison grabbing her and shoving her towards the staircase.

'It was you!' she said. 'You pushed me down the stairs that day.'

'I did,' Alison said, 'and you should have died, but you survived. You always survived, no matter what I did. Have you also remembered why I pushed you?'

'I saw a man holding a knife.'

'Peter,' Alison said.

'Yes, Peter. There was blood dripping from it. But before that, I was upstairs in my bedroom waiting for my mother to come for me. I remember now, we were going away. Then I heard her scream, so I crept downstairs.'

'That's when you came to the kitchen door. I saw you, but you didn't see me. When you ran back up the stairs I came after you and threw you down from the top stair. I thought you were dead. I was glad.'

'You said you stabbed my mother. Why? What did she do to you?'

'It was what she was going to do to me. She knew I was torturing you whenever I could. She said there was something wrong with me after she found your puppy with its neck broken. I told her you'd done it, but she didn't believe me. And she was right. I enjoyed killing that dog. Why should you get to live here and have a pet when I was passed back and forth between *my* lunatic mother and *your* mother who hated me? I wanted to live here all the time. I thought if I could get rid of you then Dad would let me stay for always.'

'But that doesn't explain why you murdered my mother.'

'Murder is such an ugly word, Sally. I acted in self-defence. It was pure luck that I was here that day. It's the one thing I have to thank my crazy mother for. Your mother was leaving, going away with her lover and taking you with her, which would have been great, but she told me she was going to leave my dad a letter telling him everything I'd been doing. She made it sound like I was crazy and needed to be shut away.'

Alison made stabbing motions. 'I was so angry; I grabbed a knife from the block and stabbed her over and over. I didn't want to stop. I enjoyed every moment of it.'

'But why did Peter have the knife?'

'Your mother had called him earlier that day after my mother dumped me here. She needed him to come and be with me because she'd planned to run away with David Carstairs. Peter arrived as I was stabbing Maggie. He took the knife from me. That was when you came down and saw him. I chased after you. Peter put the knife on the kitchen table and tried to save your mother. At least, that's what he said afterwards. Then he must have heard you screaming as you bounced down the stairs, because he came out of the kitchen to see what was going on.'

Alison smiled. 'I told him we had to bury Maggie and he said no. He said he was going to call an ambulance for you and also the police to take me away. He even picked up the phone to dial 999 but I soon put a stop to that.'

'How?' Sally asked, struggling to keep her eyes open.

'I pointed out that his fingerprints were on the knife. I would tell the police that he'd killed Maggie and they would believe me because I was only a child. He was covered in Maggie's blood from where he'd tried to help her. He insisted no one would believe he had murdered her. He had no reason to do it, but I showed him how wrong he was.'

She stood up and leaned over Sally.

'I told him that I would tell the police he had been molesting me and that he had moved on to you. I said I'd tell the police your mother had found out what he'd been doing and had been about to report him to the police.'

Alison grinned at Sally and then suddenly tears flowed from her eyes.

'Do you like my party trick? I can cry on a whim whenever I want. I let tears fall that day and told Peter I would sob in front of the police while I was telling them I was terrified of him because he'd pushed you down the stairs after you'd seen him stab Maggie and was running away from him.'

She shrugged. 'He tried to brazen it out by saying that you would be able to tell the truth to the police, but, as I pointed out, you hadn't seen me in the kitchen. The only person you'd seen holding a knife was him.'

Chapter Forty-one

'You're insane,' Sally said. 'You need help.'

Alison shrugged and continued as if Sally hadn't spoken. 'I explained to Peter that we could make Dad believe Maggie had left him, taking you with her, if we also buried the suitcases Maggie had packed. I thought we could make it look as though Maggie had driven away if Peter took the car keys, and drove her car from the garage to a secluded spot and then walked back. As it turned out, he later had a better idea and dumped it in the long-term parking at Heathrow. It's not often I can give him credit for anything, but that was a work of genius as everyone thought they'd left the country. But I'm getting ahead of things.'

Alison's voice became more gleeful with every word. She seemed to tower over Sally. She wanted to push her away but couldn't summon the strength in her arms even to lift them.

'I don't understand why he went along with you.'

'He didn't at first, but once he realised he'd be on the hook for stabbing Maggie, he finally saw things my way. He agreed to help me bury Maggie and you in the new rose bed that was

283

ready for planting, but once he realised you weren't dead he refused to put you in there with your mother. I pretended to give in and said I'd let you live and sent him to the boathouse to get some plastic to wrap Maggie's body. While he was gone, I hid the knife. I've used it to blackmail him ever since. Whenever he's tried to go his own way, I've reminded him of the power I held as long as I had that knife.'

'That's the evidence! I knew I'd heard you say that!'

Alison sighed. 'You were beginning to pick up on too much. I hadn't planned to kill you just yet, but you were starting to ask too many questions.'

Sally was glad when Alison moved back to the armchair.

'I was going to smother you with a cushion that day so that Peter would have to bury you, but the doorbell rang just as Peter came back into the kitchen with the plastic sheeting. It was Mrs Carstairs.'

Terrified, Sally tried again to move, but her body refused to obey. She was trapped on the sofa.

'Peter took off his jacket because it had too much of your mother's blood on it where he'd tried to save her, the idiot. He left it in the kitchen with the plastic sheeting and shut the door. Then I opened the front door to Mrs Carstairs. She'd just found a note her husband had left telling her he was going away with Maggie. She demanded to see Dad to see if he knew anything about where they might be.'

Alison stood up again, pacing furiously back and forth in front of Sally. 'I kept her on the doorstep as long as I could. I told her that Dad was abroad, and that Maggie had gone, but I didn't know where. Then she spotted the blood on my clothes. I had no choice but to let her come in, saying it was your blood. Peter was kneeling down next to you, feeling for your pulse or some such stupid thing.'

'Surely she must have realised something was wrong.'

'I told Mrs Carstairs that when Maggie left, you'd tried to run after her. I said you'd tripped and fell down the stairs.'

Alison punched the arm of the chair.

'She nearly ruined everything. She called for an ambulance, using the hall phone. If she'd gone into the kitchen, it would have been a disaster, but she stayed with you in the hall. She wanted to call my mother to stay with me while Peter followed the ambulance to the hospital, but I told her my mother wasn't well. Mrs Carstairs made me go with her to her house until Peter was able to leave you at the hospital.'

Sally could feel her mind drifting. She had to stay awake. *She* had to *stay awake!*

'You were in a coma, so Peter came back to get me from Mrs Carstairs'. He told her he would stay with me until Dad could return from France. We cleaned up the kitchen and waited until it got dark. I gathered up all of Maggie's toiletries and other stuff. Then I unpacked your suitcase and put all your things away, so that it would appear Maggie had left you behind.'

'You're evil,' Sally said. 'All these years I believed my mother had abandoned me when she was actually dead.'

Alison sighed. 'It was all going well. We were burying Maggie when David Carstairs arrived. He'd come to see if Maggie had left him a message in the boathouse because she hadn't picked him up where they'd arranged. He must have heard us because he came through the arch and saw what Peter was doing. I had no option but to hit him with the spade from behind – lots of times,' she said with a smile that terrified Sally.

'Peter took David Carstairs, keys and said once we'd finished he would go and find the car. It couldn't be too far away if David had walked back.' She smiled. 'I asked Peter yesterday what he actually did with the car. I've never really been curious about it, but I thought as Peter was about to die, I should ask him.' She stopped pacing and laughed. 'He'd found the car parked in a layby about a mile from here. Apparently one of Peter's gambling buddies owed him a favour. The man ran a scrap metal place that crushed cars. Peter took the car there and it disappeared, no questions asked.'

She sat down again and reached across to pat Sally's arm.

'Anyway, to get back to what happened to the star-crossed lovers. We buried both of them, together with Maggie's suitcase, and planted the roses on top. When we got back to the house the phone was ringing. It was Dad making his usual call home. Peter told him Maggie had run off with David Carstairs and you were in hospital in a coma.'

Alison leaned towards Sally. 'I hated you even more then because Dad dropped everything to come racing back home to make sure you were okay. He loved you more than he loved me! He would never have done that for me. That's one of the reasons I keep him sedated most of the time. Why should I give him any care and love when he never gave me any? I was packed off to live with my crazy mother. Did Dad ever come to visit me? No! But he went to visit you at your grandmother's, didn't he?'

Sally wanted nothing more than to drift off to sleep, but Alison kept shouting at her.

'Didn't he keep coming to see you? I know he did.'

Sally thought if only she could make Alison see that their father had also neglected her, not just Alison, then she might be able to make her sister calm down.

'He didn't come very often. I saw him sometimes on my birthdays, but not every year,' Sally said. 'He didn't come at all in the two years before Grandma Fletcher died. My grandmother always made excuses for him. She said my father was always very busy. She told me he loved me, but he had to work abroad a lot of the time. She also made excuses for my mother not coming to see me.'

'Who cares about your mother! You saw our dad far more often than I did because he loved you more than he did me!' She laughed. 'During one of my many stays in the nuthouse, when he came to visit me, I told him I wanted to kill you. That I would kill you when I got the chance. Of course, once I was so-called "cured", I pretended I no longer felt that way. He believed me, the idiot.'

She smacked the arm of her chair again. 'I've never stopped hating you. I want you to die slowly and terrified.'

'I don't understand,' Sally said. 'If you hate me so much, why didn't you let Gordon take me when he came here? Why did you offer me a safe haven so that I could escape from him?'

'Isn't it obvious? I want the satisfaction of killing you myself!'

Alison stood up and paced up and down in front of the sofa. Sally wanted to get up and run, but her limbs refused to obey her commands.

'I've always hated you, Sally,' Alison ranted. 'It's time for me to put an end to this. The therapist in the nuthouse told me I had to find a way to let go of my resentment, to get you out of my life and my mind. He was right. I've found the perfect way to do it. You're going to be buried in the garden near to your mother. The day after you arrived, I started digging a new rose bed just for you. I took you to see it, if you remember. You'll be under the Golden Opportunity arch and I've also bought some Peace roses to plant around your grave. It's appropriate, don't you think? A golden opportunity to get rid of you and, finally, peace of mind for me.'

She grinned. 'When Peter saw you here that first day, he was horrified. He guessed what I had in mind and begged me to let you leave. Even threatened me with the police. Who knew he'd finally develop a backbone this late in life? Once I realised I'd lost my control over him, he had to die. He was the only one who would know I'd killed you and I couldn't take a chance on him telling anyone else.'

Alison disappeared from Sally's eyeline. When she reappeared several minutes later, she had strong garden twine in one hand and a syringe in the other.

'I need to make sure you can't run away, Sally, so I'm going to tie you up nice and securely. Then I'm going to inject you with a little of Dad's sedative. You'll be sound asleep when I bury you, but you should wake up soon afterwards. When you're down in the hole I want you to be able to scream, knowing that no one will hear you.'

Chapter Forty-two

As she secured the knots around her ankles, Alison kept up a steady flow of words. Sally wanted to block them out, but also wanted to carry on hearing them. As long as she could hear Alison it meant she was still alive. The moment her sister stopped talking she would jab her with the sedative and then there would be no hope of escape.

'That day you came here after your grandmother died, I wanted you to stay so that I could kill you then, but Peter was here and pretended to be Dad. He sent you away, thinking that would keep you safe. He thought he could make you leave and never want to come back. I was so angry when he ruined my plan. I was going to lock you in the boathouse and then deal with you that night.'

She lifted Sally's arms and crossed them. 'There, you look nice and peaceful. I'll just tie these together. Now, where was I? Oh yes, Peter getting in my way yet again. That was one of the reasons I enjoyed killing him. He helped me bury your mother, but he wouldn't do it again when I planned to get rid of you. He knew what I was doing and tried to stop me. The biggest problem for him, though, was that he was the only one who would be able to tell on me. You see, I've thought this through. Everyone will think that revolting husband of yours came and took you away. I'm going to tell the police I woke up and you were gone. Gordon will deny it, of course he will, but after the way I've made sure you reported his behaviour, no one will believe he doesn't have you hidden away somewhere.'

She pulled so tight on the string Sally cried out in pain.

'Stop whining!'

'Alison, please, let me go. I will leave here and never come back. Your secret is safe. I'll never tell on you. Just let me go,' Sally begged, tears running unchecked down her cheeks.

Her sister continued as if Sally hadn't spoken. 'Colin Blanchett has to go as well because he might have seen that I was driving the car that ran him down. I'll have to find a way to deal with him properly. I'm sure I'll be able to get into his room at the hospital. All it will take is a little something added to his drip. I wish I'd been able to finish him off, but another car came along so I had to leave that for another day.'

She tied off another knot and then sat back.

'Unlike with Peter. I couldn't take any chances on him living to tell tales on me. Do you want to know something funny?'

Sally shook her head. 'Please, please, let me go.'

'You'll like this,' Alison said. 'It's ironic. Peter has never stopped looking for the knife with his fingerprints on. I've let him hunt all over the house for it, but it never occurred to him to look in the one place I've always claimed as my domain. It has been on display in the kitchen all along. While he was in the boathouse, I lifted some stuff out of the freezer and dumped the knife at the bottom, then put the food back on top. Then, when he went to move the cars I retrieved it, washed it, and put it back in the block where it belonged. He's walked past it more times than I could count and not realised what it was.'

She went into such a fit of giggling that Sally's heart sank even further. Her sister was completely deranged.

'As he was so obsessed with the knife, I felt it would be poetic justice if I used it to kill him. I went to his house and waited until he turned his back on me. What a fool. He thought I wouldn't hurt him. Well, I can tell you now, Sally, I'm glad I'm finally rid of him. He wouldn't let me forget the past and was always on at me to atone. Atone for what? I did what I had to do. As for the knife, it's currently in the dishwasher and will go back into the block. I do like tidy endings.'

She picked up the syringe. 'And now, Sally, it's time for you to have a nice long sleep.'

Chapter Forty-three

Sally's eyes opened to complete blackness. Where was she? *Did it matter?* She was so tired, so very tired. She'd just close her eyes for another few moments and then try to work out what was happening. When she woke again, she was still in the dark. A voice in her head was yelling, trying to tell her something. What? Something important about where she was, but she couldn't grasp the thought. Maybe it wasn't important. She just wanted to sleep, but the voice wouldn't stop yelling.

Wake up! Wake up!

But it was too hard. She just wanted to sleep. Alison had said she should sleep. Alison! Where was her sister? Alison loved her. She'd saved her from Gordon.

She wanted to sit up, but for some strange reason she couldn't manage it. She tried to move her hand, but both hands came up. They were tied together. She couldn't reach very far. Something was in the way. It felt like material. Was she wrapped in a blanket? A soft drowsy feeling crept over her as she closed her eyes again. She'd figure it out later, when she woke up properly.

Wake up! I must wake up!

She felt herself being dragged and then a falling sensation. The breath left her body as she connected with a hard surface. She must have been dropped into a hole. Why? Where? There were things she knew, but she couldn't drag them to the surface. It was something to do with her mother and Peter. No, not Peter. Peter had saved her. Had he? Alison saved her from Gordon. No, Alison wanted her to sleep.

Sally tried to call out, but no words came. She could barely move. The material was all around her. She was in a cocoon. Where was she?

Lifting her hands as far as they would go, she tried to rip her way through the material, but it wouldn't give.

'Oh no you don't! You're staying down there.'

Sally knew that voice. It was Alison. Memories of being on the sofa listening to her sister came flooding in. She knew she had to get out now or she would die here, but she couldn't move. Couldn't get her arms untangled. She had to get free. No way was she going to give in and die in this hole.

She screamed, 'Help me! Help me!'

And then she felt clumps of earth as they landed on her body.

Sally writhed and twisted, but couldn't get free of her bonds.

'Help me! Someone help me!'

'What the fuck are you doing? Sally's in that hole? Argh, you cut me, you bitch!'

That was Gordon's voice! Sally had never believed she'd be happy to hear him speak, but he could get her out of this hole.

'Gordon! Gordon, I'm down here,' she cried out, but to her own ears her words were too faint to be heard. She yelled louder, again and again, screaming for Gordon to get her out. Her hands were tied, but she scratched and ripped at the material as much as she could. She had to get herself free.

She could hear scrabbling sounds, as if a fight was taking place, but who was winning? It was impossible to tell. Then, suddenly, all sound from above stopped. Sally felt the air leave her body. She was going to suffocate. Forcing herself to breathe, she yelled again. Surely someone would hear her.

'Please, help me. I'm trapped,' she screamed again and again until her throat was raw. After what felt like eternity, she finally heard a voice.

'It's okay. I'll get you out and I've called the police!'

Mrs Carstairs? What was she doing there? Sally felt tears of relief stream from her eyes. Of all the people to come to her rescue, Mrs Carstairs was the last person she would have expected.

'Mrs Carstairs, help me. My arms and legs are tied,' Sally cried out.

'Hold on, dear,' Mrs Carstairs said. 'I need to get a ladder so that I can climb down to you. The police will be here soon. You're going to be all right.'

Sally couldn't understand what was going on, but felt the tension leave her body. If the police were on their way, there was a chance she would survive after all.

She heard the thud of something landing on the ground close by.

'I'm climbing down, dear,' Mrs Carstairs said. 'I'm not able to move very quickly, but I'm on my way.'

Sally felt hands moving the material.

'She seems to have wrapped you up very tight. It's taking

me a little longer than I would have liked. Oh, there you are!' Mrs Carstairs said as the material lifted from Sally's face.

'Oh, thank you! Thank you. I thought I was going to die down here.'

'Unfortunately, I don't think I can undo these knots. I'll have to climb out again to get something to cut the string. I'll be as quick as I possibly can.'

'Please be careful,' Sally said. 'I heard my husband's voice and he can be violent. Also, I don't know where she is, but Alison is unstable. She could attack you. She's crazy!'

Mrs Carstairs turned on the short ladder and looked back.

'I don't think you need to worry about either of them, my dear. Your husband has collapsed. Alison hit him in the stomach with the spade.'

'And Alison?'

'She's unconscious. I'm not sure what's going on, but it appears your husband came prepared with chloroform, or something similar. He seemed to have put a pad on Alison's face and she collapsed. I'm going now, but I'll be back in a minute or two.'

A few minutes later, Mrs Carstairs reappeared, secateurs in hand.

'I found these in the boathouse. I think I can use them to free you.'

Sally held herself as still as she could while Mrs Carstairs snipped at the strings binding her hands and ankles.

'You should be able to move now, my dear. I'll go up first.'

Sally struggled to free herself from the shroud Alison had wrapped her in, but finally managed to get upright. She put one foot on the ladder and collapsed. She had no sensation in her feet and her hands were numb. The string had been so tight around her wrists and ankles, the blood flow needed to return.

'Are you okay, dear? I would help you up, but I don't think I can.'

'I'll be fine in a few minutes, Mrs Carstairs. I need my circulation to return,' Sally said, massaging her limbs.

As the blood returned to her hands and feet, pain shot through her extremities. She had to grit her teeth to stop herself from crying out. Finally, as the pins and needles subsided, she tried again to climb from her grave. This time she was able to cling to the ladder and heave herself out.

Gordon's body was sprawled a few feet from the hole. It was obvious he was dead from the massive gash in his stomach. He was lying in a pool of blood. The spade Alison must have used was resting across his legs, the sharp end covered in blood. Fighting the urge to throw up, Sally crawled over to him and felt for his pulse, just to be certain, but there was nothing there.

She looked up. 'He's gone,' she said, grieving for the man she'd once loved, not for the monster he became. Then it hit her. How was it that Mrs Carstairs had come to her rescue?

'What are you doing here, Mrs Carstairs? How did you know I needed help?'

'I didn't know! I happened to be in my garden and heard a commotion. I looked through the hedge and saw your husband. Alison attacked him with the spade, but he grabbed her and put that pad on her face before he collapsed. Mrs Carstairs wrung her hands and said urgently, 'Alison's dangerous. We need to tie her up before she comes round.'

Sally nodded, pretending to accept Mrs Carstairs' word that she had just happened to be in the right place at the right time, even though it was dark, and she would not have had a valid reason for being in her garden in the dead of night. Sally had often felt she was being watched while in the garden, but had assumed it was Gordon. Now she guessed it might have been Mrs Carstairs.

Almost as if she'd read Sally's mind, Mrs Carstairs shrugged.

'The truth is, my dear, I've been spying on you since we met that day in Peterborough.'

'But why?' Sally said, unable to picture Mrs Carstairs as any kind of spy.

'I hoped you would lead me to your mother and David,' she said, her voice breaking.

Sally realised Mrs Carstairs had probably never been able to come to terms with her husband leaving her. Would telling her the truth add to her pain, or bring her some closure? She would lead the poor woman to Maggie and David, but not in the way she expected or would want.

Chapter Forty-four

Sally staggered to her feet, swaying as waves of nausea swept over her. She couldn't give in, though. Alison had to be tied up before she came round. She shook her head at the twine Mrs Carstairs held out to her.

'I don't think I can tie any knots,' Sally said, sinking down next to Alison and taking the chloroform pad away from her sister's face. 'My fingers still feel too stiff. I'll hold her wrists together and you tie her up.'

'I'll do my best, my dear,' Mrs Carstairs said, 'but what on earth has been going on?'

Sally sighed. Where to begin? 'It's a long story, Mrs Carstairs, which I'll tell you in time, but for now I need to break something to you.'

Mrs Carstairs paused in the act of tying a knot around Alison's ankles. 'What is it, my dear?'

Sally nodded, letting go of Alison's legs once she was sure the knots were tight.

'I'm sorry to say that Alison murdered your husband. He's buried in the rose bed over there, together with my mother.'

'How can that be? When did she do it?'

'The night everyone thought they'd run away together.'

'But that's not possible. They left the country. How could you have received cards and presents of money from your mother if she was already dead? Besides, David left me that note. He ran off with Maggie. I had it in black and white.'

Sally felt a bubble of hysteria rising. How could they be having this conversation next to her dead husband and murderous half-sister? It was too surreal.

'I think my grandmother must have sent the cards and money to make me think my mother cared about me. She used to make excuses for why my father didn't come to visit more often. She probably just wanted me to feel loved, so she made out my mother remembered me. In a way, I wish she'd known what had happened. She must have felt betrayed by her daughter, in the same way I felt betrayed by my mother, but that was wrong. Alison said my mother was going to take me with her.'

She looked up and saw that Mrs Carstairs had tears running down her face.

'I'm so sorry,' Sally said. 'I didn't mean to upset you.'

'It's silly,' Mrs Carstairs said, 'but all these years I'd wanted to know where David went and it turns out he never left this garden. In a way, it eases the hurt I felt that he hadn't bothered to let me know where he was. It doesn't change the fact that he was going to leave me, but who knows, maybe he would have come back eventually.'

'Do you think we can leave Alison here until the police arrive?' Sally felt a sob rise in her throat as she glanced at the hole in the ground that had almost been her grave. 'I don't feel I can bear to look on this scene for much longer.'

'I think that is an excellent idea. I, for one, could do with a reviving cup of tea.'

Sally shuddered. 'I won't go into details now,' she said, 'but I don't think I will ever again be able to drink tea without having a panic attack.'

Mrs Carstairs helped Sally to her feet.

'You poor child, what you must have gone through. I have always felt Alison was a little highly strung, but I had no idea she was so unstable.'

Almost as if she'd raised Alison with her words, Sally was horrified to hear a groan from her sister. 'I think she's coming round,' she said. 'How tight were you able to tie the knots?'

'I don't know,' Mrs Carstairs said, her face paling.

Sally didn't want to wait around to find out. They needed to get safely inside before her sister came round fully.

'Let's go,' she said.

As they raced across the lawn to the house, Sally glanced at the boathouse. So much of her life was shaped around that structure. If she stayed, which was probable because someone had to take care of their father now that Alison was going to be locked away, Sally vowed to herself that it would be pulled down and never rebuilt.

As they entered the kitchen, Sally slammed the door shut and locked it, sliding the bolts across just in case Alison was able to get herself free. She saw her phone vibrating on the kitchen table. She picked it up just as the vibration stopped. Almost immediately, it started up again. She swiped to answer the call.

'Hello?'

'Sally, thank God,' Colin Blanchett said, his voice croaky and unsteady. 'I've been calling you on and off for hours. You have to get out of that house!'

'It's okay, Colin. I'm fine,' Sally said, cutting across his words.

'No you're not!' he said. 'I've already called the police. It was Alison who ran me down. I think she might try to hurt you as well. Maybe it was her who tried to run you down. I think you're in danger. She's unstable. You must leave – now!'

'Colin, please listen to me. I know about Alison. I'm safe. Truly I am. Alison can't hurt me.'

'You don't know that,' he insisted. 'Please leave the house now!'

Sally felt a bubble of hysteria rise and had to suppress a gurgle of laughter. 'Believe me, I know I'm safe. Alison is tied up in the garden right now. I'll get a taxi tomorrow and come to the hospital to tell you everything. I take it you're now allowed visitors?'

'I am, but what do you mean about Alison being tied up in the garden?'

'She tried to hurt me, but she was overpowered by my husband. Colin, it's a very long story and far too complicated to go into over the phone. I'll tell you all about it when I see you tomorrow. I don't know what time it will be. It all depends on the situation with my father,' she said. 'I'll need to arrange for someone to care for him while I'm away.'

'I can stay with him for an hour or two,' Mrs Carstairs said.

Sally passed that on to Colin and ended the call.

While she had been on the phone, Mrs Carstairs had been busy.

'I've made myself tea and you a cup of coffee,' she said,

'although I feel you probably don't need caffeine in your system right now. I'll stay with you until the police arrive'

Sally nodded gratefully. 'Yes, please do. I'm going to go upstairs for a moment, just to make sure my father is okay. I thought she was so good at looking after him . . . but the entire time she was keeping him sedated to make her life easier.'

Chapter Forty-five

Sally climbed the stairs, wondering what life held in store for her now. One thing was certain, she would have to stay in this house for as long as her father lived here. She reached the landing and walked along to his bedroom, gently tapping on the door before opening it to go inside.

Her father was stretched out in his bed, sound asleep. Alison must have given him an extra strong dose of the sedative. Tomorrow she would have to tell him all about Alison's crimes, but for tonight she would let him sleep. Maybe he would gradually stop confusing her with her mother, maybe he wouldn't. Regardless of how it turned out, they would find a way to deal with it.

She'd hated her father for so long, blaming him for something he hadn't even done. It had been Peter who had tried to keep her from harm and out of Alison's clutches. He'd first saved her from Alison when she was a baby and had caught Alison trying to smother her. Then he'd sent her away by pretending to be her father when she'd arrived after Grandma Fletcher's death. Even recently, he'd done his best to get her to leave the house and never come back. She owed him a debt of gratitude. Without his goading, she might not have picked up on Alison's true nature. Although, to be fair, she'd realised the truth too late to save herself. Even if Gordon had stopped Alison, had Mrs Carstairs not been around to rescue her, she would probably have died in that hole.

As she walked back down the grand staircase, more memories flooded in, both good and bad. It would take time to process all of them.

She heard sirens in the distance, gradually getting closer. Maybe that was the sound of finally being able to let go of the past. She had a whole new future to look forward to and she intended to live life to the full.

Acknowledgements

I'd like to thank the team at Headline Accent for everything they do. Special thanks go to my editor, Bea Grabowska, whose suggested tweaks and excellent editing helped to refine both plot and characterisation. I hope this book does justice to your efforts.

Have you read Lorraine Mace's dark and twisting DI Sterling thrillers?

'Crime fiction at its absolute finest'
MARION TODD

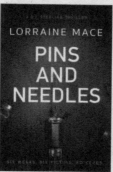

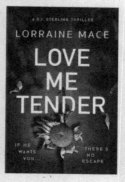